THE SHACK

ALSO BY JOANNE DEMAIO

ALSO BY JOANNE DEMAIO

Beach Cottage Series

The Beach Cottage
Back to the Beach Cottage

Standalone Novels

True Blend
Whole Latte Life

The Winter Series

Snowflakes and Coffee Cakes
Snow Deer and Cocoa Cheer
Cardinal Cabin
First Flurries
Eighteen Winters
Winter House
Winter Road
–And More Winter Books–

ISBN: 9798335483032

Joannedemaio.com

the shack

BOOK 23

JOANNE DEMAIO

one

CELIA'S UNDERWATER.

Shane knows it. That's what she's feeling right now. Panic. Unnerved. Lord knows, he's been there. Two or three times. Tossed off the lobster boat in a heaving sea. Or yanked off the boat when getting caught in the bight— that uncoiling rope snagged around his foot wrenching him overboard with it. Leaving him falling with nothing to grab on to. Nothing to stop the descent. It's happened—and is always shocking.

He never forgets the sensation, either. Can revisit it at will. That panic. The desperate attempt at even a breath before hitting that wall of water and going under.

Under to another place.

One foreign and wanting only to snuff him. To pull him deeper.

When it happens? The fleeting thought comes that his peril's gone unnoticed in the frantic busyness aboard

1

ship—the loosened, shifting lobster pots; the receding monster wave leaving large fish flopping on deck in their *own* desperation; the pitching boat; the calling voices in the gale-force wind.

Then, as the sea covers his body, there's the *unimaginable* fear that help won't come soon enough.

Real fear that the boys on deck aren't leaning over the gunwale and keeping an eye out to not lose sight of him in the massive ocean.

Fear that some life ring won't fly out from the lobster boat in time.

Something, anything, to save him from the ravages of the deep, fluid underworld.

That's where he found Celia minutes ago.

Beneath a sea of shocking emotion from which he's now lifting her.

On the city streets, noises swirl around them. Loud traffic. A cable-car bell. A truck back-up warning. Passing voices in scraps of conversation. All surge as his arms hold her safe. The late-morning sunlight glaring off windows is blinding. But that motion—the people, the cars—motion always moving.

Keeping Celia and Aria in his embrace, Shane presses his face to the side of Celia's head. Her auburn hair is soft against his skin. Her relieved sigh is audible as she exhales a shaky breath in his hold.

Yes, he leaned over the gunwale.

He kept her in his sights.

He pulled her from those waves of emotion that overtook her upon leaving a funky jewelry shop called August Dove.

Now he whispers close to her ear. *"Come on. Let's go somewhere quiet."*

He steps back and looks at her then. She's undone. Her hair is mussed. Her black blazer is disheveled over a black top and faded jeans. Aria's in her arms and touching the turquoise pendant hanging from Celia's neck.

But Celia? She looks at him. Silently nods, too.

"You good to walk?" he asks.

"I am."

As she says it, Celia kisses Aria's cheek, leans over and straps her in the stroller. When she straightens, Shane takes the stroller handles and waits as Celia loops an arm through his. Leans into him, too. He feels it. Feels it right before they start walking the crowded San Francisco sidewalks. The stroller wheels turn over the gritty concrete. The air is cool. The street, busy,

In the car's backseat, the balloons bob and bump behind Elsa. But she pays them no mind while watching Celia and Shane. "The man with Celia," she begins with a quick glance to her rideshare driver, Toby. "My God, I *know* him. Shane, his name is. He's a good person," she says, watching as Shane steps back and looks closely at Celia. A shop front's brick wall rises behind them as they stay clear of the bustling sidewalk. Celia's nodding; Aria's in her arms and toying with Celia's turquoise necklace. "Shane's a Maine lobsterman, actually. Spending time in Connecticut these past few months." She glances from Toby to Shane. *"But I can't imagine why he's here,"* she whispers more to herself than to her driver.

"Okay," she hears Toby's reassuring voice from the front seat. He'd kindly pulled over at the curb so that Elsa can get the gist of what's happening with Celia and Shane on this San Francisco street. "The man's not a stranger. So your friend ... Celia, right? She's safe?"

"Yes. She is." As Elsa says it, Celia's just put Aria in the stroller. The three of them begin walking away then, Celia's arm looped through Shane's as he wheels that stroller. And it's instinct, really, the way it happens. The way Elsa's fingers grip the door handle as Shane and Celia head off. "If you'll excuse me, Toby," Elsa says over her shoulder. "I have to go after them." Quickly, she opens the car door—slapping back those bobbing balloons, too. "I'll just be a few minutes," she calls, stepping out onto the sidewalk.

"Wait, Elsa!"

Elsa hears Toby's voice—cut off right when she slams the car door shut against those damn balloons—and hurries in Celia's direction. The sunlight is blinding; it reflects off boutique display windows and car bumpers in the Haight-Ashbury district. The whole street—with its colorful shops and that bright morning light and the sounds and people and cars—is like a nightmare fun house. People loom in front of her; unfamiliar noises startle; distorted reflections in shop windows fool the eye. Elsa pauses while squinting against the sun's glare. Taking a sharp breath then, she straightens her olive canvas jacket over distressed jeans and gets her feet moving. The navy espadrille shoes she's still wearing from her morning on the beach with Wren do the trick. No heels, no slick leather soles. The casual shoes skim over the sidewalk grit with ease.

Bringing a moment of panic, Elsa loses sight of Shane

and Celia with the baby. So Elsa trots a few steps, presses around a man ahead of her and spots Celia only a half block away. Close, *so* close. Her auburn hair falls over the back of her black blazer as she leans into Shane while walking.

Right away, Elsa quickens her pace toward them.

～

"You okay?" Shane asks Celia beside him on the busy sidewalk.

"Best I can be."

Shane glances to the street. The nearly bumper-to-bumper traffic is moving at a slow but steady pace. "Do you want me to hail a cab?"

"No." Celia glances up at him. "It's too hard with the stroller. This is fine."

"All right." They keep walking. Shane pushes the stroller ahead of them. "It's not too far now anyway."

Then? Nothing. They're quiet as they approach a congested intersection where traffic's stopped and people are crossing. Stepping off the curb, Shane and Celia make it across the street, too, just as the pedestrian signal changes to *Don't Walk*.

～

Elsa is losing them.

She arrives at the corner intersection just as the pedestrian signal there switches to *Don't Walk*. And it's clearly obvious why. Traffic at the intersection is congested but intently moving now. Driving straight on the cross street. Turning close in front of her onto her street. *Shit*.

5

There is no safe way for her to cross the road.

Oh, she *could* call out. Yell Celia's name over the din of the city.

And Elsa's voice would never be heard.

Instead, she keeps losing them. She leans to the side. She gets desperate, too. Especially now that she's decided—once and for all—to go after Shane and Celia. To stop them. To talk to them. To help. Her concern for Celia and Aria outweighs *any* earlier doubts about flagging them down.

That concern turns to frustration now as harried drivers rush to beat the light, to round the corner, to get to their destination. The moving line of cars pens her in.

Other pedestrians press close at the curb. Elsa wears a tan bandana-scarf around her neck. She lifts that fabric and dabs her face while watching first Celia's diminishing silhouette ahead—and that confounded pedestrian signal. All she can safely do, as Celia moves further away, is wait.

And watch. Watch Shane and Celia move from her sight. They're turning down a side street.

Still, Elsa can only wait.

Wait.

Wait.

"Come on, come *on*," she quietly urges the pedestrian light. "*Change* already."

And it does—right then.

So she steps off the curb and bumps around someone. Half trots now, too. Nothing will stop her. Her feet move of their own volition. Her eyes are riveted to only her destination. Shops and walkers and large potted shrubs and canopied storefronts and curbside delivery vans go unnoticed as she gets to that next street corner and turns, too.

There! Celia and Shane are way ahead of her now. For God's sake, she'll have to *run* to catch up.

Suddenly, though, a voice calls her name.

"*Elsa!* Over here!"

She turns to see Toby pulling up to the curb. He rolls down the passenger window and calls again. "Elsa! Hop in."

This stop-and-go, here-there, left-right as people mill around disorients her. With her hand to her heart, Elsa looks from the street to Toby leaning across his car's front seat.

"They're up ahead, Toby," she breathlessly says while veering his way. "It's no use!"

He stretches further and opens the front passenger door. "Come on. We'll get there," he insists as she scoots into the car. "Don't worry," he tells her.

Elsa looks from him to the street ahead. But she's lost Celia and Shane. There's no sign of them. Other people are on the sidewalk and blocking the way, so she's not sure if they're even close by. She also has to swat back those balloons persistently hovering over the seat.

$\sim$

"We're almost there." Shane nods to the city block. "My hotel's up ahead."

"Where?" Celia's tired voice asks.

They pass a small church; a bakery; a coffeehouse on the corner. When they cross the street, Shane is careful with the stroller. "There," he says once on the sidewalk again. He points to a black-and-white Victorian with a narrow black marquee at street level. "It almost blends in." When he glances at Celia, he's a little surprised to see the relief on her face. To see her eyes briefly close with a deep breath. The change in her is palpable.

She wants off these streets.

Off the streets and into the soft mute of quiet.

They turn into the hotel and stop at the front desk. There's no elevator in this old Victorian, so Shane inquires about leaving the stroller in the lobby for a bit. "We won't be long," he tells the clerk.

"Oh, that's fine," she answers. "No problem." She looks down at Aria in the stroller. "Hi there, sweetheart."

Shane lifts out the baby and gives her to Celia.

"Is that your daughter?" the clerk asks, looking at Shane.

"No. But this is Celia, my girlfriend. And that beautiful baby's hers."

"Aww." The clerk leans on the front counter. "How old is she?"

As Shane signs in Celia, he hears her answer.

"Just about five months now," she says, stepping closer.

The clerk reaches over and touches beneath Aria's chin. "Aren't you special? The cutest guest we have."

Celia offers a kind smile and gives the baby to Shane, then bends for the tote on the stroller. When she straightens, the lobby's gone quiet. Shane holds Aria in his arms and motions Celia to the nearby stairs. They pass beneath the crystal chandelier near the mahogany-trimmed settee with Queen Anne legs. Two gold tufted-back sitting chairs are near the staircase, too. Gold-framed modern art paintings hang on the white walls heading up the staircase.

Wordlessly, Shane and Celia climb those stairs to his room.

~

It takes a minute before Toby can pull away from the curb. Traffic is that heavy.

For that entire minute, for every single long, drawn out, sixty seconds of it, Elsa senses time getting away from her. Her patience wanes. But Toby finally gets the car moving and they search. They scan the sidewalks. The crosswalks. The storefront doorways. They look forward, back.

And—nothing.

There's no sign of Celia Gray and Shane Bradford.

So Toby drives around the block and they survey the very same street *again*—the street where Elsa last saw Celia.

Again—nothing.

So Elsa gets out while Toby waits curbside once more. She opens a few shop doors and looks inside for Shane in that twill bomber over rolled-hem olive pants and black combat boots. She looks for Celia's auburn hair falling against that black blazer she favors. Elsa looks for either of them bent somewhat as they push Aria's stroller.

It's as though they were never even here.

Defeated, Elsa finally gets back into the car.

Toby turns to her across the front seat.

And Elsa shakes her head. "We lost them."

"Why don't you just *call* Celia? They've *got* to be close by."

"No." Elsa sits back with a long breath. Buckles her seatbelt, too. "It's some deeply personal situation they're in, and I just can't broach it on a phone call. I'd imagine a call would be really intrusive to Celia—who was upset enough as it is. So," Elsa says with a sad smile, "no."

"You're sure?" Toby asks.

"I am."

"Well." Toby puts the car in gear now. "Where to?"

Elsa looks out the car's front window at the busy street with its every sign of life and motion and colors—but no sign of who she's desperate to see. "My hotel," she quietly tells Toby.

"Maybe that's where they're headed, Elsa."

Elsa knows by the direction Toby starts driving, and by where she last saw Celia and Shane, that they are not headed there. But she has no energy left to counter Toby's suggestion. To wonder aloud.

"Maybe," Elsa just says instead.

two

"IT'S HORRIBLE THE WAY THE body has a mind of its own." Celia's words are muffled as she's bent over the small sink and splashing water on her face.

"What do you mean?" Shane asks. He stands in his room's bathroom doorway and watches her. Or watches her reflection in the large, unframed mirror above the white sink. Celia's black blazer hangs on a wall hook. She cups her hands beneath that running faucet and bends her face into the cool water. All the while, Shane's holding Aria. He shifts the baby to his shoulder.

"I guess what I'm saying," Celia explains, pressing back strands of her damp hair, "is that I didn't count on the *physical* reaction I'd have walking into my mother's shop." She glances back at him now. "Into August Dove."

"So your body was telling you something?"

"Loud and clear. To get out. The situation was sucking the air right out of me." Celia grabs a white hand towel from the towel bar beside the sink. Gently, she pats her face dry. *"Oh, God. What was I ever thinking?"* she quietly asks herself.

"Doesn't matter."

"What?" Celia turns to him while dabbing that hand towel at the ends of her damp hair.

"You had to do it, Celia. You had to *put* yourself in that situation in order to know. And your body *let* you know—in no uncertain terms." With the baby against his shoulder, Shane keeps a hand on Aria's back and talks around her. "So you have some answer now."

"I do." Celia looks long at him before turning to her reflection. "Boy, I had a *stupid* fantasy stuck in my thick head." As she says it, she tugs that clip of tiny baby's-breath blossoms from her hair and tosses it in the wastebasket. "And now I made a fool of myself in front of the woman."

"Believe me, Celia. *You're* not the fool."

"I don't know." She exhales a long sigh. "All I *do* know is that I had this false hope watching you and Kyle bridge some gap this summer." She pauses while digging in her purse. "Thought in a crazy way that I could do the same with my mother. But there *was* no bridge there. Just … none."

Shane leans on the doorjamb. He feels Aria's small movements in his hold. Her head turning. Her arms reaching. "Sometimes you have to live it to know it."

Celia leans her hands on the small white sink top and looks directly at his reflection in the mirror. "Oh, I lived it, all right. And I regret that you had to see all that."

"Don't worry about it. I'm glad I was there." He shrugs. "Who knew how it would all play out?"

"You did." Celia's eyes tear up. She gives a sad smile, too, while turning to him. "You repeatedly told me to just hold on to the happiness I already had. Even this week, when we argued in my hotel room. And you were right."

"Not proud of that. Wish I *wasn't* right."

They quiet as Celia, standing on the black-and-white penny-tiled floor, combs her hair first, then bends close to her reflection and reapplies some makeup. A little blush; a dab of lip gloss. In the tiny bathroom—with its sink and mirror, white toilet and small white shower stall strung with a white shower curtain—there are only the cooing sounds of Aria and the muted movements of Celia at the sink. Now she straightens, puts on her black blazer and looks in the mirror again.

"Ach," she says.

"You look *fine*. Better now," Shane reassures her. And she does. Somewhat. But the morning's taken its toll.

Celia nods, turns and follows him out of the bathroom. Once in his tidied bedroom with a gray covering neatly tucked around the double bed and modern-looking globe lamps on the end tables and wall clothing shelves recently emptied, Celia motions to his luggage near the door. "When are you leaving here?"

"After lunch." Shane turns Aria in his arms now so that she sees her mama. "Got a two p.m. flight. Will be back in Connecticut around midnight. Then I'll crash at Stony Point for a few hours' sleep, before heading to Maine for a couple of days."

"Oh, Shane. You'll be tired. Please drive safe."

"I will. Need to catch up there. Talk to the captain." He pauses when Celia steps closer and squeezes his arm. "Stop home."

"I better get to my hotel, then. It's getting late for you."

She takes Aria from him, nuzzles the baby's face and holds her close. "Don't want you to miss your flight."

"We have a few minutes." Shane looks around the room. Glances out the large window, too. "Let's go on the back terrace here. It's really nice. And you'll get some sun."

"Okay." She shifts Aria to her shoulder. "Maybe Aria will nap in the stroller."

He's warm now, so first Shane takes off his twill bomber over his dark tee with the sleeves ripped off. That done, he collects Celia's bag and tote and opens the door. They step out into the long hallway with its white walls, and the same white globe lights hanging from the ceiling, and a line of guest rooms. With Celia waiting, Shane turns and checks that his door is locked behind them.

Elsa stands beneath the long brown canopy at her hotel's entrance. It's an elegant Victorian building restored to early-twentieth-century grandeur. Small potted trees flank either side of the wood-and-glass double doors behind her. Lace curtains fall in gentle folds in the large windows beside that doorway.

She made it.

She's back.

Beneath that canopy, she waits for Toby to lift her overnight bag from the car's trunk. The balloon bouquet she clutches bobs and bumps above her shoulder.

"You have my number, Elsa," Toby says as he sets her bag close by. "You call me if you need another ride. Or," he adds, giving her hand a clasp, "if there's *anything* else I can do."

"Thank you," Elsa merely says, all while thinking something else entirely. Thinking there's nothing Toby—nor *anyone* else—can do. Nothing.

"It was a pleasure meeting you. And I hope to visit your seaside inn one day."

"I hope so, too," Elsa answers with a small smile and a nod.

Toby backs up toward his parked car. "I'm sorry for the turn your trip took, Elsa. Sure hope it works out for everyone."

"Me, too."

That's all she says. But she stands there, still. Stands beneath that canopy for a second or two before lifting her overnight bag and walking to the lobby entrance. Before opening the stately door, she turns and waves goodbye to Toby. He's leaning against his car and waiting to see her get safely inside.

~⌒~

Shane makes two coffees at the self-serve coffee counter in the hotel lobby. He adds a drop of cream, stirs.

"Everything okay, Shane?" a woman's voice asks from behind him.

He looks over his shoulder while grabbing a few napkins.

"Your girlfriend looked upset before," the desk clerk mentions.

"She was." He lifts the two coffee cups. "Didn't have a good morning."

"Anything we can do?"

"No. But thanks for asking," he says, turning to the

lobby's rear door leading to the terrace. "Appreciate it."

Once shouldering that door open, Shane slows his step. Across the stone terrace, a teak bench is nestled against green shrubs. There are two teak chairs, too. A tall, lattice-topped wooden fence rises beyond the shrubs. The terrace itself is raised and enclosed by a low stone wall. Green ferns and leafy plants atop the wall spill over onto the stone. More leafy plants cascade down the sides of scattered clay pots. Small pine trees line one side of the terrace. A Japanese maple tree grows in a cut-out on the stone floor. The whole place offers a respite. A spot of the cool greens and gray stone of nature. Only dappled sunlight makes its way through all the leaves and branches and plants. Little noise does, too. This terrace is one of those rare places that lulls you into quiet.

It's worked on Celia, too. Shane sees her on that teak bench. The stroller is at her feet. Her face is tipped up to the canopy of green. Her eyes are closed.

But what he sees most is how tired she is. It shows. Even here, at ease finally, shadows circle her eyes. He walks over and hands her a coffee.

"This place is peaceful," Celia softly says. "I can breathe again."

"Thought you'd like it." Shane sits with her and sips his coffee.

"Aria does, too. She dozed off after just a few minutes of me wheeling the stroller back and forth."

Shane nods—but says nothing. He sits on the bench there in the lush greens of the terrace. Sits beside Celia and allows *her* this quiet, too. The graceful branches of the Japanese maple arch beside them as they murmur sparse words. Celia comments on how pretty a spot this is.

Then? Nothing as they sip their coffees.

Nothing until Shane talks. "So I guess you want to know what went down back at August Dove. After you left."

"I do," Celia barely says beside him.

"Okay." Shane leans his elbows on his knees. Looks over his shoulder at Celia, his beautiful Celia. "You just sit there, and I'm going to tell you—straight up—what happened." He sits back now and keeps his voice low so as not to wake Aria. "Some of it might surprise you. Some of it might hurt you."

Celia nods. "I'm ready," she says.

three

"I STUCK WITH THE SCRIPT, Celia," Shane begins on the terrace. His voice is steady; monotone, almost. "I acted like a customer in August Dove. A customer browsing for my girlfriend. But concerned, too, about what I'd seen between you and Heather."

Shane pauses here. Sitting on that teak bench, he takes a breath. Closes his eyes for a moment. When he does, the image of Heather's gorgeous jewelry shop comes to his mind in full color. The white wings—everywhere. Feathered wings and gossamer wings and beaded appliquéd wings. Sequined wings. Stained-glass wings.

And those sprigs of heather. Purple sprigs arranged in granite rock displays. Ribbon-wrapped heather bunches hanging from the ceiling.

It all comes back to him. The framed, poster-sized photographs mounted on one wall. Each picture depicted a rock star wearing Heather's custom jewelry. The mural of a white dove on a deep blue wall beside the door. The painted message there for patrons to *Try On Your Wings!*

Didn't Celia do just that? Didn't she *try on her wings*, so to speak? Try to fly on a current of hope straight into her mother's life?

And he mentions all this to Celia. Tells her how August Dove is a magical shop and he was taken with it. "With Heather, too," he assures her.

"As was I," Celia softly interrupts. "With the shop. With my mother building that fantastical world. But … I was taken only initially. Only until we slowly broached each *other's* worlds."

"Yeah. I watched. I saw the dance. You stepping this way. Heather, that way. The glances back and forth." He quiets his words. "In my mind, I was silently ordering you, too. To *do* it, damn it. To take control. To do yourself *proud* and let Heather *know* who you are."

"You're mad."

"What?"

"You're mad," Celia repeats.

"No … I … *Shit.* Yeah, I guess you're right."

"Are you mad at me?"

"No." He blows out a breath and keeps his voice level. "I'm mad that your mother didn't meet you halfway, Celia. Throw you a fuckin' bone, even. I'm mad that you're sitting here with a broken heart. *Again.* I'm mad that in Heather's shop? I stuck to that God damn script and said nothing."

Celia says nothing now, too. She just watches him talk.

"*Before* you came in, Heather asked if I was a tourist. And I gave her some story. Said I was from New Hampshire. Worked in a granite quarry there and was in town for a conference. *And* shopping for my girlfriend. So she seemed comfortable letting me browse. And trusted me once you'd left."

"*Trusted* you?"

Shane nods. "Here's what you didn't see, Celia. I'm being honest and laying it on the line. No embellishments. No bullshit. But no holding back, either."

"Please don't."

Shane sips his coffee before setting the cup on a small table beside their teak bench. He turns toward Celia beside him. Tucks her hair behind an ear and leaves his hand on her face for a long second. "When you rushed to get out of that jewelry boutique? Your back was turned as you headed to the door with Aria. But mine wasn't. I was at a countertop and looking at these wide gold necklaces in a gilded cage. Supposedly. But I was watching the two of you. And saw what you didn't. By the time you reached the door to leave, something clicked for Heather. She knew who you were."

Celia's eyes drop closed—but only for a few seconds. *"Go on,"* she whispers.

And Shane does. He tells Celia how Heather actually rushed to her. And how her long skirt got caught on one of the granite rocks in her shop displays. That she was *desperate* then. And she ripped that skirt just to quickly free herself and get to her daughter.

"To you," Shane says. "By the time she tore her skirt free and turned to the door, you were just going out through it. You and Aria. Heather gasped. And a second later, she *did* start to call out. What did she say? I couldn't tell. A panicked syllable or two that got choked back with

some emotion. Or iron will. Or change of heart. She just …
cut herself off and stopped in her tracks as the door closed
behind you. When I asked her if everything was okay, she
turned to me a little in shock. Which is when she told me
that you were her daughter. She was *sure* of it. The daughter
she hadn't seen in years."

When he stops for a swallow of coffee, Celia still says
nothing. Not until he sets his cup down in their shady glen
of peace on the hotel's terrace.

Two words.

That's all she manages then.

Two words.

"Keep going."

"*Ah*, Celia," Shane says. And he knows. Knows by the
way her eyes get moist that she hears it. Hears that *his* heart
broke for her then— and now—with what's to come.

With what he'll say when he … *keeps going*.

"Okay. I hurried to the window and told Heather I saw
you outside. Asked if she wanted me to flag you down.
Because I would've, beautiful Celia. I would've hauled you
back inside like I didn't know you. Would've tried." His
voice drops lower now. "She told me no, Celia. Gave no
explanation, either. No reason. I'm sorry to admit, but
Heather just said, *Let her go*. Those were her exact words."

Celia only presses a hand over her mouth and nods.

"Heather was still desperate. It was all over her face.
Some horrible doubt had her freeze for a long moment. I
didn't know if she would lock up quick, go out to the
streets, come upon you and give you a hug. Something.
Anything. So imagine my frustration—kept muted as I stuck
to script—when she looked to me and told me she was

21

sorry I had to witness all that. And for the personal intrusion in my shopping. She just … turned something off and got back to work without missing a beat. Asked how she could help me. If there was some style that my girlfriend would prefer. And that's it. Like you'd *never* stepped foot in that boutique. When I finally left, I glanced back from the sidewalk. Heather was just standing in her shop's open doorway. Standing there and looking out at the street."

"Was she maybe trying to decide, Shane? Decide what to do about it all while she had the chance? Decide to hurry outside and look for me?"

Shane says nothing at first. He just leans close, cradles Celia's face and kisses her lightly before whispering his answer. *"Inaction is a decision, too, Celia."*

four

SUDDENLY, NOTHING FEELS REAL.

When Elsa gets to her hotel room, she leans back against the closed door.

Here, no one sees her.

No one asks about her.

She's just Elsa alone, gripping those bumping balloons and fully leaning against that door as though it's holding her up.

What happened? To her day. To Celia. To their trip. Did *anything* happen? Or was it all a sleight of hand? Did her eyes deceive her? Was she mistaken about it all?

There's a Queen Anne-style writing table in her small room. So Elsa goes to it and loosely strings the balloon bouquet to the mahogany chair there. Among the round balloons are a cupcake balloon, a silver crescent moon and a heart. She remembers her words to Toby about the sweet surprise for her infant granddaughter. *A cute cupcake for my little cupcake!* Oh, if she could backpedal to that happiness.

Instead, she paces.

Paces in her olive canvas jacket over a fitted navy tee and distressed jeans. Navy espadrille beach shoes, too. An outfit from another *life*, it seems—*not* from just earlier this morning with Wren on the beach.

"Wren," Elsa whispers, then gets her cell phone from her purse and taps her friend's number.

And waits through the rings for an answer.

"Oh, Wren!" Elsa says while walking to the one window in her room. A window shade is half-drawn from beneath a fabric-covered cornice. *"Wren,"* she says, softer this time.

"Hey, Elsa! You make it back okay?" Wren asks.

"Yes. Yes, I did. Traffic was slow going, but … well … we still made good time," Elsa says—instead of saying that Celia's in some sort of trouble. Instead of saying that something's so wrong. "And your driver, Toby? He was a dream."

After Wren tells her she's so glad to hear this, she then asks about Elsa's plans with Celia for the afternoon.

"Well, I *just* got in," Elsa says—without mentioning she hasn't a clue where Celia even is. Because what can Wren do? Knowing any of this will just upset *her*, too. "And I wanted to call you first before the day gets away from me."

"Oh, Elsa. I'm *so* glad you made the trip. And now you and Celia and your beautiful granddaughter? You'll have a *beautiful* time together! Like we did yesterday—and this morning on the beach."

Standing at the window, Elsa listens to her friend's voice promising to one day come east. To visit Elsa's coastal New England inn. Wren's familiar, easy voice reaches Elsa's phone while all Elsa sees, behind her closed eyes, is Celia undone on the streets.

～

The clock's ticking.

Shane feels the pressure now. The need to hurry as they get back to Celia's hotel. Not only does he have an afternoon flight to catch, but Elsa is returning soon. They pass a pub. A bicycle shop. Finally, there's the brown canopy extending over the hotel's entrance. They stop beneath it a little breathless.

"When's Elsa due back?" Shane asks.

Celia checks her watch. "An hour or so."

"Okay. We have to be quick. I'll grab a cab back to my hotel and make it to the airport on time."

Celia nods. And fusses with her blazer. And checks Aria in the stroller.

"So this is it," Shane says, taking her hands in his. "Well, there's one more thing."

"What is it?"

He pauses. "Do you know what today is?" he finally asks, his eyes never leaving her gorgeous, sad, tired, hazel eyes.

"You mean, *besides* one of those days you talk about in lobstering? A real dirty day?"

"That's right. Besides that."

"I haven't a clue."

"Allow me to fill you in. *Happy anniversary, Celia Gray,*" he quietly says, then kisses her cheek. "We've been together two months, baby."

"Has it been two? Really?"

"Two months ago—today—in August? When Lauren invited me to her and my brother's vow renewal? I met you, Celia. For the first time. And I want you to know that every single day since? You've made better than I could *ever* have imagined."

Celia, eyes briefly closed, shakes her head.

"Hey." Shane touches her jaw. "Look at me."

She does, silently. Drags her fingers up and down his arm, too—right to his shoulder where his tee's sleeves are ripped off.

"I love you, Celia. And maybe *today* didn't go how you thought it might. But neither did *anything* two months ago when I first came back to Stony Point. Hell, I was waiting for Kyle, or Jason—*someone*—to take a potshot at me just to get me off their Stony Point turf. Still, that day I arrived? It turned out to be my biggest blessing … because it brought me you."

"I feel the same, Shane."

"Good." He tips up her chin. "So will you do something for me?"

"I will."

"Okay." Now he embraces her and talks near her ear. "Will you make sure you and Elsa have a good rest of your trip? Because let me tell you—you and Aria enrich *her* life, too."

"I'll be sure of it. For Elsa."

Shane kisses the top of Celia's head first, then bends down to the stroller and shakes Aria's little hand. The baby smiles at him. And kicks her legs.

When Shane straightens and backs up, he opens the hotel's double entrance door and watches Celia wheel Aria inside to the lobby. Letting the door close then, he turns away. Turns and looks out at the street.

～

And doesn't walk far.

Just a half block—to a transit shelter on the sidewalk. It's a pretty sparse structure, actually, with its steel framework around glass panels. Just a small space for people to wait for the bus. Or a cable car.

Shane steps beneath the wavy roof and sits himself down then.

Just sits there in his tee, olive canvas pants and black combat boots.

Sits right there curbside in the city shelter.

It's what he needs.

Shelter from what life served on a lousy platter this morning.

Shelter from Heather.

From Celia's sadness.

From what *could* be—but won't.

From remembering.

From picturing.

From fatigue, God damn it.

Sitting alone there, he raises his open hands to his face, massages his forehead, slides his hands down and presses his fingertips into his closed eyes and just sits there like that.

Leans forward then, too—his face in his open hands as he deeply inhales behind them. Inhales and sighs before getting up and hailing a passing taxi.

five

IN THE STONY POINT BEACH Association trailer, Cliff's having a working lunch today.

An early one, at that. Late Wednesday morning, he settles in at his tanker desk. His computer is on; a paper plate holds his double-decker ham-and-cheese sandwich stuffed with lettuce, tomato, mayo and mustard; a hot coffee is poured from his spiffy new coffee cart. And behind his four-panel room divider, an old Dean Martin record spins on the turntable. There's a fuzzy hiss in the song as the record-player needle traces along the vinyl album's grooves. An open sliding window near the trailer door lets in warm October air, too.

Everything's just … perfect. A hefty sandwich, a great tune and a *significant* Stony Point event about to be scheduled. To finish that task? He's emailing a group invitation to *all* the residents here. In mere moments, computers and cell phones and tablets will ding on every hill and valley of this coastal community. And inside every cottage and bungalow, out on decks and on the beach, residents will eagerly open their official invitation to the Guard Shack Color Reveal.

But first, he takes a bite of his sandwich. Next? Cliff reviews the invitation's time-and-place details. Satisfied, he hits *Send*. But when he sits back in his chair, sandwich in hand, he hears footsteps on the outside metal stairs. The trailer door swings open, too, and in walks fifteen-year-old Flynn. Tall and lanky, the kid's wearing a light sweatshirt over a baggy tee and long, loose shorts. He's also a little winded. Must've skateboarded to the trailer.

"What are you doing here?" Cliff asks, then takes another bite of his sandwich. "You're early by a couple of hours."

"Had a half-day." Flynn drags a hand through his dark, moppy hair. "Thought I'd start painting the shack. You know, get going on my community service hours."

"Good thinking." Cliff pulls in his chair and sips his coffee at his desk. "We lost a full day yesterday with the hardware store's paint-mixing machine on the fritz. But I called there and everything's up and running." He shuts down his computer and stands now. "So we're taking a field trip to pick up the shack's final paint." As he says it, Cliff stuffs the rest of his sandwich in his mouth and wipes his hands on a napkin.

"You mean, I have to go *with* you?" Flynn asks.

Cliff nods, then drops his lunch plate and napkin into the trash. "You're not staying *here* alone," he says, squeezing through the folding accordion door to the back of the trailer. "Last time that happened?" he calls to Flynn while

29

turning off his record player. "You locked innocent people in the supply shed." When Cliff returns to the office area and lifts his *Commissioner* windbreaker from the back of his desk chair, Flynn's pouring himself a cup of coffee. "Who knows what kind of pandemonium would ensue in one hour's time with you left to your own devices again." Pulling his keys from his pocket, Cliff motions Flynn and his coffee to the trailer door. "So let's go."

⌒‿

Paint, paint is everywhere.

Cans and cans of it. Cans arranged by color. By size. Quarts. Gallons. Shelves are stacked left to right, top to bottom.

Then there are the cans of wood stains. Walnuts and maples and oaks.

And the paintbrushes. Natural bristles. Nylon bristles. Narrow brushes, wide brushes. Angled. Flat.

There are pad applicators and rollers, too.

Flynn manages to stop at it all. And ask endless questions.

"Never mind that," Cliff says, prodding him along. "Our paint brushes were all bought and paid for when I picked up the primer. We're good. And we have to get a move on. The shack reveal is happening at the end of this week. Once Elsa's back from California."

"Why can't we just spray the guard shack?" Flynn asks. "It'd be a lot faster than those brushes, Commissioner."

Cliff's standing at the paint counter now. "Because if there's any wind, paint goes everywhere. It floats through the air and lands on cars. On cottages. On *people*. No, we can't take that chance. Brushes, it is." With that, he turns and places his order for the shack's highly voted, most popular, custom paint color.

"Be a few minutes," the paint clerk tells him before heading to the color-match machine.

Flynn stands beside Cliff. He leans an arm on the counter. And looks around. *"I can't believe I'm here,"* he mutters. *"Being babysat!"*

"Listen, Flynn. Why don't you go to the popcorn machine while I wait for the paint? Grab a couple of cones." As Flynn takes his attitude with him and wanders away, Cliff's cell phone rings. It's Flynn's mother calling. "Sarah?" Cliff asks into the phone.

"Oh, Cliff! I'm *so* sorry to bother you. But by *any* chance do you know where Flynn might be?"

"Flynn?" Cliff looks off in the popcorn machine direction. "Why, he's right here with me. At the hardware store picking up the guard shack paint. Getting some free popcorn as we speak."

"What?" Sarah asks.

"Yes. Your son arrived early for his community service—which I thought was very admirable of him." Cliff turns back to see the clerk prepping the color-mixing machine. "Said he had a half-day at school."

"He most certainly did *not*," Sarah insists on the phone. "He skateboarded off the school premises and cut *all* his afternoon classes."

"He *didn't*. Are you *sure*?"

"Yes! The high school called me to report his unexcused absences. Flynn's not answering his cell phone—and I've been frantic looking for him."

31

Flynn moseys back to Cliff just then and hands him a cone of fresh popcorn. As he does, Cliff harshly whispers to him, *"What gives? Your mother's on the phone looking for you. I thought you had a half-day today."*

Behind the counter, the paint clerk is entering color codes into the mixing machine.

But Cliff sees it. The clerk's also watching this customer commotion. He's looking over his shoulder from that mixing machine. Looking at moppy-haired, skater-dressed Flynn and his blasé attitude before resuming the paint-color coding.

All while Flynn gives a wry smile to a few customers waiting behind them. "I *did* have a half-day, Commissioner. Decided to leave at the halfway mark."

"But … why?" Cliff presses. "And don't be a smart aleck about it."

Flynn shrugs and tips his cone of popcorn to his mouth. "Felt like it," he says around the food.

Sarah is still at it on the phone, too. "Cliff? *Cliff?* Is Flynn right there?"

"Yes. Yes, Sarah."

"Can you put him on?"

Cliff looks over at the clerk—who's keeping a nosy eye on the drama at the paint counter. The clerk removes the first can of paint from the color-mixer and gets it going in the paint-shaker now. "Listen," Cliff tells Sarah as the can in the shaker flips and turns over and over. "My paint's about ready. I'll talk to Flynn on the way back to the guard shack and get to the bottom of this." When Sarah agrees, Cliff pockets his phone and grabs a handful of popcorn.

And sees Flynn start ambling away.

"One second, young man," Cliff calls, then tosses more popcorn in his mouth. When Flynn turns back—with an eye roll, no less—Cliff motions him to the counter. "If you think your community service is *done* this week …" Cliff quietly says around the popcorn. "You can just think again."

Meanwhile, the paint clerk watches while entering the second gallon's custom code into the color-mixer.

Which is when the questions, lies and accusations start firing. They go back and forth between Flynn—still tipping his popcorn cone to his mouth—and Cliff.

Cliff seriously tells Flynn he has to assume more responsibility in his life.

Flynn says responsibility is for adults.

The paint clerk asks if everything is okay over there.

To which Cliff nods, then discreetly suggests to Flynn that he needs to *act* more adult with his father away on such dedicated service to our great country.

To which Flynn shrugs.

So Cliff tells Flynn his mother has enough on her mind worrying about Flynn's father stationed in a foreign land.

At which point, the clerk sets the second can of custom-color paint in the shaker machine—all while keeping a watchful eye on the paint-counter argument. The clerk looks a little *worried* at the ruckus now. Especially when other folks begin offering advice to Cliff. *And* to Flynn.

From an older man: *Commissioner, maybe you could be a father figure while his dad is away.*

To which Cliff says he'd be honored. "But I'm afraid I just don't have the necessary time. That Stony Point community manages to claim every minute of it! And so any fatherly help from me might be inadequate."

A middle-aged woman is next: *But then you could ground the boy for cutting his classes.*

And Cliff: *Now, now. That's not my place.*

From Flynn: *It's all because I hate my history class. And my teacher was giving a pop quiz. Which I never studied for.*

Back to the older man: *Do you have a study group? It helps to learn if you're having fun with other students, too. I remember when I was in high school—*

Interrupted by Flynn: *How about it, Commissioner? A study group while we paint? Nick and Carol can maybe quiz me?*

Cliff again: *And when would they get the shack painted then? Now do you see how your behavior is having a detrimental effect on an important situation?*

Again the middle-aged woman—with a shake of her head: *Tsk-tsk.*

Now the paint clerk chimes in. The paint clerk who's resting an elbow on Cliff's second gallon of paint. He's drumming the fingers of his other hand on the paint counter, too.

"Paint's all ready for you, Mr. Raines." After he says it, he rings up the total on the register—right as Flynn plunks his empty paper cone on top of Cliff's head.

"What?" Cliff asks, swiping off and crumpling that cone before finishing the last of *his* popcorn. "Seventy dollars?"

"Per gallon," the clerk explains. "Prices on *everything* have gone through the roof."

Well, what can Cliff do? Nothing. So he pays for the paint.

All while the older gentleman behind him counsels Flynn to do well in school if he wants to one day afford the finer things in life.

"Finer things. Like paint?" Flynn asks as he picks up the two custom paint cans.

"Good luck," Cliff hears someone say as he and Flynn walk away.

"Wait!" the clerk calls out. Cliff turns back to see him holding a handful of paint sticks. "Stir well before painting. And have a nice day!"

When Cliff takes one of the paint cans from Flynn, Flynn pushes through the hardware store door out to the sunny day. Side by side, they cross the parking lot.

"You lost radio privilege this time," Cliff quietly tells him while opening the car trunk. "*I'm* picking the station while we paint."

"Whatever." As he says it, Flynn carefully lifts a can of paint to the trunk. He takes Cliff's paint can, too, and sets it firmly beside the first.

six

ONCE CELIA'S BACK IN HER hotel room, she's back to her old life. First she warms a bottle for Aria in the tidy kitchenette. Sitting on a wood chair at the small table, she feeds the baby, then changes her and puts her in her bassinet for a much-needed nap.

Moving, keep moving.

It's an easy way to not think.

Until she has to think about *this*.

Celia looks at a photograph on her cell phone now.

At a picture of her efficiently packed carry-on prior to this trip. Who knew filling a carry-on could be so ... complicated? But they're leaving California tonight, so she has to pack. And Shane, he knew—telling her to photograph the carry-on he packed *for* her before this trip. It would make repacking that much easier.

Yep. And there everything is in the photo. Everything she's worn the past few days. Her black blazer, rolled and tucked here. Rolled burgundy midi skirt on the bottom. Today's jeans, too. Rolled tees atop. Today's chunky loafers in plastic bags. Belt coiled and tucked in netted pocket. In the photo, it's all perfectly folded, rolled, aligned and fitted together like complicated puzzle pieces.

And it's exhausting—just realizing the packing ahead of her.

But she begins. Quietly, she goes to the small hotel closet and lifts her burgundy midi skirt. Drops it on the bed. Sits beside that skirt, too.

Just sits with fatigue.

And picks up her cell phone again to study the carry-on Shane expertly packed just last Friday. It was a rainy day when he slipped into the guest cottage for a brief visit while Elsa was out buying doughnuts for her boardwalk meeting. Celia was frazzled with her packing attempts when Shane arrived. And he took right over, neatly packing *everything* into her one carry-on.

She thinks now of how she sat and watched Shane pack. She was giddy with anticipation for this trip. Oh, on that rainy day, she had so much *hope*. It practically hummed inside of her. Hope for the impossible. Delusional hope.

But still, it was hope.

Now? Now she's just tired.

⁓

Shane toys with the dove.

The bird was no doubt hand-carved by a master silversmith.

By Heather.

Celia's mother.

Sitting in the gray, nailhead-trimmed chair in his hotel room Wednesday noontime, he glances out the window to the San Francisco streets. Streets where so much went down just this morning. A whole spectrum of emotion was laid bare on those sidewalks.

And in August Dove Jewelry Boutique.

As he looks outside, his hands toy with the sterling-silver arm cuff he bought from Heather before he left her shop. The cuff, meant for Celia, dangles from his fingers. He turns it. Spins it. Sets it on the small wooden table beside him. Looks at it.

The carved silver bird is on one end of the arm cuff. Its silver band extends from the dove's tail and wraps around in a gentle curve to a curlicue of silver at the other end. The thing is, the piece of jewelry is so Celia. Understated. Gentle.

Finally, he picks up that arm cuff and packs it in the duffel on his bed. Zips the duffel. Drops it at his door. Turns to be sure the room is in order. His bed neatly made. The two gray chairs arranged just so near the window. Clothing shelves on the wall cleared of his things. Wristwatch on. Bathroom toiletries packed. He puts on his black twill bomber jacket, too.

Good to go—and just in time.

Except right as he's half-in and half-out his hotel room door, his cell phone rings. So with his one free hand, he pulls his phone from his pocket while holding the door ajar with his foot.

"Jason," he says when he sees who's calling.

"Yeah, Shane. Checking in with you, guy. I'm outside

The Dockside about to see your brother. Thought I'd give you a quick call first. How'd everything go this morning? With Celia and her mother."

"Oh, man," Shane says, then pauses and glances inside his room from where he's standing in the propped-open doorway.

"That doesn't sound good."

"It wasn't. But listen, Barlow. It's too complicated to get into on the phone." He glances at the wristwatch on his hand holding his duffel. "And I'm outta time. My flight home's taking off in a couple of hours, and I'm actually out the door. Have a cab to the airport waiting downstairs." As he says it, Shane heads out, his room door closing behind him.

"No problem. We'll catch up later. But everyone's okay?"

"Yeah. Barely," Shane says, hurrying beneath those modern globe lights mounted from the ceiling of the long, narrow hallway. "But, listen," Shane adds, rushing down the black carpeted stairs to the hotel lobby. "Meet me for breakfast in the morning? Stop by my cottage."

"You're headed back here, then?"

"I am. My flight lands at Bradley around midnight. So I'll crash at my rented cottage for a few hours, then I'm off to Maine."

"Shit, that was a fast trip west," Jason remarks.

"Roger that. It's all a blur."

Everything is right now. The beautiful hotel lobby—a study of contrasts with its vintage Victorian furniture set against framed modern artwork; the minutes he spends checking out at the desk; his trot out the door toward his taxi waiting at the curb; the noise of the city as he veers around passersby while crossing the sidewalk; the glare of midday sunlight; the motion of tossing his duffel in the cab's backseat and climbing in behind it; and finally, the thud of closing the taxi's door.

A blur.

Even as the cab takes off for the airport.

A wavering ribbon of distorted colors, shapes and shadows flies past the car's windows as Shane just sits back and breathes.

⁓

A sound comes to Celia.

She's asleep on her hotel bed. But when she hears a muffled sound, she somewhat opens her eyes. And sees her nearly packed carry-on beside her on the bed. Aria's close by, too, asleep in her bassinet. Grogginess takes over then, and Celia's right back to sleep. It feels so good. Her breathing is deep and slow.

Until that sound comes again.

Shit, it's a knock at the door.

So she bolts up on the bed. She'd just started packing, but *had* to close her eyes and rest. Just for a minute. But when she checks her watch, it's obvious. One minute turned into fifteen. So she rushes across the room while sweeping back her hair and straightening her clothes. Is it Shane at the door? Could it be her mother?

Well, who knows?

Because when Celia pulls open the door, all she sees are balloons.

⁓

Elsa's not sure what to make of *anything* anymore.

At least, not since this morning, she's not. Not since seeing Celia so upset on the city sidewalk.

And now? To see her like *this*?

"Elsa!" Celia exclaims when Elsa moves aside the balloon bouquet.

Then? It's hugs and smiles and a few *shushes* because the baby's asleep.

But Celia looks … happy. In her stocking feet, she's dressed in the same faded jeans and mockneck top of this morning. Her turquoise pendant hangs on her neck. Gone is the distress from just a few hours past. Was it ever even there? Did Elsa misread what she saw? She carefully feels Celia out before making any decision to broach the subject.

"The balloons are for Aria," Elsa tells her now.

"Oh, she's still napping," Celia whispers. "Come on." She motions Elsa to follow. "Let's go on the balcony."

"Good. We'll tie the balloons out there. And plan our afternoon while Aria's asleep."

Celia quietly points to her dresser top. "Grab the baby monitor. I have some things in the fridge," she half whispers. "I'll bring out lunch, and then you can tell me all about your time with Wren."

The thing is? In the golden midday sunshine on the hotel balcony, it's hard for Elsa to convince herself that something bad happened to Celia this morning. The sun is warm; Celia carries out cucumber sandwiches she brought upstairs earlier from the hotel restaurant. She pours sparkling water. They split a small cup of fresh coleslaw.

And they talk.

Elsa's *problem* is this. She's carrying on a double conversation:

41

one with Celia, and one with herself—in her mind.

"When did you get back?" Celia asks when she sits at the bistro table on the balcony.

"Oh, just a little while ago," Elsa lies.

Celia's lifting a sandwich half now. "Did you have a good time with Wren?"

"Did we ever," Elsa tells her.

And you? Elsa thinks. *What about your time with Shane? Where is he now?*

"Tell me about it," Celia prompts her. "What'd you two do?"

Over their lunch, interrupted by Celia's *Mm-hmms* and *Wonderful!* and encouraging nods, Elsa shares her new memories.

"My time with Wren was beautiful."

Why was Shane here?

"We made a happiness jar on an amazing beach this morning."

What happened to you out on the streets this morning?

"And we went *horseback* riding yesterday. *On* the beach!"

Are you actually seeing him?

"And oh! The cypress tunnel we walked through! It was magical, Celia."

Did I witness a breakup earlier?

"I'd love to take you to that spot sometime. Then we walked the quaint downtown where Wren lives. Shopped in some boutiques."

How can you show no distress now? Nothing! No evidence of a clearly distraught morning. It's wiped clean. Am I going crazy?

"Oh my gosh, *Elsa!*" Celia says, setting down her last sandwich piece.

"What?" This is it, Elsa thinks. Celia's about to reveal something.

Now Celia leans close over the table. She reaches to Elsa's hair and brushes it aside. "Your ears!"

"My what?"

"You got a double!" Celia says with a laugh. "How fun!"

"Oh, those. Yes. Me and Wren both." Elsa lifts her hair to show the diamond studs in her second hole. "We wanted to be a little wild. You know, tap into our old college-days vibe." Elsa reaches into her tote on the floor. "And I got something for you, too," she's saying. When she straightens, she gives Celia her silver dream-catcher earrings with tiny silver feathers and turquoise stones dangling from the woven silver web.

"*Aww*, Elsa. You are so thoughtful." Celia stretches over and gives her a light hug. "Thank you, love."

Elsa nods and watches dear Celia across from her.

Dear, mysterious Celia.

Celia with a secret she's *not* letting on. Some sad secret. But right now, her hazel eyes sparkle as she sits with Elsa in the California sunshine. Celia easily chats and holds the dream-catcher earrings to the light. Traffic sounds rise from the San Francisco streets below. A breeze blows off the distant Bay.

And a part of Elsa's heart feels for Celia. *Something* happened today that had brought her to sad tears. Something that involved Shane Bradford. Something that maybe one day—or not—will be revealed to Elsa.

So Elsa tries to comfort Celia without letting on any of what she'd witnessed.

"I know you always say you're not much of a dreamer,

43

Celia," Elsa begins, her voice kind. "But I still want you to catch any dreams you desire. Like I did on this trip."

For a brief moment, Celia gives her a smile. A sad one, if Elsa had to say so.

And it's obvious—that smile is the *most* she'll get out of Celia that might have anything to do with the morning.

seven

JASON HAD PARKED HIS SUV at the small loading bay behind the Dockside Diner. After his phone call to Shane, he finds the key Kyle gave him to the diner's back door and goes in that way. Jerry's at the stoves when he passes the kitchen. "Kyle around?" Jason asks him.

"Out front. Good to see you, Jason."

"You, too, Jerry," Jason tosses back while headed to the front of the diner. As he nears, he hears voices. Kyle's. Lauren's. A few customers', too. They're all worked up while talking about Harvest Night and something about a blind date and fix-ups.

"Yo, Bradford," Jason says when he turns to the diner counter. That's where Kyle's huddled. He's leaning right over the counter while talking to two men and a woman eating there. Lauren has a string of orange twinkle lights draped around her shoulders while doing autumn decorating. "When you asked me to grab your delivery from the farm stand,"

Jason tells Kyle as he nears, "I thought it would be apple pies for your pastry case. Not a truckload of *pumpkins.*"

"Yeah, man." Kyle, wearing his white apron over black pants and black tee, straightens. "Did you get the hay bales, too?"

"I did. Which means I'll be vacuuming my vehicle later."

"Sorry, dude." Kyle turns right back to the counter. "But I knew you were driving by that farm stand for your White Sands shotgun job today. *Totally* saved me a trip," he says over his shoulder.

"No prob." Okay, so something's up with Kyle. He's *really* into whatever talk's going down. "What's with the pumpkins, anyway? Decorating the diner for fall?"

"Kind of. Doing another Harvest Night Saturday. Had one already last month and people *loved* it."

Jason wanders around the counter and sits at an empty stool. Which is when he sees Kyle's cell phone, along with a second phone, on that counter. And it's the phones that have Kyle and his three customers there riveted. Oh, and Lauren too, as she swings closer. While unzipping his thermal sweatshirt over a tee and brown cargo pants, Jason looks around the diner then. "You didn't get too far decorating," he says, noting the half-strung orange lights and a pile of straw scarecrows propped in the far corner.

"We're a little preoccupied, Jason," Lauren says—not even giving him a glance as she slides close a phone and looks at a photo on it. "Right, Irene?" she asks the lady beside her.

Irene nods. "And how."

"Preoccupied? With what?" Jason asks, leaning over. "Wait. Is that Shane?"

"It is." Lauren flicks to another photo for Irene, then

46

gets on a stepstool and begins stringing those orange lights between vintage buoys dangling from the ceiling. "We're trying to fix him up with someone."

The older man sitting there pulls over Lauren's phone. "This Shane looks like a nice-enough fellow, Kyle."

"He is, Smithy. That's my kid brother. Thirty-seven now," Kyle tells him while getting Jason a brownie from the pastry case.

Jason leans his elbows on the diner counter, moves aside a silver napkin dispenser and just takes in the apparent matchmaking going on.

"Shane's a hard worker, too," Kyle says while sliding over Jason's brownie plate. "A lonely lobsterman from Maine. But he's here enough to date someone."

"I might have an available neighbor," the other guy seated at the counter muses, flicking through pictures on Kyle's phone. "But if your brother's such a good guy, Kyle, why isn't he taken?"

"Eh. He practically lives on the Atlantic. Says it's tough on relationships. But you know something, Dunk? I figure, with the right woman …"

"But why would we fix up someone we know," Irene asks from her stool, "with somebody never around?"

"Oh, he's around *enough*," Lauren insists. "And the industry's changing these days. Lobstering's feeling a pinch, so who knows how long he'll even *be* out on the boats."

Kyle, arms crossed, leans back on a counter behind him. "He even mentioned leaving lobstering and farming seaweed, instead."

"Kelp farming?" Jason asks around a mouthful of fudge brownie.

47

"Yep." Kyle draws a hand down his jaw. "A few of his buddies are considering it."

Well. This is something new for Jason. The folks here are on a *mission* to hitch some female to the lonely lobsterman. Jason's seriously amused as he watches the customers show pictures on *their* phones now. Photos of neighbors. Relatives.

"Here's a picture of my niece," this Irene says. Irene wears a thin cardigan over her outfit, and her silver hair is coiffed. "She's a real sweetheart. And in graduate school now for social work, so she's busy with that. Hasn't had time for dating. Same way your brother hasn't had time." Irene slides her phone to Kyle—who scrutinizes the young niece.

Meanwhile, Dunk mentions that divorced neighbor. Smithy asks if there aren't any single *regulars* Kyle can pair up with his brother. On and on come the suggestions. Cell phones get slid this way, that way. Until a voice calls out from the kitchen.

"Kyle!" Jerry says. "Grab these plates. We got customers waiting."

"Right away," Kyle says, telling the others he'll keep them posted as he takes back his cell phone and heads to the kitchen.

"Wait up." While finishing his brownie, Jason hops off the stool and follows after Kyle. "Help me unload your haul from my truck, too."

So as soon as Kyle carries a few late-lunch dishes around the counter, and behind still-decorating Lauren, and delivers the dishes to a couple of booths, he heads out back with Jason. In the midday sunlight, they heft pumpkins from the cargo space of Jason's SUV and set the pumpkins on the concrete loading dock against the back of the diner. One by one, large pumpkins, misshapen pumpkins and perfectly round pumpkins get all lined up.

"They'll be okay out here," Kyle says as he takes a hay bale from Jason now. "Until we decide how to decorate the place for Harvest Night."

Jason lifts out a few more mini hay bales, hefting them up by the twine wrapped around them.

"Hey, Barlow," Kyle says. "Stop by Saturday night. You and Maris," he tells him as he takes the bales from Jason. "See the fruits of our labor here."

Later Wednesday afternoon, they're all clustered beside the guard shack.

The whole motley crew is there—Cliff, Nick and Flynn. Carol's off to the side planting a shrub.

But it's almost two o'clock and time to start painting.

"Let's get a move on," Cliff says, motioning them close. Until a horn beeps over at the trestle.

"I'll check it out," Nick says, jogging to the trestle from behind the privacy panels surrounding the shack.

"Make sure you get the license plate," Cliff calls after him. "You've been getting careless, Nicholas."

When Nick returns minutes later, he says it was just Barlow. "Taylor was behind him. Eva's daughter."

"So she got her driver's license, then?" Cliff asks.

Nick nods. "This week."

"I remember getting my license. What a feeling!" Cliff reminisces. "*Ah*, freedom."

Flynn swipes back a lock of dark hair. "When was that, Commissioner? A hundred years ago?"

"Watch it," Cliff warns him. "With those kinds of remarks, your parents won't let you get *your* license next year."

Carol walks over just then. She's got on a faded red sweatshirt over a black tank top, black canvas pants covered with assorted pockets and tool loops, and lace-up work boots. "So what color finally won the paint vote, Commish?" she asks.

"Well, I guess it's the moment of truth," Cliff announces to all of them. "Let's pop the lid and you'll see for yourselves. Flynn," Cliff goes on, handing Flynn a flathead screwdriver. "I'll give you the honor of opening a can and painting the first swath."

"Sweet." In his baggy tee, long shorts and loosely tied skate sneakers, Flynn kneels at one of the paint cans. It's set beside the primered shack behind those privacy panels installed days ago now. Flynn works the screwdriver's flat head beneath the paint lid. Pressing down on the screwdriver, he lifts the lid *just* a little here, and here, and here. He inches around the entire paint can this way—each time lifting the lid a bit more. Finally, that lid is loose and ready to come off. Gingerly, Flynn lifts it from the can.

To silence.

"Whoa." Nick says first.

Cliff leans closer. "This isn't right ... That's the wrong color!"

"Actually ..." Carol lifts her green-tinted circle sunglasses and squints closely at the paint. "That's not even *any* of the color contenders." She straightens and turns up her hands at Cliff.

"Well," he says, then clears his throat. "How did *this* ever happen?"

Flynn stands and nods. "I know how. It was when Cliff was at the paint counter and—"

"No!" Cliff interrupts. "It's because *your* mother called me when *we* were at the paint counter. She asked if I knew where you were because you'd *obviously* cut classes to get here early." He turns to Nick and Carol now. "Then the paint clerk got all distracted when we argued right there, at the same time Flynn's mother was upset on the phone, and Flynn was running around with … with *popcorn*!"

"Really?" Nick turns to Flynn. "You skipped school—for us?"

"I guess," Flynn tells him.

Nick grins. "Hey, you like hanging out here that much?"

"Sure beats my history class."

"All right!" Carol says, shoving Flynn's shoulder. "Chillin' with the cool kids here."

"Now don't be rewarding delinquent behavior, Carol. Flynn's truancy has cost us dearly. Because this paint is a non-returnable custom color!"

Flynn grabs a paint stick. "Maybe mix it, Commissioner. Could *our* color have settled on the bottom?"

Cliff tries. He dips that stick deep into the can. Slowly, and methodically, he twists and turns and lifts that stick. Lifts it dripping right over the full can.

To no avail. It's *so* the wrong color.

"Just buy the *right* color, boss," Nick says, squinting at the dripping paint stick. "And we can change the unveil date."

"That's a no on so many levels, Nicholas. Invitations

have already been sent out for the big reveal on Friday. And there's no money left in the budget for more paint. This," he says, motioning to the clearly wrong color paint, "was purchased with a BOG stipend. And … do you know how much money a gallon of paint costs these days?"

"Sure do," Flynn answers. "Seventy dollars—each!"

"What?" Carol asks, nearly falling back with that number.

"Well, let's calm down here," Nick says, looking from Carol to the shocking paint color. "Let's just pause. And … think."

"Hmm." Flynn bends closer to the open paint can that has them in a pickle. "Do you guys *like* the color?" he asks, looking from Cliff to Nick to Carol.

"Do you?" Carol asks, bending and giving the paint stick a stir.

"Kind of," Flynn quietly answers. He reaches for a brush then, dips it in the can, turns and sweeps a stroke of paint on the white-primered shack.

"Hey!" Cliff turns to the shack. "What are you doing?"

"Painting the first swath," Flynn huffs. "Like you said I could."

Behind those tall privacy panels, they each inch closer to the wet strip of paint on the guard shack.

"It's not what I *expected*," Carol says. From beneath long blonde bangs sweeping her eyes, she looks at the unplanned paint color. "But it *is* complementary to the area."

Nick moves beside her. "Actually, it maybe looks … rad," he says.

Carol looks from him to the shack. "Yeah."

Cliff tips his head. "I don't *hate* it."

Flynn dips the brush into the can and drags another swath

of paint on the guard shack. "I have to process this," he flatly says while doing so. Then he steps back and squints at the paint. "Yeah … *yeah*." Turning to Cliff, he asks, "Can't we just use it?"

"Use it?" Cliff shoves up the sleeve of his *Commissioner* windbreaker and checks the time, then looks at the wide streak of paint on the shack. "Problem is, that color is *not* officially sanctioned by a BOG-required vote."

"Let's just vote *again*, then," Carol suggests. "As representatives of the community. We'll make that color official ourselves!"

And heck, Cliff's run out of options, time, money and, God knows, patience—so he agrees. "All those in favor, raise your hand."

Shockingly, it's the easiest decision Cliff's *ever* come to governing this confounded community. A community all tied up in knots dithering over paint color. Because the vote is … unanimous!

No time is wasted then. Brushes are distributed. Drop cloths are spread over landscaping. Painter caps, donned.

And just like that—it happens.

Brushes are dipped; the crew bends and reaches and sweeps paint on the old shack; a quiet falls on them; the autumn air is cool; the midafternoon sun, golden.

And the guard shack? It's transformed—before their very eyes.

⌒

The hay went everywhere.

Jason stands in the driveway behind his house now. After plucking strands of straw from his SUV, he hauled his shop vac out of the garage. Now he attaches the car nozzle and plugs in the vac with an extension cord. The vacuum roars to life. Bending into his SUV, he pushes and pulls that sucking nozzle over the cargo area so every damn piece of straw and hay are removed. Little pieces of it click against the vacuum hose. Back and forth, back and forth, he pushes and pulls that nozzle to get every *bit* of straw. Dirt, too. Clumps and pieces of *that* fell from all those pumpkins. When he's done in the cargo area, he drags the droning shop vac around to the side of his SUV, opens the rear passenger doors and vacuums the floor and seats there, too. Over and over. It's surprising how much farm debris was left behind here from Kyle's Harvest Night haul.

Finally, Jason's done.

Well, almost.

Because as he straightens and shuts off the shop vac, Maris opens the deck door from the kitchen to let Maddy out. The German shepherd bounds down the stone steps to Jason in the driveway.

"Hey! Come here, girl," he tells her. After checking the deck to be sure Maris went back inside, he switches on the shop vac again. When he does, Maddy drops low on her front legs and barks—just once—at the *whooshing* machine. The dog's tail's wagging; she happily whines.

So Jason does it. With the vacuum roaring, he moves it closer to Maddy.

Starts vacuuming the dog, too, like he did at Ted's cottage this summer. He gently drags the nozzle across her back. Her shoulders. Down her flanks.

And she loves it. She lies down and he vacuums her throat, her chest. She motions her paws at him. Half sits up

54

when he does her back again. He changes the nozzle to a brush attachment this time. The brush fluffs up her thick coat of fur as the vacuum sucks at it. For crying out loud, the dog looks like she just had a wash and rinse at the groomer's. The dry fur of her undercoat is sucked right off.

When he's done, Jason gives her a good shoulder rubbing. "Don't tell Maris now. *That's* your brushing for today." He bends to Maddy and fluffs the scruff of her neck as she tries to lick his face. "Get you ready for those Christmas cards," he says, scratching her ears then. "Just like Maris wants."

eight

As DIFFICULT AS THE DAY'S been, Celia has one promise to keep.

A promise to Shane.

She still hears the words he whispered close outside her hotel. *Will you make sure you and Elsa have a good rest of your trip? Because let me tell you—you and Aria enrich her life, too.*

Celia's going to keep that promise—now that she's finished packing. Their flight leaves tonight, just after ten. So over lunch on the balcony, with those balloons bobbing, she and Elsa made special plans for this final afternoon in San Francisco. And they agreed to pack *first* so that nothing would be on their minds during their last excursion here.

They could just be in the moment.

"Oh, I'm stuck in a moment, all right," Celia whispers while finishing up with her carry-on. *"A moment in August Dove."*

Before meeting up with Elsa, though, Celia does one more thing. She empties Shane's sea glass pieces from her

56

blazer pocket into her open hand. The glass clinks together; each piece is salt-coated. Bringing them to her face and closing her eyes, she can almost smell the sea. Feel it. She strokes a dulled glass piece to her cheek. To Aria's sweet face, too. The baby, in her bassinet, smiles and pedals her hands and feet.

But Celia feels some sadness, then.

Because with Elsa's unexpected early return, and with their lunch together before packing up *everything* in her hotel room, Celia's been too busy to even think.

Now, though? As she tucks the sea glass pieces into her carry-on, closes the luggage and sets it near the door, those thoughts catch up to her.

Especially with the packing done, with the baby changed and rested, and with a few spare minutes to herself in the straightened-up hotel room. So she walks to the large window near her bed, lifts the blinds all the way up and looks outside.

But she doesn't see the street below.

No. Celia sees instead August Dove Jewelry Boutique.

Sees feathered and gossamer and painted wings.

And bunches of pale purple heather. Sprigs of heather tucked among granite stones.

And jewelry. Gorgeous, custom jewelry pieces.

And she sees her mother. Her blonde hair in a loose chignon. Wide silver hoops on her ears.

Looking outside now, something else hits Celia—full force.

It's all those *what-ifs* that the day's busyness kept at bay.

In this still, quiet moment, here they come.

What if she didn't sit on Shane's terrace this morning?

57

What if she'd instead summoned the nerve, the emotion, and just … tried?

One more time.

What if she and Shane went back to August Dove? If they got there *quick*.

Oh, Celia's thoughts swirl with possibilities as she leans against the window frame and gazes outside.

What if the shop was closed when they arrived again? All the lights were switched off. The door locked tight. That would mean something, right? Maybe that her mother was upset.

What if they waited a little while? Then knocked on the locked door. Cupped their hands to their eyes and leaned close to the glass window. Peered inside. Saw the white-dove mural on the blue wall beside the door. Saw the heather bunches hanging from the ceiling. Saw the gilded birdcages. The framed musician portraits. Maybe her mother would be somewhere in the back of the shop—but would open the door. Just for them.

Oh, the relief that might flood them.

Or what if Celia went back to the jewelry boutique *alone*? If Aria stayed with Shane at his hotel. And it was just Celia and Heather in the shop—a mother and child reunion. If she had ten minutes alone with her mother, what would she say to her? Celia's questions are so vast and many, it's hard to know. Which would have been given voice?

But what if she went back to August Dove and her mother was simply going about her routine as if nothing had happened? And her expression dropped when Celia walked in again. What then?

Celia takes a long breath. *Is* her mother upset now? Or

is she glad Celia left her shop? Or does she wish, pray, *hope* that Celia will come back? Does Heather step out onto the busy sidewalk and try to spot her daughter?

Alas, Celia thinks as she shifts at the window. *I'll never know.*

~

Elsa packs her San Francisco souvenirs into one bag. A turquoise ring; a couple of fashion scarves. She tucks the bag into her carry-on and turns. Her scarf-blanket—just like the one she'd given to Celia—is on her dresser. So she lifts the scarf's frayed edge and, yes, she wipes away a tear. Because she'd hoped, really hoped, that when Celia opened her door before lunch? Elsa hoped she'd hear her story. She even hoped Shane would have been in Celia's room.

Elsa would've simply welcomed the truth.

Now Elsa does something else. She doubts herself while making sure her own room is in order. Oh, she can't stop those doubts—the way they just roll one after the other through her mind.

Why didn't she get out of Toby's car quicker?

Bolt out of it and immediately call out to Celia and Shane.

Why didn't she run to them? Call out as her espadrilles skimmed the sidewalk.

Why didn't she demand answers, even?

So what if Celia and Shane would be as shocked as she was?

So what?

They'd all go back to the hotel, tie the balloons on the

balcony, sit there together and tell the story.

But as Elsa checks her closet, she thinks that maybe a part of her doesn't want to *know* that story. Because when life finally—*finally*—settled down … when it got good, even? Well, knowing Celia's story would surely change it again.

But what about dear Celia's tears—oh, those distraught tears—that Elsa silently witnessed on the San Francisco street? What about Celia's pain? *Should* Elsa have confronted her then?

Opening a dresser drawer now, Elsa checks to be sure she'd emptied everything. She also wonders if she should have confronted Celia over lunch on the balcony. With those balloons bouncing and bobbing in the gentle breeze. It was just the two of them. Celia could feel comfortable talking. Could have a heart-to-heart with Elsa. Elsa would listen, and nod, and squeeze Celia's hand.

But at that lunch, Elsa didn't see a single hint, clue, slipped word or *any* sign at all of Celia's emotional morning.

Nothing.

Nor did she see any sign of Celia *wanting* to share her story.

Which is unsettling to Elsa.

Did she make the right decision—over and over again? On the city streets, on the hotel balcony?

In the bathroom, Elsa pours herself a cup of cold water. Sipping it, she thinks her reflection in the mirror looks pale. And it's no wonder, with all her worrying.

Well, she'll just get on with things then. She didn't flag down Celia and Shane on the street. Didn't mention anything to Celia at lunch.

So now, here in her hotel room, Elsa can only pack.

Standing at her open carry-on, she tucks in the beach espadrilles from Wren. What a magical time she had walking along the edge of the Pacific Ocean with her friend. Elsa turns now and rolls up the psychedelic tapestry she bought with Celia on their hippie-van tour Monday. The blues and greens of the tapestry evoke the sea, the beautiful sea that Elsa loves. The sea back home. The sea here. She folds that rolled tapestry into her tote now.

Beauty. Magic. Nostalgia. She had it all here.

But since this morning? Everything just feels wrong.

When the plane reaches cruising altitude, Shane gives in to his fatigue. Sitting in his window seat, he rests his head and closes his eyes. A few hours' sleep will do him damn good. Everything seems, feels, looks better—rested.

Problem is, as soon as his eyes close, his mind goes into out-of-control overdrive.

Every possible scenario that he *could* have done in August Dove today plays out.

Hell, *this* could've happened. It really could have—and the scene unfurls in his thoughts.

After Celia and Aria leave the shop, Shane confronts Heather. He admits who he is and explains what a beautiful person Celia is. He stands there and quietly talks with Celia's mother. Tells her that he's in love with her daughter. Her *daughter*. And that his heart's broken with this hole in Celia's life. Maybe in Heather's life, too.

Or is there no hole? he asks Heather.

Asks only in his mind.

Wouldn't he like to know the answer to that question.

Or ... *this* could've happened.

After dropping off Celia and Aria at their hotel, he returns to August Dove. Alone. Admits his relationship with Celia. He leaves his name and phone number. Asks Heather to please get in touch once she processes the day.

Or hell, *this* could've happened. This is the one that's hard to think about now because he *thought* about it in August Dove. It was a close possibility—but he didn't do it. What if he did, though? What if he went off-script? Took the script Celia requested and tossed it. Threw it aside. Dumped it on the streets of San Francisco, wrote his own God damn script—and then this happened.

Celia wheels the stroller through August Dove. She looks striking in her black blazer, black mockneck and faded jeans. Her auburn hair is swept off her face. And when Heather is taken with little Aria, and Celia is explaining the baby's name, Shane walks over. Stands beside Celia and slips his arm around her waist. Tells Heather she might like to know *this* beautiful woman, too. This Celia Gray.

Off-script.

It would've saved Celia. Aria wouldn't have dropped her fuzzy lion rattle. Celia wouldn't have bent to pick it up and lost her footing, her balance and her nerve all at once. She might've gotten annoyed with Shane, but hell, he'd smooth it over later.

And the decades-old ice would've been broken. Talk between Celia and Heather would've taken off in a different direction.

Things would not have fallen apart. He'd have seen to it.

Celia would not have come undone. Shane can *just* picture it. She'd have smiled her gorgeous smile; hugs and affection would've gone down; the day would've spun differently.

Shane opens his eyes now. Shifting in his airplane seat, he turns and looks out the window to the vast sky beyond.

nine

THEY'RE HIGH ABOVE THE BAY.

Below, the water is blue. A cool breeze blows off of it, too. Celia and Elsa both tied back their hair. Against that wind, Celia's black blazer is buttoned; Elsa's olive canvas jacket is half-zipped. And in her stroller, Aria wears a button-up tan corduroy jacket and her wide leopard-print headband with its loopy bow.

Best of all? Beneath the afternoon sunlight, they're walking in a place Celia never dreamt she'd ever walk. Ever.

They walk across the Golden Gate Bridge.

What's surprising is that Celia imagined idle chat would fill their walk. That there would be mention of the things Wren and Elsa did together. And more talk of their *own* San Francisco adventures earlier this week.

But mostly, they don't chat. Because it's especially noisy on the bridge—what with the wind and passing traffic. Their quietness doesn't seem to matter, though. For either of them. Maybe they needed this type of California afternoon. Needed these hours to just remember the past few days. To soak in thoughts of them.

This is the place to do it. San Francisco Bay is an estuary, just like Long Island Sound back home. And today, Celia feels it, smells it—that salty sense of the sea. The Pacific Ocean is so near, there's no mistaking it. If she closes her eyes, the wind off the Bay feels reminiscent of the winds on the sea. Winds that Shane's told her about—Atlantic Ocean winds kicking up waves, tossing the lobster boats.

So this is it. Their last hours in California. She and Elsa walk. Celia pushes Aria's stroller. The salty breeze touches their faces. The bridge's orange towers slice high into the blue sky above. Angel Island is ahead. Its gentle green curves rising from the Bay's blue waters evoke a sense of peace for Celia.

Peace.

That thought, along with the sights of beauty from the bridge? All of it has Celia deeply inhale. Soak in that sweet, fleeting peace, *peace*. Oh, it's what she had prior to this trip—and what she's trying to recover after her walk into August Dove this morning.

Elsa's voice comes to her now as they stroll. She mentions more of her horseback ride with Wren, and how the horses walked right *in* the sea. Nodding their heads, those horses splashed through the shallows while the wind lifted their long manes. And the wonder of it all, feeling the horse move beneath her while the sea sprayed up at her, gave Elsa a sense of the wild.

"It sometimes felt like a simple miracle," she muses, tucking back an escaped wisp of her hair. "Like I was walking on water."

Celia mentions another horse that stole her and Aria's hearts—a carousel horse. How the two of them spent a lazy afternoon in Golden Gate Park. "Wouldn't it be nice," she asks, "to bottle peaceful days like that?"

And when Elsa agrees, Celia sees it. Sees the pockets of peace Elsa *herself* holds on to before returning to Stony Point. She clutches them like a special pendant, or a wildflower bouquet that one might clasp near. Might close their eyes and dip their face to.

They keep moving. The stroller's tires turn on the gritty walkway. Other people pass close. To their left, cars drive by; their tires rhythmically *thunk-thunk* over the bridge's expansion joints. And to their right, beyond the orange railing, vast waters of the Bay shimmer in those wavering shades of blue.

Celia points to the sunlight glimmering atop the water. "Bay stars?" she asks, to which Elsa only nods.

But it's at the bridge's far end where they stop and snap a few pictures. Elsa takes one of Celia holding Aria close. In the photo, the Golden Gate Bridge vista rises behind them on this beautiful autumn afternoon. The slightest mist paints the air with a whisper of a haze. Elsa holds the baby then, and presses her face to Aria's as Celia snaps *their* picture. Once Celia settles Aria back in her stroller, they start the return walk across the stunning bridge. Elsa suddenly stops, though. She pauses right there and gives Celia's hand a squeeze.

"Today?" Elsa begins, nodding to the misty panorama. "It feels like all that salt air rolling off the water? *It* cures what ails you, too—just like at home."

Celia looks long at her, a little puzzled at what prompted

the remark. But she follows Elsa's gaze as she nods to the view. The bridge's cables and two towers frame the massive structure. To either side, the Bay water ripples. A froth of gently breaking waves washes onto the rocky shore below. And that thin, salty mist hovers.

Cures what ails you.

Celia looks with a small smile. But she's not too sure about those words here. Doesn't *really* feel them. Because atop the bridge, she's feeling something else.

Feels not Long Island Sound's scant breeze, but rather the Bay wind.

Hears it as it skims her tipped-up face.

Today, that wind—more than anything—whispers sadness for her.

Sadness as Celia closes the door on the morning. As she *accepts* those few hours of sadness. Then, as the wind cries all around her, she lets go of *that* feeling, too. Let's the wind steal her sadness right from her heart and scatter it somewhere far out over the distant Pacific Ocean.

ten

CLIFF STOPPED SHAVING ON WEDNESDAYS.

This Wednesday included. He quit with the razor to get a scruffy vibe for his line dancing class. All the students are *that* into it. The women in frayed shorts and cowboy boots. The men in their Western-style shirts and brimmed cowboy hats.

"You got this," their instructor Nash yells that evening. He also throws up his hands and steps back as the group of dancers takes over. A rollicking tune blasts through the community center. Sneakered and booted feet shuffle and stomp on the gleaming hardwood floors. Hands clap and bodies pivot at exactly the right count.

All in unison.

That's how good they've gotten.

Almost as a formality, Nash gets back in. "Now *kick* it … two, three, four," he calls out.

And Cliff does. Jaunty heel then toe, heel, toe, *five, six, seven, eight.*

The difference between tonight's class and the first class is that all the steps come naturally now. Naturally enough for Cliff to talk some to Paisley dancing beside him.

"Now tell me," she says, swaying left, *two, three, four.* "What the heck paint color won the guard shack vote? Inquiring minds *must* know."

Cliff laughs while keeping up with her sway, but doesn't give. "Loose lips sink ships," he tells Paisley. "But—what I can tell you is this," he says, now swaying right, *five, six, seven, eight.* "The final color certainly isn't what *any* of us thought it'd be."

And as Cliff takes his cue from Nash and walks it—*with attitude*—he does something else, too. He realizes that life is *never* what any of us think. Because isn't that *his* life, lately? Not what he'd ever think. Who knew he'd have had the *briefest* liaison with this pretty Paisley during the past few weeks? A liaison now over.

"And, pivot!" Nash yells—and claps—over the music.

Cliff pivots. Yes, who knew he'd go from that situation—to now. To looking after delinquent Flynn. To picking up Elsa—of newfound heart-emoji fame—from the airport tomorrow. To—*what?*

He was so busy charting his life just now, he almost missed Nash's announcement of a dance recital.

"We'll be performing the numbers you've all been practicing. And *keep* practicing, too. Not just the steps, but the swagger and fun imbued *in* those steps," Nash reminds them. "I'd also like to assign some students a solo dance— but can only choose the best."

This is where Cliff fades.

Until.

Until the day turns into a, well … a *humdinger*.

Especially when *his* name is called for the few solo dances.

"Yes. Cliff Raines," Nash says, motioning him to the front of the room with the other two solo students.

Well. Will wonders never cease. Even better? Cliff has to choose his solo number from a brief list—right now. And when he sees that list, he doesn't hesitate. The song he chooses is—perfect.

"Now," Nash says, "for these last few classes, we'll all learn simple steps for each solo number. And for the recital, I'll choose *two* backup dancers to accompany each soloist onstage," he tells the class. "Let's begin. We'll start with Cliff's number."

A moment later, the *club* version begins of an old standard Dean Martin's sung on Cliff's turntable.

Here it is, a line-dancing version.

The snappy, rhythmic drums.

The jangling piano tune.

The vocalist singing, "Hey, mam-bo!"

Nash guiding their footwork, "To the right. One-two-three … *point*. Five-six-seven … *point*."

Oh, yes, Cliff thinks again, five-six-seven … kick. *This is my life lately. Never—ever—what I think it'll be.*

⁓

That evening, Jason sits on the sofa in his shadowed living room. His forearm crutches lean against the nearby club chair. A cluster of candles flickers in the stone fireplace. The wide candles, some tall and some short, are set right on the grate. Burning flames cast a wavering glow on the room.

This is just where he wants to be. After he vacuumed the dog, he'd come inside, took off his prosthesis and changed into this faded concert tee and pair of sweatpants. The pants' left leg had been altered short by Maris. So everything fits—and feels—just right at the end of the day.

Especially now, after dinner. And with a bottle of Chianti on the coffee table.

Even better? Maris walks in just then. She's got on a soft beige sweater over cropped jeans. Her stocking feet pad over the hardwood floor. She also holds two goblets in one hand, a plate of brownies in the other.

"The glasses are chilled," she says while setting them on the coffee table. "For the wine."

"Okay, good." Jason leans forward, picks up the bottle and gives it a slight swirl.

"And I have to talk to Kyle about not loading you up with goodies again," Maris goes on.

"So you're not having any?"

Maris lightly swats him. "That's the problem. I'm going right down the rabbit hole *with* you," she says, setting down Kyle's fudge brownies and sitting beside Jason on the couch.

"Say when," Jason tells her as she lifts her chilled goblet to the tipped Chianti bottle he holds.

"When," she whispers when the glass is half-filled. She takes a sip, too. *"Mmm.* Nice." Sitting back on the couch then, she lifts her stocking feet to the table.

And it *is* nice, Jason thinks.

All of it. The candlelit living room; the evening relaxing;

71

the wine; the jukebox in the alcove playing a quiet, bluesy number; Maris beside him.

Just stop everything, right here. That's the order he'd give to the powers that be if he could. Stop it all. For a little while, just let the world spin without them. For an hour or two, anyway.

It feels like maybe someone does freeze time. Like someone heard his plea. Because no intrusions come into the room. Into his sanctuary. No cell phones ring; no text messages ding. He and Maris just sit there and sip wine and nibble brownies and talk. About the day. About Maris' writing. About everything and about nothing. As Jason settles back on the couch and bites into one of Kyle's fudge brownies, he hears Maris' voice beside him.

"Did you brush Maddy today?" she's asking, then sipping her wine before curling her feet beneath her. She faces him now.

Jason nods while chewing. "Brush, vacuum. Same thing."

"What?"

"After I vacuumed all Kyle's pumpkin debris from my SUV, I vacuumed the dog."

"You *vacuumed* Maddy?"

"I did. Used to do that at Ted's, too. He had some canister vacuum, and Maddy would always be at my heels for a sweep." Jason reaches to the coffee table for his wine goblet. "So I gave her a vacuum-and-brushing combo today. With my shop vac."

"Jason!"

"No, wait." He sips his wine, sets his glass down and sits back again. "I was very gentle and used the brush attachment. She's looking pretty glossy, no?" he asks, nodding to the dog on her big bed-cushion beside his club chair. "And when's this Christmas card photo shoot happening?"

Maris drags her fingers through his hair. Kisses his cheek, too. "Soon. So don't slack on Maddy's grooming— or your own."

"Yeah, yeah," Jason says. "Listen, I told Shane about your Christmas card plan before he left for California. He couldn't *believe* you're thinking Christmas in October."

"That's because he doesn't have a holiday card that needs him to plan a wardrobe, stage a space, gauge the right lighting, decorate, primp. You know. He'll see—*if* he ever gets himself married."

"Ha! That might be happening sooner than anyone thinks, sweetheart."

"What?" Maris sits up straight. "Wait. Is there a California proposal I don't know about?"

"Hardly. But when I delivered Kyle's pumpkins to the diner today? He and Lauren were on a *mission* to fix up Shane."

"No!"

"Oh, yeah. The two of them were in a huddle at the counter. Even Kyle's regulars were in on it. And I mean, *into* it. Showing pictures of ladies they know, talking personalities."

"What about Celia?"

"Listen to this," Jason lets on while biting into his brownie. "She was a contender on their list—until Lauren discounted the possibility."

"Jason! Shane will *kill* them if they go through with this."

"Which is why I'm not even going to warn him. What a hoot that'll be."

In the softly lit living room, with a gentle October breeze lifting the curtains, Maris sits back beside Jason. She lifts her stocking feet to the table again, cups her wine goblet and leans close.

"Have you even *heard* from Shane? I'm dying to know how things went with Celia meeting her mother out there."

"I called him earlier," Jason tells Maris, then reaches an arm around her shoulders and pulls her closer. "And it didn't sound too good."

"Really? What happened?"

"Don't know. When I called, he was just catching a taxi to the airport and couldn't talk. Got the feeling there's a helluva story there."

"I hope Celia's okay." As Maris quietly says it, she reaches to Jason's hand on her shoulder and entwines her fingers in his.

"Me, too."

"I'd *thought* it would all go well—knowing Celia—and started a little project for her. On one of the denim jackets I made a few years back when I was designing. You know, just to show my support for Celia reaching out to her mother."

"Is that what I saw you stitching up in the barn loft?"

Maris just nods.

"Well, I'm having breakfast at Shane's cottage in the morning."

"Here? At Stony Point?"

"Yeah. Said he'll catch me up on San Fran then. Guess he's headed to Maine for a few days afterward."

Maris nods again. They talk some about Heather Gray and her status as a celebrity jeweler. The musicians she's worked with. What her life must be like.

But they eventually quiet in the dim room. The jukebox stopped; the couch is comfortable; their wineglasses, nearly empty. Maris reaches for the remote on the coffee table and turns on the TV.

And as she flips a few channels—no doubt distracted with concern for Celia—Jason leans over and kisses the top of Maris' head, his fingers touching strands of her silky brown hair as he does.

eleven

THURSDAY MORNING, THE GODS MUST'VE gotten Jason's life spinning with the rest of the world again. His quiet evening with Maris is behind him. Gone.

Now? He's at the kitchen island while packing his work things, answering two contractor emails, back and forth feeding the dog, then looking at the planner app on his phone. After breakfast at Shane's, most of his day will be spent filming for *Castaway Cottage*. Then it's back to his barn studio for print-drawing for his latest reno here.

He looks up when Maris walks into the room. Her hair is in a low chignon. Thin gold hoops hang from her ears. She wears a cropped camel tweed jacket over a navy shell, ripped jeans and leather mules. Gold chains loop around her neck.

Sleek. She's sleek and beautiful.

So Jason gives a low wolf whistle.

"Jason!"

"All dressed up with nowhere to go?" he asks.

"I have somewhere to go. *Work*, Jason. Doesn't matter if people are around. I put myself together for *myself*, every day." As she says it, she grabs a plate and slices a cranberry English muffin in half. "If I were to write unshowered and in my sweats," she goes on while pouring herself a glass of orange juice, "the book would be as much of a mess as I'd be." Orange juice carton back in fridge, butter pulled out. "Because it makes a world of difference getting dressed—even just for yourself," she says while lifting her OJ glass. "When I feel good, look good … Then, you know what?" Okay, long sip of juice swallowed. "I write good."

"You mean well."

"What?"

"You write *well*," Jason repeats. "Good is an adjective. Well is an adverb."

"Ooh, Jason Barlow!" She flicks his shoulder before turning to the counter for a banana now.

"That's all right. You just put that Fenwick editor of yours to work." Standing there at the island, Jason takes in all of Maris. Okay, he's maybe smiling a little, too, at her grammar huff and dressing rant. Which she's not done with—evidenced by the quick breath she takes while squinting over at him.

"Speaking of getting all dressed up, Mr. Yalie?" she goes on, eyebrow raised.

"What?" He looks down at his navy hoodie over beat-up blue jeans and dusty work boots—then back at Maris. "I'm just having breakfast with Shane."

"No, no, no. You're *filming* at Mitch's today, too. And that is *not* a filming outfit," she insists, then sets aside the banana she was about to slice. "I mean," she continues while approaching him, her leather mules scuffing across the kitchen floor, "you're going to be filmed for *TV*, Jason." A pause as she hikes up a shoulder of his sweatshirt. "In a hoodie?"

He turns up his hands. "I have to get down and dirty on a demo segment. Couldn't wear my good threads."

"But this look doesn't exactly say serious *architect*." Maris bends to cuff his jeans, then straightens and brushes her fingers across his unkempt hair. "Wait." She backs up a step. "Just wait a second."

So he does. And his life is spinning with the planet again, that's for sure—between answering a work text message now, pocketing his phone, checking his watch, then letting the whining dog outside. "You can come with me for breakfast, Maddy. Then right back home," he tells her.

When he turns around, Maris is a blur rushing back into the kitchen. She's holding his heathered-brown blazer and reaching behind him. "Come on," she says, nudging an arm.

So he holds out one arm, then the other as she slips on that fall blazer—one sleeve at a time—over his navy hoodie. "Once a fashion designer, always a fashion designer," Jason says, turning to her and tugging down the blazer sleeves.

"That's right." Maris adjusts the blazer's shoulders and lifts out the sweatshirt hood. She presses it flat on his back, then brushes off his lapels before looking at him and nodding. "You can take that blazer off later—when you get down and dirty."

Jason pulls her close and kisses her goodbye. "We can get down and dirty, too," he says into the kiss, then hefts up his work duffel and heads out the slider. "Later tonight, sweetheart," he calls back while crossing the deck.

～

"You look like shit, man," Jason says ten minutes later when climbing the seven olive-painted steps to Shane's open-air back porch. Maddy rushes past him and nearly swipes a tall, tarnished-bronze candle-lantern on the side of the top stair.

"Yep." Shane jumps off the half-wall where he'd been sitting with a coffee. He's got on a long-sleeve thermal tee over black jeans and hiking boots. His face is unshaven; shadows darken his eyes. "Feel like shit, too."

"What's going on?"

Shane gives Maddy's shoulder a rub, then opens the squeaking screen door and motions Jason inside. "We'll talk over a bagel. I'll tell you all about how things went belly-up out west."

For the next few minutes, though, they're back and forth to the porch—bringing out flatware, napkins, juice, a plate of fresh Granny Smith apple slices and a bottle of honey. Shane grabs a box of dog biscuits he has on hand to stock his tool belt.

"For when Maddy keeps me company working on your stairs," he explains.

They set everything on the faded white table out there. Dried beach grasses sweep from a rusted milk can nearby. Jason brings out a saucer of water for the dog.

Back inside, Shane tells Jason to grab some dishes. "In that cupboard, there."

Jason turns to a tall, aqua-painted cupboard. Behind the sticking door is a hodgepodge of chipped and faded dinnerware. He delivers two dingy white plates to the counter where Shane's set the cream cheese.

"Listen. I need a distraction before I get into the California shit or I won't have an appetite," Shane's saying while getting a bag of frozen bagels from the freezer. "So fill me in on the doings here that I missed." At the counter, he pulls out a couple of bagels, thaws them in the microwave, then separates them with a butter knife.

Jason sits at an old kitchen table. "Oh, man. One thing and one thing *only* has been going on here. The guard-shack painting. Hell, there's been lots of whispering and paint-rolling behind those privacy panels. But that's all I know. The unveil's tomorrow."

"Really?"

"Yeah. Late afternoon. I guess Cliff's making a big to-do out of it."

Shane moves the toaster closer on the counter. "Maybe I'll make it back from Maine in time. And what about you, Barlow?" he asks over his shoulder. "What are you up to today?"

"Mostly filming at Fenwick's. Doing a little deck work first, then some demo moving around walls for Mitch's new office. I'm headed there straight from here."

"That's decent. Job shaping up?"

"Yeah, it's coming along. And hey, Trent loved that abandoned mansion clip we did in your neck of the woods up north. He's been after me for more segments like that—with you in the clips, too. Says it's a nice angle for the show. You know, exploring actual castaway places in New England."

"No shit."

"Yeah, so I thought I could really expand on the idea of architecture collaborating with time. You know, how a building evolves over the years. Sometimes into ruins—no matter how solid the blueprints."

"So now I'm the man of the hour," Shane remarks, dropping two bagel halves into the toaster. "Got to finish your stairs. Then Trent wants me." Shane presses down the toaster lever, but the bagels pop right back up. "Captain's after me to finish the local season with the boys. Federal fishing's on tap, too." Again, Shane presses down the toaster lever—to no avail. "So I'll keep your *Castaway* offer in mind, guy," he tosses back from the counter.

"You know where to find me." Jason watches him struggle with the toaster. Shane lifts out the bagel halves and swaps the slots he drops them into again. When he presses down the toaster lever *this* time? It's with agitation. His fingers repeatedly slam that lever down as it repeatedly pops up the unheated bagel halves.

"Damn toaster's just about busted. Piece of crap in these rental cottages. Pay good money for shit," he says, jamming down the lever *again* and slapping the cold toaster when the bagel halves pop back up.

"Helps if you plug it in," Jason informs him from the table.

"Shit." Shane takes a breath and jams the plug into the outlet.

"I get it," Jason says. "One of those days, man."

"Nah. One of those *weeks*, months." Shane then mentions he's leaving for Maine after breakfast. "I'm still tired," he says as the bagels toast now. "Felt like me and

Celia both hit a brick wall in San Francisco—after all that friggin' buildup to reconnect with her mother."

Once the bagel halves are toasted, they bring their plates and cream cheese out onto the back porch and sit at the old table. They pull in their mismatched chairs. Maddy settles with a few biscuits at the top of the seven porch steps. The salt air lifts off Long Island Sound. All as there's a flurry of clicking knives and slathering cream cheese. Shane layers the thin green apple slices atop the cream cheese on his bagel, then squeezes the honey bottle over it for a generous drizzle. "Try some," he says, nudging the apple plate Jason's way.

So Jason does, topping his thick layer of cream cheese with a few apple wedges and sweetening it all with a dash of honey. And for a minute or two, there's only them digging in and eating. Sipping orange juice. Eating more before Shane begins his story.

"What a mess it turned into," he says around a mouthful of bagel. "I needed more than a dustpan to clean it up, too."

Jason takes a double bite of his toasted bagel as Shane talks. As Shane tells him that initially, everything went to plan. *He* walked into August Dove first. Celia, a little later. Heather was there, working. All was good. No surprises.

"And hell, what a shop. Wings everywhere, Barlow. Feathered wings and gossamer. Painted and beaded. Hanging from the ceiling. Tucked into gilded birdcages. All among these incredible jewelry designs. Then there were the heather bunches set in granite stone arrangements. Nice stuff."

"Sounds impressive."

"It was. So Heather and I innocuously talked before Celia

arrived. Heather said all the wings are a way of tapping into the white dove of peace. It all goes back to Woodstock, man. From when her parents actually brought her to that festival when she was just a kid. It's undeniable, the influence."

"That shop must be something to see."

"Definitely. Problem is, once Celia walked in, nothing peaceful—like the bird of peace would suggest— happened. Nothing magical—like the enchanted décor of Heather's shop—happened. There was no *wonder* like the gilded cages strung with necklaces and bracelets. Or like the bunches of purple heather tucked into granite displays. Or like the framed photos of rock stars onstage wearing her custom jewelry." Shane sits back in his chair and sets down his bagel piece. Looks out at Long Island Sound as the morning sun's rising over it, then looks to Jason across the table. "Nothing uplifting happened. Nothing hopeful happened," Shane's level voice says. "Nothing at all."

Shane sees it on Jason. Sees it when Jason turns up his hands and sits back in his chair. Sees the same frustration Shane felt in August Dove yesterday morning.

"Well, what the hell *did* happen?" Jason presses him.

Shane holds up a finger. "Let's get coffee first," he says, pushing back his chair and standing.

Jason follows him inside and they do. They pour two steaming cups and return to the porch. This time, Shane sits on that half-wall facing Long Island Sound. As the sun's rising higher, the water ripples beneath its morning light.

Jason leans against that same half-wall and sips his

coffee. "So what gives, man? Because *something* went down in that jewelry shop yesterday."

"Damn straight it did." Shane looks from the blue water of the Sound to Jason. "Went down like this." He hesitates, then lets it all go. "Celia came in the shop. She was right there. Right where she'd wanted to be. She was dressed good. Looked good. Had the baby in her stroller. And everything skidded to a stop."

"What do you mean?" Jason asks, his coffee steaming.

"She couldn't do it. Couldn't bridge that fracture with her mother. And I'll tell you, Barlow. As much as I finally *wanted* it for Celia, if only to show Heather how far Celia had come, who she was … my heart broke when Celia just could *not* do it. At the same time, I wanted to punch a fuckin' wall. I'd bounce between anger and sorrow watching this reunion possibility fade. Over and over again—I'd ricochet from anger to sadness. Still do—when I think about it too much."

"I can see that," Jason says.

Shane nods before taking a swallow of coffee. "Even that Heather annoyed me."

"Heather did?"

"Hell, yeah. Because I was just a customer watching this all unfold. And I *saw* that bitch put together the pieces. The pieces of her own personal *life*, for Christ's sake—the biggest piece right in front of her. She *recognized* Celia. Knew *exactly* who she was. Saw Celia struggling, too. And I thought, *Throw your daughter a God damn bone, why don't you.* But … she wouldn't."

"And Celia wouldn't make a move, either?"

"She already *did*, man. Walking into that shop cold was

a pretty bold move." Shane shakes his head. "But just as fast, she made a move to get the hell out of there. And did."

"But I thought she was set on doing this," Jason says, still leaning on the porch railing. "*What* changed her mind?"

"I did. Me."

"*You?* How?"

Shane draws a hand down his jaw. "By what I gave Celia the day before. The glorious afternoon at Hippie Hill."

"I don't get it, Shane."

Shane takes a quick breath. "Listen. For Celia? That afternoon in the park had her feel so *complete*. She wanted for *nothing* on our Hippie Hill day. The sun was warm; the drum circle was playing down the hill; Celia held Aria and swayed so easy to the music; she'd hold her baby close and slow-twirl right there on the hill; the three of us lounged on a blanket on the grass; the baby dozed right between us; Celia and I had a little picnic; drank some wine. There was no worry. No stress. No home. No chores or bills or arguments or fatigue. Up on that hill? It's like we were lifted on some fuckin' cloud and floating above all the earth's strife. You ever have a day like that?"

"A few. Not enough, though."

Shane nods. "*That's* what changed Celia's mind about her mother. Because Celia couldn't fathom being on Hippie Hill in the Haight like that, especially with her baby—and *not* having it be enough. And seeking something … *more*. Her life, Tuesday afternoon, couldn't get better. Literally. And walking into August Dove the next morning? It just hit her that her mother never felt that with her. And it broke Celia up, too. So when I found her on the street afterward, that's what she told me. She was *legit* distraught—crying, upset—and it just came out. She could *not* ever imagine feeling like that with Aria. That her beautiful daughter wasn't ... *enough*. The way Heather apparently felt about her. And so a meeting of the minds, of the mother and daughter, was never to be."

"Shit. Tough decision for Celia—to just walk away. Walk out of that shop."

"It was. I held back, though. Once Celia left August Dove, I talked more with Heather—without letting on my identity. I was a stranger—as far as she was concerned. But I wanted to see what I could get out of her, you know? And she admitted to me that she recognized her daughter just then. *Admitted* it. A daughter she hadn't seen in decades. So I looked out the window, saw Celia still close by, and asked Heather if she wanted me to go after her. To flag Celia down and ask her to come back." Shane blows out a breath and tosses up a hand then.

"Don't tell me," Jason says, then sips his coffee.

"You got it. *No. Let her go.* Those were Heather's exact words. I even asked if she was sure, and she nodded. Told me yes. So what could I do? I bought some jewelry and left."

"Wait." Jason sets his coffee cup on the half-wall and hoists himself up on it. Looks at Shane across from him then, too. "You're telling me you actually *bought* something of Heather's? You could justify giving her your money?"

"Had to."

"So what'd you get?" Jason motions to his wrist. "A cuff, maybe? Or ... a signet ring?"

"No, I'm not really a ring guy."

"Why not?"

"You never know." Shane flexes his fists as though about

to clobber someone. "Got to be ready. On the lobster boats … around. Shit happens. Then you got to throw a punch at some loser."

"Ha! Like you did at The Sand Bar last month?"

"Exactly. Asshole called you a peg leg."

"And you and Kyle were right on it."

"Sure as hell were." From where Shane leans against a porch post on the half-wall, he raises a clenched fist. "And if I had on a ring that night? Would've damaged my finger with a few of those hits. Bought this, instead." He reaches around his neck, unclasps a leather choker and tosses it to Jason.

"Pretty dope," Jason says. "A Heather Gray original?"

"That it is. Leather, brass and stone. Typical style of hers." Shane sips his coffee. "Grabbed anything I could there, actually. Then I got myself out on the city streets and found Celia and the baby. Got out the dustpan like you told me and calmed Celia down."

"Well …" Jason toys with the leather choker. "Before you write Heather off, or condemn her. Is there *any* chance … even a slight one—"

"Of what?"

"That maybe—just *maybe*—the woman's *not* who you made her out to be?"

"What are you getting at, Barlow?"

"Hey. I've been there, you know. Thinking one thing about someone—and being dead wrong. Because that's how I felt about Ted Sullivan—*before* I met him in person." Jason pauses. He looks out at the blue sea stretching to the horizon, then at Shane. "Ted Sullivan was the God damn enemy, as far as I was concerned. He killed my brother, took my mobility."

"Shit," Shane quietly utters.

"Yep. The man ended my life as I knew it. For a long time, he *was* the enemy."

"And now?"

"Ted's a good friend. One of the very few people I can count on."

"Oh, man. Who'd have thought?"

"Not me. So listen. I'm *not* trying to defend Heather." Jason leans over from his perch on that half-wall and tosses Shane his leather choker. "Just playing devil's advocate. You know, can Heather ever be that to Celia? A mother in some *different* capacity? And not just be a *stranger* in her life."

"Don't know." Shane sets that funky choker on top of the half-wall. Looks from the choker, to Jason. Takes a breath of the morning's salt-laden air. "Hebrews 13:2 might have a say on it, though."

"Let me hear it."

Shane nods. *"Be not forgetful to entertain strangers: for thereby some have entertained angels unawares."*

A long beat of silence passes. There's only the splash of Long Island Sound's gentle waves lapping at the private beach beyond Shane's yard.

Until Shane hears Jason's one question.

"Is Heather actually the angel?"

twelve

HOME, HOME, HOME.

Celia can't get there fast enough. The closer they get to Stony Point, it feels like it'll never happen. Traffic is light this Thursday morning. She's sitting in the backseat of Cliff's car. Aria is strapped in her infant seat beside her while Elsa and Cliff chat in the front. And for every mile Cliff drives on Shore Road, past every marsh with sweeping golden grasses edging serene blue saltwater inlets, past every shingled cottage facing the distant Long Island Sound, past the bait-and-tackle shop and a take-out seafood joint and another inlet—this one with a few rowboats anchored there—Celia gets more excited to reach her destination.

To get home.

Elsa seems to be in her own world, though. She's mentioning all that went on in San Francisco. The sights they saw. Her fun excursions with Wren. So it's a perfect time right now. A perfect time for Celia to get out her cell phone and sneak in a text message to Shane.

We're back, she types from her hideaway spot behind Elsa.

While she waits for a response, she first brushes a finger across Aria's cheek before looking out the car window again. There's the local farm stand. Pumpkins cover a long table beneath the yellow-and-white striped awning. Bunches of tied cornstalks lean against a tall rack.

So they're getting close.

Celia's phone vibrates in her hand. It's Shane, texting her back.

Glad you made it okay. On highway, just pulled over.

Highway?

Headed to Maine. Back tomorrow night.

In the backseat, Celia discreetly types on the phone in her lap. *In Cliff's car on Shore Road. Nearing Scoop Shop.*

All's good?

It is.

Love you.

Same here, Celia types, then drops her phone in her purse.

Because there it is up ahead—the stone train trestle. She drinks in the sight. The brown stone tunnel. The leafy autumn brush cascading down the hill upon which the train tracks run. The allure of what's on the other side of that shadowed tunnel.

"What is it legend says?" Elsa asks over the seatback. "You drive through the tunnel with a ring, a baby or—"

"A broken heart," Celia finishes—right as they pass beneath the tunnel. And she silently decides she'll claim that one today. Because doesn't her heart have a *little* crack in it—for what never came to be in August Dove.

Meanwhile, Cliff's thinking otherwise. "I certainly hope you ladies haven't left your hearts in San Francisco," he says, glancing at Celia in the rearview mirror.

Celia smiles, leans over and looks out the window when they emerge from the tunnel. "What the heck are *those*?" she asks.

"Privacy barriers," Cliff explains, stopping his car on the other side of the trestle. "We installed them around the guard shack."

"Why?" Elsa asks, squinting at the large panels.

"To keep out prying eyes, Mrs. DeLuca. We've been painting behind those panels all week. And the shack looks mighty fine. But no peeking," he says, waggling a finger. "Once I drop you two off, it's all hands on deck finishing up with the crew. Me, Nick, Carol and Flynn."

"*Oh!* That Flynn." Elsa shakes her head. "How's his community service going?"

"Flynn keeps us on our toes, that's for sure. He'll be here painting this afternoon, after school. Carol's wrapping up the landscaping. She put some solar lights around the shack, too. It's very … atmospheric now."

"And what color won the vote?" Celia asks from the backseat.

"Yet to be revealed," Cliff says, still pulled over roadside. "So it's good you're back today. You can get settled in before the big unveil tomorrow afternoon. We'll be roping off the street in the morning."

"Roping it off?" Elsa turns in her seat toward him.

Cliff nods. "It's an important affair. Whole community's going to line the street. Hope you'll both be there," he says to Elsa, with a glance back at Celia, too.

"Absolutely," Celia assures him.

"Wouldn't miss it," Elsa says as Cliff starts to drive past the barricaded shack.

"Oh my goodness! Would you look at that!" Elsa leans forward in her seat. "Did you do that, Cliff?"

"With a little help from Flynn," he admits while pausing the car again.

Which gives Celia a chance to look at the colorful banner strung across the road. A banner just for them. She points to it and whispers the words to her baby daughter, *"Welcome home, Elsa, Celia and Aria!"*

And wow, Celia only thinks as they drive beneath that banner. *Am I ever glad to just be … home.*

~

It's cooler right on the water this morning.

And Jason might as well *be* on the water. The tide is high, the waves practically lapping at Mitch Fenwick's cottage on the beach. Jason, Mitch and Carol are on the elevated deck; filming is underway for *Castaway Cottage*; Zach's following them around with a CT-TV camera on his shoulder while deck options are laid out.

"Thought you might like this metal mesh instead of balusters between the railings, Mitch," Jason says, holding a large, framed mesh sample. "The mesh is really strong *and* durable. Even better, it mirrors actual fishing net."

"Very cool," Carol says, reaching for Jason's framed sample. The mesh's thin wire crisscrosses in the same grid-like pattern as traditional fisherman nets. "What do you think, Dad?"

"Now I *like* that," Mitch says with a slow nod. "Really dig it."

"And because you switched to vinyl shake shingles on the *cottage*, it's probably good you're opting for composite decking, too," Jason tells them, nudging a sample floor plank with his dusty work boot. "A lot less maintenance for all of it—with your cottage being right *on* the beach and taking the brunt of the coastal elements."

"My thoughts, too," Carol says. Wearing a distressed-and-ripped denim jacket loose over a gray tee and gray skinny jeans, she's standing nearby. Silver chains loop around her neck; her ankle boots are scuffed to hell.

"But," Jason goes on, circling the laid-out decking samples, "a *composite* deck, especially with your very large wraparound deck? It'll blow your bank account, Mitch. So beware."

"Duly noted." Mitch draws a hand down his goatee. His fading blond hair is slicked back beneath his beat-up safari hat. His fleece-lined field jacket hangs open over a beige tee and faded jeans. "I'm not sure about the color, either," he muses, looking at the varying laid-out planks. There are shades of browns, shades of gray. "Maybe I'll just go with wood."

"Really, Dad?" Carol picks up a gray plank and moves it so that it's more in the sunlight. "With your schedule of college classes *and* editing Maris' book, now you're going to stain a wood deck every year, too? A *big* wood deck?"

"No, *I* won't." Mitch leans against the deck railing and crosses his arms. "But I can certainly hire a crew to maintain this here deck."

"Well … *I'll* just stain it, then." Carol clomps her booted feet back to the expensive decking samples and starts stacking them as though they're done. Decision's made. Wood deck. Her blonde hair falls in a blunt cut; her sun-bleached bangs sweep her eyes. "I've been painting the guard shack—and doing a fine job. So I can handle a deck every now and then, too."

"No, no, no." When Mitch tosses up his hands, Zach repositions himself for a better camera angle. The sandy beach stretches out behind where Mitch is standing. "You need a *life* plan, Carol," Mitch tells his daughter. "Not more idle time filled up with home maintenance. You can't just be selling flowers and painting decks."

"Dad!" Carol scolds, hands on hips. *And* with an eye roll to Jason.

"Listen, Carol." Mitch pulls out a chair from the patio table and leans his folded arms on the top of it.

Which is when Jason backs away … just a little.

Right as Zach zooms in some.

"You have so much potential—and you're wasting it," Mitch tells his daughter while tipping up his safari hat to better see her. "Not using *any* of it."

"What do you mean?" Carol squints at her father through the late-morning sunlight. A salty breeze lifts off the water and blows her sweeping bangs aside. Behind her, ripples on the Sound sparkle beneath the sun. "I'm living my *passion*," she argues. "With my flower cart. And the plantings and gardens I manage."

Mitch's hands are clasped together over that chairback. He lowers his voice now. "That's not enough, though."

"I beg to differ, Dad. I plant and grow the flowers. Gardens of them. Prune them. Cut them. Design the bouquets." Leaning her elbows back on the deck railing, she

94

crosses her booted feet and eyes Mitch. "I create the tin-can vases. The Mason jar arrangements. I plan my inventory. Paint rocks to accompany the bouquets. Transport the goods to fairs and events. Market. Sell my wares."

Now this is something Jason never saw coming. Neither did Zach or Trent. Today's filming was supposed to be standard fare: decking options, with Jason explaining heat-mitigating technology, and railing choices, and streaked colors versus monochromatic colors. But Jason sees Trent motioning Zach to keep filming now. So they *like* this family tension thrown into a typical design-choice scene.

"But Carol," Mitch is persisting, then exhaling a long breath. "I've been in the working world many more years than you have. Have seen many businesses rise—and fall."

"So you're saying my business will fall?" Carol asks.

"No. What I'm saying is that you must *grow* it to be successful. Otherwise? It's merely a hobby. And I do *not* want to add staining a deck to your roster if it *keeps* you from expanding your business in some meaningful way. It's time to find a focus in your life. Your days. Since Mom died, you've been … adrift."

"I'm *working* on it, Dad."

"And I'll help." Mitch walks to the sample composite deck planks and chooses a medium gray color. He picks it up and turns to Jason—now standing way back. "We'll go with the composite deck, actually," Mitch tells him. "This color." Then Mitch turns to Carol. "*Not* having a deck to stain will free up your time to *find* your potential and let it … blossom."

When Jason sees Carol tear up—whether out of appreciation for her father's concern or out of embarrassment of being on-camera, he can't tell. But he steps in, anyway. He crosses the deck and stands between the two battling family members. "Tune in *next* time," Jason says to the camera now—his arms outstretched between dad and daughter, "to see if Mitch and Carol work out their issues. Decking options, life plans. We cover it all on *Castaway Cottage*. For now," Jason says, standing there in his blazer over hoodie and jeans as the wind picks up off the water, "I'm Jason Barlow."

When Trent motions to Carol, Zach turns the camera on her.

"And I'm an *irritated* Carol Fenwick."

"And I'm her overbearing father, Mitch Fenwick," Mitch concedes when Zach gets him in his camera sights.

Jason closes the segment. "Time will tell if this cottage—and its family—will survive the renovation."

As Jason says it, Carol punches him in the arm, Mitch laughs and tips his safari hat, and Trent calls, "Cut!"

~

It's late.

After midnight, so ... hell, it's late enough to be morning. Which works for his meal. The two bagel halves he toasted in the fireplace serve as an early breakfast. And when he opens the fridge, it's natural the way you just expect the interior to illuminate. The way you expect light—not darkness. Not pitch blackness. But the whole damn cottage is black now. The hurricane snuffed out every stinkin' light—including the refrigerator's. Blew down every power line. Cracked in half how many utility poles.

But the thief knows darkness well. How many nights in 'Nam did he live in it? Open his eyes and be blinded by black. Blink—and panic—as he felt for his rucksack, his rifle. As he shot at only a noise.

Still, he needs a candle now. One burns beside a vase of saltspray roses in a tin can on the kitchen counter. He takes the candle to the open refrigerator and finds the container he's looking for. Leaving the candle in the kitchen, he grabs a knife and the chipped plate with his toasted bagel on it, and turns. A few candles flicker on the dining room table, so he walks there through shadows. He can also make out some details in the candlelight. The table is white, as are the blue-padded chairs. And they all face a wall of windows to the sea.

Problem is, planks of plywood have been nailed over those windows. But he sits there facing the windows anyway. Facing the sea. And looks at the half-dozen candles with flames flickering. Wax dribbles down each taper, each pillar. Wasteful, wasteful. He learned that in the jungle, too. Nothing goes to waste. Not supplies. Not fresh water. Not ammunition. Not dope. Not a flask of liquor. Not food. Not sleep. Not words. Not prayers. Nothing.

So now? One at a time, his dampened fingertips close around five of the six flames there. "Waste not, want not," he whispers. In Vietnam, he wasted nothing. How many times did he trade half a joint for mosquito repellent. Or give a dying comrade a sip of whiskey. Everything hoarded got put to good use. He learned that in 'Nam and lives it to this day. So by only one candle flame now, he spreads cream cheese on his charred bagel halves. That done, he pinches out the final candle flame and just sits there.

Funny how he hears better in the black. Hears how the sea spray whipping the plywood-covered windows carries pieces of sand. The grit of those sand grains pelting the wood is audible at his table in the dark. The waves sloshing beneath the floor of this cottage-on-stilts comes to him, too. A muffled, slight sound of rushing water.

And he just sits alone there and eats. Takes a cream-cheese-laden bite of that bagel and tries to silence his thoughts. Quiet voices come to him from other rooms, though. At some card game played by candlelight. There's also a low, serious conversation happening in the kitchen.

But the thief just sits in the blackness. Becomes a part of it. And eats his early, early breakfast.

He hears something else then, too.

Hears the damp hem of bell-bottoms brush across the wood floor behind him.

Hears the chair beside him being pulled out.

Hears Princess whisper, "Hey."

He just nods and digs into that bagel.

"What are you doing sitting here like this?" Princess asks.

"Like what?"

"Well. Like alone in the dark. Staring into space." She pauses and whispers the rest. "Like you're worried."

"I am worried." He turns to her beside him but barely, barely sees her. "My brother … he'll be dead to me one way or another."

She touches her fingers to his arm. He only feels that touch. Doesn't see it. Feels it. Feels that touch saying it's okay about before. When he heaved the vase. The touch saying she understands why he did it.

So he keeps talking at the table beside the boarded-up windows where the sea is just on the other side. "Whether my kid brother goes to Vietnam or dodges the draft and goes to Canada, he'll be dead to me, kind of. Because either way, I probably won't see him again."

"But isn't that what you wanted? For him not to fight this awful war? I heard you scaring the shit out of him before with those glass pieces. Telling him about the punji-stick traps just to get him to go north. Who wouldn't pack their bags and bolt with your horror stories?"

Nothing, then. Just blackness as the thief takes another bite of that bagel. Chews it. Swallows. And hears every miniscule movement, every muscle of his eating. Hears the ravaging wind-driven sea slapping the cottage. Hears Princess' voice once more.

"When you were called to serve, well, why didn't you *dodge the draft? Go to Canada?" her voice asks.*

He looks at her but can't really see her. He only sees blackness and hears terror outside the windows. A terrified sea being whipped by an angry wind. The same terror his brother is surely feeling with his imminent departure to a jungle ten thousand miles away.

Why didn't *he go to Canada? the thief silently wonders.*

And he hoards his answer. Wastes not, wants not. Yes, because the answer he just came up with that he keeps to himself? It gave him something. Shit, something he really needs. Just like the rolled joints gave him bug spray. Just like the flask gave a dying man calm.

Why didn't he go to Canada when he was drafted? Well, who says he's not going? It's never crossed his mind, but how about it? How about it if he goes a little late?

How about if he goes to Canada now?

How about if he goes for his brother?

With *his brother.*

Yeah.

The thief thinks of how he already served his country. Did his tour. Did it for America.

Realized soon as his boots hit the ground—it was for nothing.

It wasn't worth it.

So how about this?

In the darkness here in the boarded-up cottage, everything takes shape.

How about if he does it now? Ditches the USA for Canada.

Yeah.

Ditches the USA for the USB.

For the United State of Brotherhood.

～

Maris pauses her typing. She raises her fingers off the keyboard and looks at the laptop screen. Is that the right angle for *Driftline*? Sitting there, she slips off her cropped tweed jacket and hangs it over her chairback. Late-morning rays of sun push into the writing shack. Neil's battery-operated radio and two-burner kerosene camping stove sit on nearby shelves. An old black sweatshirt of his hangs from a nail in the wall. Baskets of salt-coated seashells are on dusty wooden shelves, too. Neil's hands painted these wood-boarded walls white. His hands lit the foggy glass-domed hurricane lanterns here.

Neil.

Neil.

Jason's kid brother.

What if Jason served like his father did in that war—served in the nightmare—and barely survived?

But did.

And then what if Neil was drafted, too. What would Jason do to protect him?

Maris looks at what she just wrote and nods.

"Everything," she whispers. *"Absolutely everything."*

thirteen

ELSA'S STAINLESS-STEEL WASHER IS SLOSHING. Once Cliff dropped her home later Thursday morning, she'd showered and changed out of her flight clothes. In her robe now, she's sitting in the striped upholstered chair in her laundry room. Everything around her—the gray beadboard paneling; the commercial-grade inn washer and dryer, as well as her own personal units; the big sink with its coiled-spring faucet; the twig wreaths on the wall—is spotless. Sunlight falls through the paned windows as she's loaded all her California clothes into the washer.

And while sitting on that chair in the corner of her laundry room, her mind is still *in* California. So she's scrolling her cell phone photos now. For the past day, she'd given Celia space just to see if something would come to light about what happened on the streets of San Francisco.

About what Elsa witnessed between Celia Gray and Shane Bradford.

Nothing has. No light was shed—on anything. Celia won't say a word.

So Elsa swipes through her phone photos and does a comparison test. Celia *pre-Shane incident* in Haight-Ashbury at the Grateful Dead stoop versus Celia *post-Shane incident* on the Golden Gate Bridge. Elsa's eyes go back and forth between the two sets of pictures. She looks at Celia's smiles, pre-Shane. Looks at her body language. The way she holds Aria close. Is there some secret behind Celia's happy eyes? Did Celia know when they took their hippie-van tour that Shane was even *in* California? What was he doing there? Did he conduct some business? Was he visiting a friend? But he would've *mentioned* this to Elsa if that were the case. Would've *said* he'd be in California, too.

Well. One thing Elsa does know is that fretting accomplishes nothing.

Waiting out an explanation accomplishes nothing, too.

So she gets busy.

She changes into cropped wide-leg olive pants with a fitted black sweater. Dabs cleaning solution on her second piercings, puts thin gold hoops in the first hole and begins with her busyness.

But who says that busyness can't be *about* Celia and Shane? Clipping along in her chunky clogs, Elsa hurries to her inn reservation desk at the end of the hallway and hauls out her big leather calendar-ledger. Even with the inn still unopened, she makes calendar notes on many days. Mostly it's to chart zoning progress on her stalled marsh rowboat rides. Or to jot chore reminders. Or to log simple journal entries of a day's activities. So maybe this calendar will tell her something. Maybe some Shane-Celia connection clue will show in her notes. After hefting that ledger back to her large marble kitchen island, she lifts the leather cover and begins.

"Okay," she vaguely whispers. *"What do I know?"* she asks while flipping the marked calendar pages two months back. *"What do I know? Hmm."*

Flip.
Friday, August 12
Shane Bradford check-in.

"For Kyle and Lauren's vow renewal. That was the first I knew of Shane," Elsa murmurs. "And that night, I thought he was Kyle's cousin."

Flip.
Sunday, August 14
Sunday Dinner with gang.

Topic of conversation at inn dining room table: Shane Bradford's arrival.

In which, Elsa remembers now, Celia admitted that Shane helped her remove all the flowers from the vow-renewal rowboat the night before. The night of the cancelled event.

Flip.
Thursday, August 18
Penciled in: *Sand Bar.*

"Oh, yes," Elsa tells herself. "One of Celia's acoustic night gigs. When Shane gave an impromptu jam with her on his harmonica."

Flip.

Tuesday, August 23

Penciled in: *Mason jar delivery.*

Elsa can picture it now. Shane pulled up in *his* pickup truck loaded with jars for the inn opening. Yet it was Celia who was getting them the day before. So their paths somehow crossed. Again.

Flip.

Sunday, August 28

Penciled in: *Neil's Memorial Mass and brunch.*

When Celia was AWOL with some flimsy excuse. Something about her father's car being in the shop and she helping him with errands that day. Elsa looks at that ledger page again. "Maybe true, maybe not," she quietly admits. "Wasn't like Celia to skip that Mass."

Flip, flip, flip.

Early September pages of Celia's spotty absences from Stony Point—all coinciding with Shane's lobstering life resuming up north.

Flip.

Wednesday, September 7

Penciled in: *Shane stopped by. Dinner together!*

And Elsa remembers it was when he'd returned from Maine when his captain's boat was laid up in the boatyard. Back Shane came with gifts for all—including an anchor tote for Elsa. Returned from a Maine trip that happened during Celia's spotty absences.

Flip.

Saturday and Sunday, September 17 and 18

From her notes, Elsa sees it. Oh, yes. Shane was all in with her and Celia's moose-head hijinks. And he was *really* into it. "All for someone he really didn't know?" Elsa asks herself. "*Or* for someone he was falling in love with?"

Flip.

There's the late-September week when Celia said she was in Addison for a few days. For a child's birthday party at her old neighbor's house. "The same week Shane was in Maine while devastated to lose his crewmate?" Elsa asks, then shakes her head. "How could I not have seen this?" The answer to that, she realizes, is obvious. With the inn delay and the fissure it caused between her and Celia, and getting entangled with Mitch, then getting untangled, to repairing the hurt with Cliff and seeking his forgiveness, to impromptu California trip-planning, to privately grappling with the one-year loss of her son—of her beloved Salvatore—Elsa hasn't been seeing much of *anything* clearly these past few months.

Now, she does.

Flip, flip, flip.

Elsa keeps the large ledger pages turning. She tries to piece together the hints. The coincidences. The links between Shane and Celia. Were they all happenstance? Is her mind just playing tricks on her? She only wonders until finally stopping on—and tapping—Wednesday, October 12.

Yesterday.

Yesterday, when she saw such unmistakable grief on dear Celia's face.

Yesterday, when she saw Shane embracing Celia and Aria right on the San Francisco streets.

Sitting alone at her marble kitchen island, Elsa can only think one thing. *Nothing* else makes sense. She sits back and glances at the ledger as her vintage rope-wrapped wall clock quietly ticks away the seconds.

Was what Elsa witnessed yesterday … a goodbye?

If there's one thing Celia's gotten good at these days, it's this: convincing herself of things. Of truths. Of lies. Of reasons. Of the ways they twist together.

She's about to do it again, too.

Now, after giving Aria her bottle and putting her in her crib for an afternoon nap.

Now, as she starts to call her father then quickly changes her mind—three times.

She's still in her airplane outfit—cargo trouser pants, white tee and black denim jacket. With Aria asleep, Celia thought she'd manage a quick shower and change.

But she can't.

Because surely her father, Gavin, is waiting for her full California report.

Or at least, her full report on reuniting with Heather in August Dove.

Which is why Celia's convincing herself again. Convincing herself that if she *withholds* some of the truth, that's not really lying. Because the last thing she wants to do is lie to her father. But she also can't bring herself to tell him that her emotions got the best of her. That she couldn't go through with the reunion with Heather. Especially after her father persistently told her he *didn't* agree with the plan.

Celia settles on her screened-in back porch to make the call now. At least here, she can sense the distant sea. Can smell the salt air lifting off Long Island Sound. Hear the cry of a swooping seagull. The early-afternoon sun shines brightly outside. Golden mums spill from clay pots on her stone patio.

Sitting on a painted wicker chair beside a large Boston fern, she finally places the call.

"Here we go," she whispers as her father's phone rings in her ear.

The pleasantries are the easy part. The talk of sightseeing, and mentions of Aria, and updates on Elsa's time with Wren.

Then comes the hard part.

"I actually decided not to go through with it, Dad. With meeting Mom. At the very last minute." Truth, all truth. Just the truth cut short. So—not a lie.

"But Celia," her father persists. "You were *intent* on this. There was no talking you out of it. And … Shane was there to help, too."

"I know, Dad. I just had a change of heart."

"You're serious?" Gavin quietly asks.

"I am." More of the same. Truth. The truth stopped short of saying that her change of heart happened upon seeing her mother up close. Upon standing with her in August Dove. *That* truth has stinging tears burn her eyes right now.

"Listen, Dad," she goes on. "When Elsa was away with

Wren, Shane and I had a *beautiful* day in Golden Gate Park."
She stands and walks to the porch door. Leans there and
looks out while talking. "It was the kind of magical day
when I realized what matters in my life. *And* I realized that
I already have it. Have sweet Aria. And Shane. You, too, of
course. And Elsa. But fully realizing that, Dad? It had me
think differently." Truth, all truth. Now Celia nearly
whispers her next words. "I have all I need, Dad. *I'm actually
blessed to have so much.* So I let things stay as they are." Truth;
she just isn't sharing that, okay, she decided all that in the
middle of a breakdown.

Instead, she finishes the conversation with her father.
She answers his questions. Reassures him. Tells him Shane
was good with everything, too. And she doesn't lie.

After their talk, she makes herself a cup of tea and sits
on her front porch rocker. What comes to her, sitting there,
is a memory from last weekend. She and Shane had dinner
with her father in Addison. And Gavin asked Celia what
she was looking for—exactly.

*I'm looking to not have my last memory of my mother be from
when I was a young child ... At the very least, I'm looking to have
some adult perception of her.*

Well, she got what she wanted, didn't she? Sitting on her
porch rocker, in her little world at Stony Point, with the
Ocean Star Inn just a front yard away, she sips her tea and
breathes in the cool autumn air.

Yes, she has a new memory of her mother: a woman in
control; poised; successful; aware, even, of her.

And it's enough; Celia knows.

Enough to carry with her. She needs no more.

She knew that when she'd stood face-to-face with

Heather Gray yesterday morning.

In the middle of August Dove, Celia barely creaked open Pandora's box. And after seeing all that started to come out—she quickly shut the lid.

Rushed out of that shop—the door swinging closed behind her.

fourteen

SHANE'S FLOWER BOXES CHANGE WITH the seasons.

That's why he grabbed a few more mum plants. Bought them on his drive north Thursday morning, after breakfast with Barlow. This way, he can replace the wilting geraniums at his shingled house in Rockport, Maine.

Standing at the flower box beneath his front paned window now, he waters the soil where he just dropped in the golden mums. As he does, his neighbor Bruno stops by with the mail he picked up the past week and a half. So Shane sits on the front granite step, tips up his newsboy cap and they bullshit some. They talk about Shane getting back to lobstering. A little about his trip to San Francisco. A little about how he has to do some lawn mowing and straightening up.

Once inside, Shane flings off his cap and thumbs through the envelopes and flyers Bruno delivered. He sets down the bills; the rest is junk he tosses. Minutes pass in the quiet house.

It's time to get things done. So he finds a pen, grabs his checkbook and stamps, then drops them—with his unpaid bills—on his wooden kitchen table. But the house got stuffy being all closed up, so he turns to open a window. When he opens the door to his deck, too, salt air drifts in.

And like it always does, that briny scent draws him outside—bill-paying be damned. The screen door squeaks when he pushes through and slams shut behind him. He walks to the deck's far railing and has a clear view of the distant docks and harbor. Few lobster boats are there today—they're all out hauling as much as they can to finish up the local fishing season. Seagulls swoop and cry; the sky is blue; that salt air, pungent.

Shane misses it, too. Misses being on the sea. Misses feeling its spray on his skin. Misses its wind in his hair. He didn't realize how much until standing right here within the sea's sights and scent and salty breeze. Damn, not too much can cast a spell on him and his hardened ways. But the sea is right up there.

So he stays out on the deck and decides to call his brother. Kyle believes he's been in Maine all *week*—and Shane needs to present an ironclad alibi. So he sits himself on the custom white-planked bench he and Shiloh built and snaps a picture. It's of the harbor view Kyle really dug when he was here. He texts Kyle the photo. Then he calls him.

"Yo, Shane!" Kyle answers. "What's doing up there? You out on the boat?"

And so it begins—Shane's alibi.

His alibi of lies. Of how he's talked to the captain. Even went out on the boat earlier in the week.

Lies, bullshit, crap. But all of it's his cover. An alibi keeping his San Francisco trip under wraps from the rest of the world.

An alibi that, as he goes on and on to Kyle, has Shane feeling *criminal*, for God's sake. Shit, sneaking around, lying, doing things on the sly. The last time he lived like that? It was during his juvie days. Times when he was a punk teen breaking and entering cottages to raid liquor cabinets. Swiping cash from the register drawer when he was working part-time scooping ice cream.

And here he is doing it again. A grown man. Sneaking away on a plane west. Spending clandestine time with the woman he loves. Privately worrying about her more than anything else.

"Hey, listen. While you've been gone?" Kyle's saying now. "I sealed the deal on my new mower. She's a sweet machine, man. I'm actually *stoked* to do some lawn work."

"No shit. Did you get it yet?"

"The dealer's delivering it today. I'm home now, expecting it any minute. And when are *you* coming back?" Kyle asks him.

"Later tomorrow, bro."

"Okay, good. Come by the diner Saturday. I'll cook you up a hearty supper. On the house."

Shane lifts a foot to his knee and sits back on that bench. "Yeah, sure. I'll stop by. Fix me something amazing, guy— with no hidden peppers this time."

Kyle laughs. "Don't worry, you're good. Actually got another Harvest Night going on Saturday. Diner will be all decorated. I want you to see it. We went all out, you know. Should be a rad night."

Everything's stacked up.

That's what Shane sees when he goes back inside. He was last here a week and a half ago for Shiloh's memorial at sea. And in those ten days, bills rolled in, dirty laundry from his trip accumulated, the grass grew, and musty dust filled his Maine abode.

Maine. Stony Point. He's got places in both. His home here, his cottage rental there.

Yet a part of him still feels stuck on the streets of San Francisco. Like the city still swirls around him. Like Celia's still upset.

Hell, he can't get yesterday morning out of his head. And it agitates him. He's in a bad mood. He wanted a different outcome for Celia.

So he kind of slams his way through his chores. Unzips his duffel of dirty clothes from San Francisco. Tucked in that duffel, he sees the sterling-silver arm cuff he also bought at August Dove. Someday, he'll give it to Celia. For now, he lifts it out. Looks at the carved silver dove on one end. Puts two of his fingers through the looped cuff and spins it around them. Leaves the cuff dangling on a drawer knob in the kitchen and brings his clothes duffel to his washing machine. Gets the laundry going and returns to the kitchen. Sits at the wooden table, picks up his pen, pays his bills, tears checks from his checkbook, stuffs and stamps envelopes.

Done.

He fills a glass with cold water and quaffs that down.

Done.

Puts on his newsboy cap, heads outside, wheels his mower from the shed, fires up the machine and cuts his grass.

Back and forth.

Back and forth.

Over and over again beneath the afternoon sun.

Gets his leaf blower, fires that up and clears some grass clippings from the gravel driveway. The front granite step. The deck.

Inside, he tries to open a sticking living room window. "I said, *open* already," he growls as he gives it a hard shove—nearly breaking the window when it flies up.

He drags a dust rag over some furniture, over the frames of his stolen paintings.

Beats a rag rug outside on the deck. Beats the hell out of it.

Opens the refrigerator to find something for dinner.

"Fuckin' empty," he says, slamming the fridge door shut.

Puts his newsboy cap back on, brushes off his jeans and tee grimy from the mowing, grabs a jacket and his pickup keys and heads out.

Ten minutes later, Shane pushes open the door to Red Boat Tavern and nears the buccaneer statue in the front alcove. How many times has he done this in the past fifteen years? Walked straight off the lobster boat, straight across the Rockport Harbor docks and landed here. Famished from a hard day's labor. Happy to just sit with some of the boys and chow down.

Not today.

Today, he just wants some quick nourishment. Wants

food he doesn't have to prepare. Doesn't have to cut, season, cook, clean up after. Doesn't want to socialize, either. He just wants to eat. So he veers across the tavern, past the bearded swashbuckler statue and café-style tables and shelves of model schooners before grabbing a seat alone at the bar. It's late afternoon. The tavern's dark paneled walls are shadowy. A few locals sit here, there. Voices talk. Silverware clinks on plates.

"Hey there, pirate," the waitress says as she walks closer.

"Mandy." Shane just nods at her.

Mandy stands there dressed in a fitted maroon tee and black denim skirt. Her blonde hair is in a loose braid; her smile, easy. "You alone today?" she asks.

Shane looks long at her. "Give me the meatloaf club with cheddar and fried onions. Potato wedges, too," he says evenly—instead of answering her question that's nothing but trouble. "A side of fried zucchini chips with that. And a cold beer."

Mandy looks equally long back at him. "Got it," she finally says, pulling her order pad from her half-apron and briskly jotting the order. She doesn't bother with a second look before breezing off.

Shane just sits there on the barstool. Props his elbows on the bar top and looks at nothing, really. Just kind of zones out until Landon delivers his food.

"There's my boy," the bar owner says, setting down Shane's plates before pulling a draft for him.

"How's everything, Landon?" Shane asks. "Good?"

"Ayuh." Landon stands behind the bar. He crosses his arms over his maroon apron and eyes Shane. "You?"

"Good enough, I guess," Shane says, lifting the top

bread off his meatloaf sandwich. The melted cheddar sticks some, but he manages to salt the food and dig in.

"You ain't been around. Back to work now?" Landon asks.

Shane shakes his head and wipes the back of his hand over his mouth. "Maybe next week. Pretty soon, anyway."

"That's good. Get yourself back out on the water. Just what the doctor ordered?"

"Come again?" Shane asks around a mouthful of potato wedge.

"You know. After everything with Shiloh."

Shane says nothing. He just nods, throws down a swallow of beer and lifts his sandwich again.

"Okay, my friend," Landon tells him. He's about fifty with a shaved head, a manicured close beard. A face full of salty wisdom, too, from decades of watching contentious fishermen walk through his tavern doors. Now he reaches over and slaps Shane's shoulder. "Hope things look up for you."

"Yeah. Thanks, Landon."

As the bar owner walks away, another familiar voice calls Shane's name. It's Todd, a fisherman from another lobster boat in the fleet. He just walked in looking straight off the job. His hair's a mess. He's dirty. His clothes, tired.

"Where you been, loser?" Todd asks, settling on the stool beside Shane. "Heard from your crew the catches been down without you on board."

Shane glances at him, then takes another swallow of beer. "What difference does it make?" he says then. "Catches will be *permanently* down with the new regulations."

"What are you talking about?" Todd leans an arm on the bar. "The gauge changes?"

"Damn straight. Come on, increasing the minimum lobster catch size? Shit, we'll be throwing those lobsters overboard only to have the Canadians scoop them up. Their fuckin' rules don't match ours. On top of warming waters, might as well pack it up and move to Canada if we want to keep making a living."

Todd squints at Shane, then stands—nearly getting his barstool tumbling. "Jeez," Todd says. "Just asked how it's going," he gripes before straightening the stool and walking away.

"Yeah." Shane waves him off. "It's going."

And that's the last thing he says in the tavern. Doesn't utter another word. He just sits there and finishes his meal in silence at the bar.

～

An hour and a half later, Shane's kicked off his boots and sits on his couch. Lifts his stocking feet to the leather ottoman. The laundry's done; dinner's been had. So he holds the remote and flips through some TV channels. Shuts off the TV, lowers his feet and grabs his cell phone from the coffee table. Fidgets with the phone. Leans his arms on his knees and scrolls through his contacts. He wants to talk to someone. Work something out, maybe.

But he's not going to bother Jason. He talked off Barlow's ear enough over bagels this morning.

"Not going to bother my brother," Shane whispers when he scrolls past Kyle's number. *"He's clueless about the situation."*

And he's certainly not going to bother Celia. She'll be busy with the baby *and* with her own unsettled thoughts, he's sure.

Tossing aside his phone, Shane puts his boots back on and walks to the front door. It's open to the night outside, so he just leans there against the doorjamb. The sun's gone down now. Shadows are long and dark. In the distant harbor, a bell buoy clangs. Salt air off the Atlantic presses close.

Standing quietly there, he realizes something. Realizes there *is* somebody he can bother, actually. Someone who'll listen, too.

So he grabs his sweatshirt off the end of the couch, pushes out the front door, locks up and drives down the night roads in his pickup.

The streets are black. Shane drives a stretch where there are few streetlights. And the towering pine trees silhouette the roadside in even more black. If it wasn't for the half-moon directly overhead dropping some pale light, he'd have missed the turnoff. He swerves to it just in time.

Once he parks and gets out of his truck, he's on familiar ground. Hell, he could maneuver it blindfolded. Still, he's careful walking through the garden and around moss-covered granite ledges. The stone stairs are a little damp underfoot, too. He climbs them to the wood-framed structure sitting atop an ancient stone foundation.

"I know you're here," he says when he walks in. "And we need to talk."

There's no answer.

So Shane takes a few more steps. "I got nowhere else to turn, man."

In the ensuing silence, he stops. Around him in the open-air chapel, wide, peaked cutouts in the wood walls look out onto the night. There are dark shadows of gardens out there. And black smudges of stone walls. And more murky stone staircases surrounding the chapel.

But you can only see them during the day.

Now, he sees only variations of darkness. That half-moon hasn't risen high enough yet to drop any pale light on those gardens and rock.

Darkness, darkness.

Shit, it feels like he's been in some darkness all day.

So he turns in the chapel. It's late, and the place is empty, so he sits himself on one of the wooden benches serving as pews. Leans his elbows on his knees and bows his head. *"Our Father,"* he whispers, *"who art in heaven. Hallowed be Thy name."* A pause, then, *"Thy kingdom come, Thy will be done … Oh, man,"* Shane says, sitting up straight and running a hand through his hair. *"On earth as it is in heaven."*

Which is where his prayer stops. Because talking to God like this, maybe he just got his answer. Maybe he knows now *why* he's so mad. Shane stands and walks to what he considers an altar. It's the soaring open-air arch in the entire front wall of this wooden chapel. A tall, narrow cross is mounted in the upper curve of the arch.

Tonight—right now—it's the only place where Shane sees light.

Because on the other side of that open, arched wall is the sea. The vast and glorious sea. And the golden half-moon hangs low over it. Pale lunar light drops through the skies onto the dark water.

"I thought I was mad at Celia," Shane says, his low voice

barely audible in the empty chapel. "Dear God, I'm sorry I even let her *think* that. Think that I was mad at her for not going through with her plan. For not talking to her mother. For not taking control." Shane shakes his head. "But maybe she did control things."

Standing at that massive arch open to the October night, Shane hikes up his sweatshirt around his shoulders. Takes a breath. "Thought I was mad at Heather, too. For not reaching out. She knew, damn it. She *knew* Celia was her daughter standing right there in her beautiful jewelry boutique. And she did nothing? *Nothing*?" he repeats, his voice rising. Jason's one haunting question comes to him now, too: *Is Heather actually the angel?*

"An angel?" Shane whispers. *"Like shit."*

But he stops then while dipping his head and closing his eyes. Squeezing them shut, actually, against burning tears. He turns quickly away from his altar-to-the-sea. Walks across the damp stone floor to the wooden benches and sits again.

And feels too ashamed to say any more.

Too ashamed to admit *who* he's mad at.

Too ashamed to say it's himself.

Actually? He's *really* angry at himself. Angry that he didn't take the opportunity yesterday to say something to Heather in August Dove.

Angry because he *didn't* let on who the hell he really was.

Angry that he didn't tell Heather what a *blessed* mistake she made years ago.

"Ach," he says now. *"Mistake after mistake after mistake after mistake.* When will I *ever* stop fucking up my life? Do I *ever* learn?" he asks, then walks to his ocean-altar once more

and looks at the sky. The moon. The sea. Breathes the salt-heavy air. Gasps it in as though it's saving him. "Why didn't I just *do* it? Just go off-script."

He pauses then, as though some answer will come to him. Come from above. Or from the sea. The heavenly skies. His own conscience, even.

None does. There's only silence this cold October night in this sparse, open-air structure practically in the woods, not far from the sea.

"Thy will be done—on earth as it is in heaven?" Shane finally asks. "So I let You down, God. What else is new, right? I let You down—*again*. Because I couldn't do it. I didn't let *Your* will *be* done on earth. *Your* will to love one another. Because I didn't defend the woman I love. Didn't defend Celia to Heather. I didn't lift Celia in Heather's eyes." Shane swallows around a knot in his throat. *"I was afraid, don't You get it?"* he whispers to the night sky. *"Afraid to go against Celia's wishes."* He slaps an escaped tear off his face. "Afraid to go off-script. I stuck to every stinkin' word of that script. Every stinkin' inflection. Every pause, every intonation. I stuck *only* to the script. In the moment? I believed it was right. And what did it get me? What did it get Celia on one of the most important days she's lived? *What?* It got her a mother who just watched her daughter come undone. Watched some weakness, maybe. Some flaw as Celia wavered. That … *That's* what sticking to the damn script got me. *Nothing.*"

Shane stops now. He stops his rant. Stops his words. But he circles the empty open-air chapel. Walks past the meager benches. The peaked cutouts in the wooden side walls. And circles around again to his soaring open-air altar.

Loosens his sweatshirt. Shoves up its sleeves.

Listens.

To silence.

"Well, right now?" he quietly goes on. "I don't give a damn about that script," he says, his voice level. "Not one bloody damn," he tells the sky, the sea. "I'm so mad at myself and wish, just *wish* I'd behaved differently. Controlled, but differently. Took Heather aside … and said … a few phrases, even."

When he realizes that his last words are broken up by some crying, he looks out at the sea one last time. He swipes at his face but can't shake a deep-seated regret.

Regret is the worst of it. Regret means it's *done*. He missed his chance and made his mistake. There's no going back and changing that San Francisco script. No changing his own decision. His own behavior in August Dove.

No changing what he said—or didn't say—to Heather.

No changing how Celia's emotional exodus from that shop left Heather feeling.

No changing anything.

It's done.

Turning away from the sea view now, he slips on the damp stone floor. But he regains his balance and finds his way to the bench pews. There, in this chapel in the night, he drops to his knees, rests his elbows on the bench and bows his head against his clasped fists.

fifteen

ELSA'S HIDING.

Okay, so no one knows it. But hiding she is behind her dark cat-eye sunglasses. Because early Friday morning, she has to make the rounds. While she was in California, people here looked after her inn, her car, her flowers. Her *life*—truth be told. Now she has to collect her personal belongings from them.

Thus, the sunglasses to hide her persistent worry about Celia. Because folks today—Maris, Eva, Jason especially— they'll home right in on that worry. They'll see something in Elsa's eyes and squint at her. Drop their voices and ask if everything's okay. They'll press her for details. They'll pull her aside, sit her down, clasp her arm, lean in and listen.

And she'll have none of that.

So sunglasses on. Innocuous outfit, too: black jogger pants with a ribbed cream mockneck top. Before leaving the inn, she also loops a geometric-patterned silk scarf around her neck. Steps into dark slip-on sneakers. Easy on, easy to rush off in. Lastly, she hops in her golf cart.

The rest is a blur.

A weaving blur as she stops at the Bradford house to pick up her and Celia's spare car keys from Kyle—hoping to catch him before he goes to the diner. But alas, he's gone. So Lauren retrieves those keys from inside. She also manages to squeeze in some questions—all as Elsa grabs the keys, rattles off a few enthused responses, gets into her golf cart and *put-putts* away to Eva's house.

Where Eva hands her a pile of her mail—all while she's on a business call on her front-porch realty office. *Perfect— no time for questions!*

Next Elsa gets her watering can from Maris—who informs her that Jason's working in his barn studio when Elsa asks if the extra inn keys are around, too. The ones she gave Jason so he could check on her place while she was away. Problem is, Jason's so damn perceptive, he'll see right through her sunglasses, her words, to the truth that something's on her mind.

And oh, something is.

Celia is. Celia and Shane and some private heartbreak she witnessed. So Elsa silently decides in another blur to get her key ring from Jason some other time. When Maris heads back inside the house, Elsa takes that as her cue— hopping on her golf cart, tucking away the watering can and zipping off yet again. Just not to the barn studio, like Maris thought.

It all works, too. Her rushing off; those big sunglasses; her bluff of busyness. It keeps her on the move so she can't talk much. Oh, when Maris and Eva and Lauren asked about her trip, of course Elsa flashed a quick San Francisco photo or two on her cell phone. But then she sped off in her golf cart and called out, *The trip was fabulous!* Or, *Peace and love!*

Yes. Her sunglasses hid her troubled eyes.

Yes. She kept *moving-moving-moving* before anyone at all had a chance to say: *Oh, you look tired!*

Or, *You're quiet today.*

Or—even worse? *Everything all right, Elsa?*

⁓

Okay, something's different.

Celia notices it right away after settling Aria beside her. They're at a booth in the Dockside Diner, and Aria's car seat is nestled next to her on the bench. But while Celia turns up the cuffs of a corduroy blazer she wears over her brown sweater vest and straight-leg jeans, she looks around. It must be the home stager in her—because she notices some décor changes. Hurricane lanterns sit in the windows now instead of dangling fishing globes. Orange harvest lights frame the dessert case, the doorway, and are even looped around the colorful buoys that hang like pendant lights from the ceiling. A cornstalk tied in rust-colored ribbon leans near the diner's *Specials* chalkboard; small pumpkin centerpieces are on the booth tables.

"Hey, there's the hippies!" Kyle's voice says then.

With a smile, Celia looks over right as he sits in the booth seat across from her. Dressed in his white chef apron over black tee and pants, he reaches over and tickles Aria under her chin. "And you're the little flower child," he softly tells the cooing baby.

"She was such a good girl out in San Francisco," Celia says.

"I'll bet. And what brings you here this fine morning?"

"Breakfast! I'm low on food at home and thought I'd grab a bite before stopping at Maritime Market to stock my kitchen."

"Got it. How *was* the trip, anyway? Outtasight?"

"Definitely," Celia answers with a laugh. "It was really fun," she adds while showing some of their Haight-Ashbury tourist photos on her phone. "We had a blast. Took a genuine hippie-van tour to sightsee. Wove flowers in our hair for dinner. Walked the Golden Gate Bridge. And when Elsa spent some time with her friend? Me and this one," Celia says, touching little Aria's hand, "hung out on the hotel balcony. Walked in the park. I even channeled the West Coast vibes for some songwriting."

"That sounds *great*." Kyle sits back in the booth while drawing a hand down his jaw. "And listen. Speaking of songwriting …" he goes on while squinting across the table at her. "Any chance you're free tomorrow night?"

"Saturday?"

"Yeah."

"Might be. What's going on?"

"Well, as you can see by the decorations, we're having another Harvest Night here. And it'd be even better with live music."

"Are you asking me to play?"

"I am. Because, heck. You've done acoustic night here already. Know the ropes and all that." Kyle turns up a hand. "So you up for another gig? A paying gig. You'd get your standard rate."

"Yeah." Celia nods. "Yeah, I think I'd like that. I'll play some old favorites. Throw in a new song or two."

"You'll do it?" Kyle asks. "Seriously?"

"Sure. Just have to get a babysitter."

"Awesome! Hey," Kyle goes on while getting out of the booth. "Give me a sec, would you?"

Celia does and watches as he brings over his A-frame chalkboard.

"Before I take your breakfast order, let me add you to the Harvest Night lineup." Kyle picks up a piece of chalk. He says each word as he block prints them on the blackboard. "Special Appearance by acoustic singer-songwriter Ce—"

"Wait!" Celia interrupts. "Erase that name."

"What?"

"I want to try out a new stage name."

"Really …" Kyle says while erasing her first name. "Okay. Let me have it."

In the morning hubbub of the diner, amidst flatware clicking on dishes, and voices chatting, and kitchen griddles sizzling, Celia tries it out. She says her new hippie name bestowed in a jetliner high, high up in the sky—*Lady Blue Heart*—all while watching the chalked words take shape on the board.

~

"Do my eyes deceive me, Mrs. DeLuca?" Cliff asks Friday morning. He's sitting at his desktop computer and leans back in his office chair. Elsa just walked into the trailer and is carrying some bag. Her big sunglasses are propped atop her head and holding back her thick brown hair. "Or are those twinkling *stars* in your lobes?"

"What?" Elsa asks, shifting that bag in her arm and touching an ear. "Oh, those."

"Yes, *those*. They look very fine—if I do say so myself."

"Thank you, Cliff." Elsa brushes aside papers on his tanker desk and sets her bag down there. "I got a double piercing with Wren on our trip."

"And I like the look."

Elsa simply reaches into her shopping bag—and veers off-topic. "Before I left, though, I promised to spruce up your coffee cart. And bring goodies." As she says it, she's lifting something from that bag. "I've had no time to bake anything yet. But this," she goes on while setting a box on his desk. "Well, it's store-bought, but it's a good template for how your cart can be. You know, very ... *welcoming* ... to clients. Residents. BOG members."

Cliff slides over what looks like a raspberry Danish.

"I brought a glass pastry dish to slice it on," Elsa says, lifting that dish from the bag, too. "You should probably get yourself a cake stand so you can change up the offerings." She sets the glass dish on the coffee cart, then lifts the raspberry Danish from the box and sets it on that dish. "Keep in mind things like, well, fanning out your napkins. Don't just stack them," she calls out while rushing behind the accordion door to his kitchenette. Moments later, she's back with a knife. "And order yourself a wicker utensil basket online. You know," she instructs while carefully slicing that Danish into guest-size strips. "So things aren't a mess here." She glances at him still leaned back and observing her in action. "Organized. Things should be ... organized." Slowly, she just draws that knife through the pastry now.

Cliff keeps watching. And noticing those diamond studs in her second piercing. And the sassy way she slung a mod silk scarf around her neck.

All as she arranges pastry pieces and prattles on about needing a supply of paper doilies and a small wastebasket for his business guests—until she looks at him silently watching her.

"What are you doing?" she asks, stopping her knife mid-pastry-slicing.

"Me?"

"Yes."

"I'm observing that you seem *distracted* this morning."

"Distracted?"

"Yes. You're here, there," he says, motioning to the accordion door she left open. "Talking pastry, decorating. Flitting about. You seem … distracted."

"Well, I'm not. I'm just busy. Shouldn't you have Association things keeping *you* busy?" she deflects.

Cliff looks from her to his computer screen. He sits up straight then, too. "I *was* checking RSVPs to the Guard Shack Paint Reveal event later today. *And* estimating how much of the street to close off for the BYOC."

"BYOC?"

Cliff nods. "Bring your own chairs. *Sand* chairs. Lawn chairs. I need to estimate how many will be lined up so that Nick can put out road barriers." Cliff shuffles through loose papers on his desk. He pulls some out from beneath Elsa's pastry bag. "The megaphone has to be dusted off, too." Setting aside those papers, he looks at Elsa. "Wait until you see that guard shack. It's really something," he says. "You know that Flynn who locked us in the shed?"

"Don't remind me."

"He's actually a *meticulous* painter." Just then, Cliff's cell phone dings with a text message. He turns the phone atop his desk to read it. "Excellent," he says, then types a return text. "Flynn's mother messaged me she'll bring dessert for the event." Now he looks up at Elsa again. "Can we use your folding table? The one from your boardwalk meetings?"

"Sure." Elsa's wiping her fingers on a paper napkin now. "Just send someone for it. It's in the storage space beneath my deck. I'll leave it open." She pauses her finger-dabbing and straightens a piece of pastry on the glass dish.

Again, Cliff leans back in his office chair. He crosses his arms this time and watches her at that coffee cart. Something seems off. She's not herself. "Listen," he begins now, reaching for his cell phone again. "Speaking of text messages, I've been meaning to ask you something." He flashes her the heart emoji text she sent him from her California balcony. "I don't suppose this was sent in error?"

Elsa takes the phone, looks at his saved text, then gives back his phone. "No," she says. "No error."

"Really?"

"Yes. Celia was *very* sure when she tapped that heart."

"Wait." Cliff looks at that heart that's entertained his thoughts these past days. *"Celia?"*

"Yes. Celia."

"You mean, *you* didn't send it?"

"No. Celia did. When you texted me that day, she reached over the table and was fresh. Said that heart was what I *should* be texting you back."

Again, Cliff looks at the text—this time with disappointment. "So we're back to square one?"

"Oh," Elsa says, waving him off. She takes that now-empty pastry bag and folds it into her tote.

Cliff, dejectedly, deletes his long-held-on-to text. "I guess we'll have to decide *what* exactly we are, then."

"Or," Elsa declares while pulling her keys from her tote now. "As I often read in the BOG meeting minutes, we can just *pause* the issue."

"Pause it?"

Elsa nods. "Like the BOG does when it can't make a decision and dithers too long on a topic. They ... *pause* it."

"Meaning, as in most BOG instances ..." Cliff says, standing when he hears a noise outside the trailer. "Most likely never to be resolved or come back to?" Now he's glancing outside, then excuses himself and rushes to the trailer's metal door. He opens it to see several people setting up early to reserve their sand-chair spots for the day's big event. One man leaves a mini grill, too. Another arranges cornhole boards behind the open chairs. And a ring toss. Someone deposits a couple of Frisbees. And ... *wait*. Cliff hurries down the four metal stairs to the trailer's yard. "Is that a tic-tac-toe board—in the *street?*" he asks himself. He also lifts his walkie-talkie from his belt clip and tells Nick to get here. Fast!

"I read you, boss," Nick's voice comes over the walkie-talkie. "On my way," he says, followed by a fuzzy chirp.

"We need to close the road to traffic," Cliff explains into the mouthpiece. "Set up the sawhorses. Make a temporary detour onto Hillcrest Road only. ASAP." As Cliff talks and approaches the early spectators opening sand chairs, Elsa passes him and climbs into her nearby golf cart. "It's imperative that the Paint Color Reveal is a safe community event," Cliff says to Nick via walkie-talkie—all while watching Elsa. "We're going to have a big crowd."

Nick's voice squawks back. "Of course it's going to be big." Static blasts from Cliff's walkie-talkie before Nick's squawking voice comes again. "*Any* event here is a hoopla."

When Elsa carefully steers her golf cart onto the street and gives a light horn-toot, Cliff calls out to her. "See you tonight, Mrs. DeLuca! Got a special sand chair reserved for you!"

⁓

Cliff was right.

She *is* distracted. Case in point? As Elsa zips off, she realizes she forgot to mail Wren's thank-you note earlier when she was buying pastry. The envelope is still in her golf cart. So she puts her cat-eye sunglasses back on before making a U-turn.

And keeps moving.

Her cart zips along beneath the stone train trestle *again*, hangs a left and turns into the Scoop Shop plaza. This time she passes the convenience store and stops in front of the post office's satellite branch further down.

But she also pauses—right there. Holding Wren's thank-you note in her hand, Elsa feels a little nostalgia. Why, it was just *days* ago that she rode horseback through the Pacific Ocean with Wren. And walked the perfectly serene Cypress Tree Tunnel.

"Oh, if only my life were serene," she whispers while stepping out of the golf cart. It's midmorning. The sky is that crisp October blue. The air, cool. So she takes her time walking

to the mailbox outside the post office. Carefully then, she feels for the mailbox handle to pull open. Reaches left, right. Lifts her sunglasses to the top of her head again and bends low. Looks and feels for that darn handle.

"Need some help with that?" a familiar voice calls out.

A familiar voice Elsa recognizes. A voice that has her briefly drop her eyes closed before straightening to see the man who goes *with* that soothing voice. The man wearing a brown tweed jacket open over a denim button-down and khaki pants. The man whose faded blond hair is pulled back into a small ponytail. The man with a double rawhide choker around his neck.

"Oh, Mitch," Elsa says with an easy smile. "I was trying to open this mailbox as though it had a handle. Old habits just die hard sometimes," she admits, then plunks the thank-you card into the mailbox *slot*.

"Well." Mitch crosses his arms and leans against his safari-style vehicle parked there. "Aren't you a sight for sore eyes. Haven't seen you around these parts lately."

Elsa nods and steps closer. "I've been away, actually. Visiting a friend."

"Anywhere exciting?"

"California. San Francisco and the Bay Area. Spent some time with my old college roommate."

Mitch says nothing. But he cautiously squints at her with those astute eyes of his.

"What's the matter?" Elsa asks, leaning beside him on that safari vehicle of his now. And returning the squint, too.

"Well …" Mitch slowly begins. "Your trip sounds *fun* … So why do you look so sad, Elsa?"

"Damn it." She hikes her tote up on her shoulder and

looks away, then back at him. "Is it that obvious?"

"Afraid so. Anything I can do?"

Elsa considers him for a long moment, then motions him to one of the bistro tables set outside the plaza. Sweeping ornamental dune grasses cascade behind it. Mitch follows her and they both sit at the tiny black-mesh table.

"If you have a minute, I believe you *can* help," Elsa tells him now.

"Shoot. Let me hear it."

"Okay." Elsa pulls her chair in closer. The sun shines bright around them. Cars drive in and out of the nearby parking lot. "The thing is, Mitch? I really could use an unbiased opinion about something that happened. So do you think you might give me some advice, friend to friend?"

Mitch draws a hand down his goatee. "I'll certainly try."

"That works for me. What I'm wondering is, well … Okay. What would *you* do if you witnessed something you weren't meant to see? Something—unsettling—yet private. From someone you care about. And it made you very worried about them."

Mitch shifts in his chair. "Someone here?"

Elsa gives a quick smile. "I can't go into details. But I'm wondering … Would you *approach* them? Or see if they come to *you* about the situation. I mean," Elsa presses, "is it your place to say anything at *all*? Because I'm honestly at a standstill and don't know *what* to do. How to handle this emotional situation I saw. What steps—if any—to take."

"So you're only a witness, then. Correct?"

"That's right. Purely."

"And not privy to details of what sounds like a *difficult* situation."

"For sure."

"Well, Elsa." Mitch takes a long, regretful breath. "I learned the hard way recently … that you have to let people live their *own* lives. The lives *they* choose."

Again, Elsa briefly closes her eyes. Because she hears what Mitch *isn't* saying. She hears the innuendo suggesting *she* was the person who dealt that hard lesson during their breakup. *"Go on,"* she whispers—not sure if she really wants him to.

But he does.

"I speak from experience, dear Elsa, that no intervention can change someone's heart. You can only … hope for the best for them." He stands now. "I'll hope that for you in *this* situation, too." With that, he squeezes her hand for a moment, turns and walks away.

sixteen

FRIDAY MORNING, SHANE ALMOST MISSES his captain. But at sunrise, he calls out and trots to him on the docks. They both grab a coffee from the little harbor shed there. And linger by the railing. And talk. Fishing days are running out and his captain wants him back—for at least the final week.

"You've been off the water since Shiloh died. Been nearly a month now," the grizzled captain tells him. "It's time for you to get back, Shane. Get on with it. With your life, your work."

He's right, Shane knows. And he *will* get on with it. But not yet—which annoys the captain. Shane picks up on it.

"Don't keep me waiting too long, Shane. I need a deck boss. If not you, it'll have to be someone else."

"It'll be me, I swear," Shane explains. "Just need more time, sir. Still have things to get done. Obligations."

Obligations like this.

Like later that morning, approaching a home Shane didn't know if he'd ever see again. The old white clapboard farmhouse has a steep-pitched roof and open front porch. Close by, on a slightly sloping hill, there's also a little white farm stand selling a scattering of pumpkins and gourds. Potted mums dangle from the farm stand's roof overhang.

So does a cluster of faded fishing buoys.

Which breaks Shane's heart all over again. Because he knows. The buoys are there in honor of Shiloh.

While turning into the long driveway to the farmhouse, he sees more. Fresh pumpkin pie and coffee are set up on the front porch. Once out of his pickup, Shane straightens his dark green cardigan hanging open over an untucked brown flannel and cuffed jeans. Takes a breath. And walks to that porch. Dried leaves crunch beneath his beat-up trail shoes. A farm dog lopes closer and follows him to the front door. It's obvious by the pie and coffee that Shane's welcome here. So he clears his throat and knocks at the door.

Tammy and Keith, Shiloh's parents, rush out and hug him right there on the porch. There are shoulder claps and close murmurs telling Shane they're so glad he called.

"It's really good to see you," Keith tells him. "We've been thinking of you."

"Shiloh and both of you are never far from my thoughts, either," Shane tells them as they settle on rockers and a wicker settee on the porch. A huge maple tree close by sheds its red leaves. They float and swirl to the leaf-strewn yard. A cornstalk on the front porch leans near the screen door. That farm dog sits on the top step. And beside Shane, Tammy and Keith are dressed in sweaters and jeans.

Tammy's shoulder-length, silvery-blonde hair is down and brushed back. Keith's close-cut goatee matches his closely shorn black hair. This time, their grief isn't as palpable as when Shane last saw them.

This time, they're coping.

Part of that, Shane sees, is by keeping busy. Selling pumpkins from their farm stand. Tammy baking the pumpkin pie she's now slicing. And dropping a dollop of whipped cream on. And turning to hand Shane the pie-laden plate.

He takes a bite of that pie and sips hot coffee on this mid-October morning. Though the sun's shining, there's a hint of winter coming now, too. They're quiet as they just sit together. Eat together.

Shane asks them, then, a question most difficult. But he has to ask. Has to let them talk, vent, cry, whisper—whatever they choose.

"How are you both doing?" he asks, his voice low.

"Oh, as expected, I guess," Tammy's soft voice confesses. "We try to fill the hours. To have some routine. Tend the farm. Go into town for groceries. Talk to folks who stop by for a pumpkin or two. Folks who don't *know* what happened to us and are just glad to be out for a scenic drive."

Keith squeezes Tammy's hand, then sips his coffee. "Honestly, Shane? We go through the motions," he admits. "We do that other stuff all as Shiloh's *foremost* in our minds. But really? We just … go through those motions. Put up a front, in a way."

"If I didn't keep myself busy," Tammy explains, "I'd be crying much more. Looking at old pictures. Remembering my Shiloh."

"I hear you," Shane says, nodding.

When they ask about *him*, Shane fills them in on all he's been doing—from rebuilding a grand stairway to the sea for an old friend, to his spontaneous trip with Celia to San Francisco earlier that week.

"No lobstering?" Keith asks.

"No. Not since we lost Shi. But Captain wants me back to close out the season. So I'll be there soon, on the boat. And the whole time? It's to do right by Shiloh."

They talk a little while more. Shane has a second piece of pumpkin pie. Takes a refill on the coffee. Sits and listens to their even voices talking of the farm, and of their son. Tammy says how she misses Shiloh's booted steps coming up the front porch stairs at the end of the day. She vaguely mentions how he liked to get the firepit going on cool October evenings. And Keith? He pats the farm dog sitting there and tells Shane how the dog misses Shiloh, too. They can tell. The dog sits like that on the step and watches the driveway … like it's waiting for him. That this was Shiloh's dog. Tammy nods, her eyes moist.

And Shane sees that it's those kinds of small things— the mundane stuff of life—that aren't mundane at all. They're monumental.

Hanging out at a firepit.

The footsteps of someone coming home at the end of the day. Steps one must listen for—though now they'll never be heard again.

A guy and his dog.

Shane can't help it, either. When he sees Tammy's tears of grief for the son she lost just weeks ago … sees how she would give *anything* for more time with Shiloh, he thinks of another mother.

139

Of Heather.

Of Heather who *doesn't* feel that way toward her own daughter—very much here and alive.

⌒

Which leaves Shane with a sudden sense of urgency.

He has to get back to Stony Point.

Back to Celia.

If someone's ever going to *be* there for her, it's him.

So once back at his shingled harborside home, he finishes up some odds and ends. Finds lobster stuff for Evan's fourth-grade class presentation—coiled rope and extra gauges and a fake lobster and an old gaff hook used to snare the trap-line buoys. He tosses it all in a cardboard carton. Now, one more thing.

"Buoys, buoys," he whispers, looking around. "Ah, yes. The shed." He hurries to the kitchen. First he sees the dove arm cuff he'd left dangling on a cabinet knob. So he drops that sterling-silver cuff into his duffel before searching his kitchen junk drawer. The key to his shed is somewhere in there. His hand brushes through old paper menus and matchbooks and pens and notepads until—*yes*—got it. A single key on an old metal key ring.

Pushing the drawer closed, he turns away.

Then turns back and opens the drawer again. Something caught his eye just now. So he fishes it out—an old roll of film. It's Neil's and has been sitting in that darn drawer for ten years now. Shane's seen it but never bothered doing anything with it. Hell, he'd thought Neil was still alive until just a couple of months ago. He joggles the film canister in his hand. Okay, the film *might* be unused, just a blank extra roll Neil left behind on his last visit here.

Or the film has undeveloped photographs on it.

So Shane tosses that film in his duffel, too.

Quickly then, he goes to the shed outside, unlocks it and swats away a few cobwebs as he pokes around on the rear shelves. Yep. There they are. Old fishing buoys strung on tangles of salt-coated rope. The kids in Evan's class will love this.

So Shane's good. And he's rushing. Back in the house, he adjusts the timers on a few lights. Texts his neighbor Bruno that he's off again. Tells him there's a brew with his name on it if he can keep an eye on things still. Puts the carton of gear and the old faded buoys in his truck bed. Tosses his repacked duffel in the front passenger seat. Trots back to the house. Goes inside, checks the back door, the stove, windows. Closes some curtains. Relieves himself. Locks up.

And splits.

Gets in his pickup and pushes the speed limit on the winding Maine roads.

Takes the quickest route to the highway.

Keeps an eye on the speedometer.

The coastline view of harbors and lobster-trap stacks veers to more country-rural.

To woods and swampy wetlands.

Forest presses close to the roads now.

Shane's booted foot is heavier than it should be on the gas pedal.

His hands grip the steering wheel as his truck barrels along, taking the curves with ease.

On the rural byways, the roadside forest is blurring past.

Another check of the speedometer.

That urgency hasn't let up to see Celia. To be with her. Hold her.

The past week just broke his heart for her.

So that's all he wants now—to get to Celia.

To go to Stony Point.

To go.

Go.

~

And he'd get there—except for the moose.

The massive, majestic bull moose.

A temperamental bull moose in the heart of mating season.

So an animal *not* to be messed with.

And the animal is standing *exactly* in the middle of the road.

Shane lets up on the gas. Quickly presses the brakes. And stops the pickup within several feet of the huge animal. He's not sure he's ever seen a bull moose this close.

But one thing's for sure. If anything's going to stop Shane from quickly getting three hundred miles south, it could only be this Maine mammal.

This easily thousand pound, six-foot-tall moose.

A moose whose antlers must spread four feet, at *least*.

This moose whose tall legs and humped back and rack of antlers are *nothing* Shane wants to challenge.

Some water drips from the animal. Its legs and underside are wet. Damp, reedy grass blades cling to its hefty sides. So the moose must've just emerged from some swampy pool of water in the nearby woods.

Okay. Shane's got no choice, really. He just idles his pickup—right there. Silently. He doesn't move. Doesn't hit the horn. Oh, he slaps the steering wheel. Says a few choice words, too. Then grabs his cell phone and snaps some pictures. The moose takes a step or two. Turns its enormous head toward Shane. Freezes like that for a few seconds, then walks a couple of steps in his direction.

"You son of a bitch," Shane mutters. He could've been picking up the highway right now—if it weren't for the moose. Could've flipped down the visor against the midday sun and been gunning it seventy miles per hour south. Could've been feeling those miles of pavement roll beneath his truck tires.

Instead of this.

Instead of being in a full-blown standoff with one of God's greatest creatures.

"All right, big boy," Shane says, sitting back with a long breath. "Whenever the spirit moves you."

seventeen

IF THE TRESTLE GIVETH AND the trestle taketh away, one thing's for certain.

This time, it's all giveth.

Because five hours later, there it is—that stone trestle with golden and red brush cascading down its embankment. And that railroad trestle is giving Shane the only world he wants right now.

The world of Celia.

She's somewhere on the other side of that big, beautiful, dank, shadowed stone tunnel. So he slowly cruises beneath it and feels better than he's felt the past few days.

Well, he *did* feel better.

Until he's stopped to find the entrance to Stony Point blocked. Except this time, it's not a moose blocking his way. It's multiple sawhorses. And sand chairs set out roadside. And cornhole games.

And Nick in full guard uniform—black security visor with khaki button-down over black pants, a walkie-talkie

144

clipped to his belt. He's also holding his official Stony Point clipboard while standing at the privacy panels blocking the guard shack across the street. When he sees Shane just this side of the trestle, he fast approaches.

"Hey, hey. How're the seas treating you, lobsterman?" Nick asks as Shane rolls down his window.

"Not bad," Shane tells him from the pickup's driver's seat. "But what's this shit I'm seeing? A *detour*?"

"Sure is. One day only. The Guard Shack Paint Color Reveal's later today." Nick hitches his head to the completely barricaded shack. "Expecting a big crowd, so let me get your deets to keep the boss happy." Nick holds his pen aloft over some form on his clipboard. "Name?" he asks, without looking up.

"What?" Shane asks.

"Okay, okay. *Shane Bradford*," Nick whispers while jotting the name. "What's the address of that bungalow you're renting?"

"Don't know the number. It's on Sea View. Place called This Will Do."

"Good enough. Let me get your license plate." Nick walks to the front of the pickup, then returns to Shane's open window. "How long you here this time?"

"Not sure. But the cottage is rented through the end of the month."

Nick notes that. "Well, come by later," he says, rapping a knuckle on the side of Shane's pickup. "Bring a sand chair, too."

Shane nods while Nick waves him through, pointing clearly for Shane to veer left to the detour route.

Shane does veer left. But he doesn't turn onto Sea View Road. Doesn't head to his little beach bungalow. No. He stays put on Hillcrest for another few blocks. Shingled shanties and gabled colonials and cottage charmers line the road. Front gardens are strewn with yellow and orange leaves. Pumpkins sit on cottage porch stoops; stuffed scarecrows are tied to lampposts. Finally, he veers his pickup right into the sandy beach parking lot. After five hours of barreling down the interstate, there's only one thing to do right now: stretch his cramped legs and breathe that salt air.

He doesn't waste any time, either. Doesn't stop on the boardwalk and take in the sight—the blues of Long Island Sound rippling beneath the October sunshine; the stretch of golden beach reaching down to the rambling Fenwick cottage and the rocky ledge beyond.

No, instead he just walks across the sand and sits himself right on it. Takes off his socks and beat-up trail shoes, rolls up his pant legs and starts walking.

Starts skimming, too.

The sand feels warm beneath his bare feet as he scoops up flat stones and flings them out to sea. Each stone skips and jumps over the calm Sound. Small silver plumes of water spray up beneath each skimming rock.

Something else happens, too.

With each stone he skims, a thought skims out to sea. Thoughts of Heather Gray. Thoughts of Celia distraught on the streets of San Francisco. Hours of worry. Anger. Sadness.

Skim it away.

Skim it all.

Skim it to the sea and let the current take the angst with it.

He crosses the beach and doesn't let up with his sandy stones. Each one spins out of his hand in a side-armed pitch.

Until moments later, someone out-skims him.

Shane turns to see Kyle standing there in some greasy black diner tee over swim trunks. "Hey, loser," Shane says, shoving his brother. "Aren't you supposed to be behind the stoves?"

"I was," Kyle tells him, then skims another stone. "Since the crack of dawn. Left early to bring the kids to the Guard Shack Paint Reveal."

"That's decent."

Kyle peels off his diner tee, tosses it on the sand and does some stretching.

"You're going swimming?" Shane asks. "It's October, man."

"Best time. Water's still warm and I have the Sound to myself, dude. So I take a dip while I can. Seriously lowers my blood pressure, too," Kyle says while wading in.

"Have a good swim, then."

"Come on in, the water's fine. Could be the last warm day." As he says it, Kyle touches his fingers to the salt water and vaguely blesses himself with his dripping fingers before turning to Shane. "Race you to the rock, slowpoke."

"Can't."

"Why not?"

Shane shoves up his flannel shirtsleeve and shows Kyle his new tattoo. "Can't go swimming until this heals up."

"Lemme see that." Kyle sloshes closer and lifts Shane's arm. "A bison? You got a tat of a *bison*—in Maine?"

Shane bluffs his way through some bullshit reason about

tapping into the animal's strength, then backs further up onto the dry sand. "Catch you around," he tells Kyle. "Don't drown."

Kyle just waves him off before running into the blue water and diving beneath it. When he emerges, brushing water from his sopping face, he calls out to Shane. "Yo, guy! See you tonight. Set up your chair next to ours."

Shane nods, scoops up his shoes and walks back to his truck. The very first thing he does there is lift his cell phone and text Celia.

Just got back, he types. *Can you steal away?*

Yes. Will take baby for walk, comes Celia's answer a minute later. *Meet you at your place.*

Safe? Shane types.

From Celia, *I'll scope things out on the way.*

⁓

Shane wastes no time.

After parking alongside his rented bungalow, he leaves the piles of old roped buoys in his pickup.

Grabs up the classroom carton of lobster gear from the truck bed, then his duffel from the passenger seat.

Trots along the narrow footpath of boardwalk planks flanked by scrubby beach grasses.

Takes the seven back porch steps two at a time.

Unlocks the door to the kitchen and drops his things inside.

Throws a handful of cold water on his face.

And heads back out to the cottage shed.

On the way, lifts a newsboy cap off the coat hook, too, and puts it on.

In no time then, he's stabbing a dusty beach umbrella into the sandy area behind his cottage. The umbrella is rusty from dampness in the musty shed. He clears a spiderweb off the grimy spokes, wipes his hands on his jeans and places two sand chairs beneath the now-open umbrella.

And then there's Celia.

She must've spotted him when she wheeled Aria beside the cottage, because she's crossing his backyard now. She wears a beige Henley sweatshirt-tunic over a white tee and black leggings with her beige trainer sneakers. Her hair is in a low ponytail; his gold mariner chain loops around her neck.

"Hey there, little one," Shane says to Aria first as he lifts her from the stroller. The baby's got on her pink *Mama's Girl* sweatsuit with a light jacket. She smiles and brings her fisted hands to her face as he turns her in his hold. Turns to Celia, too. "And you," he says, stepping closer to her. He leaves a kiss on her lips. "*So* good to see you, Celia."

"*Oh, you, too,*" she whispers into his kiss.

"The coast was clear?"

"It was," she answers with a second quick kiss, then a third. "How was the drive?"

"Long."

When she sits on her sand chair, Shane puts Aria in her lap and they settle in. Celia pulls a few things from her tote: a rattle ring filled with beads, as well as Aria's favorite lion rattle. The baby clutches her beaded ring. With it in her fingers' grip, her little arm rises and falls.

Shane sits, too, beside Celia. The talk is light at first.

Celia asks about Maine.

Shane tells her things he did. Chores. California laundry.

149

Talked to Bruno. The captain. Went to town to eat. Visited Shiloh's parents.

When he tells her that, she reaches around Aria and squeezes his hand.

Shane asks about her time, then. Asks what she's been up to.

"I called my father," Celia admits. "Filled him in on things that happened out west."

"And how'd it go?"

"Not bad, Shane. I was just honest—but vague. Didn't want to get into everything with him."

"Celia. Really? Maybe you should've."

She shakes her head. "Like I said, I *was* honest. I told him that at the last minute, I decided to let things be and not pursue anything with Heather. And that's all true. He just thinks I changed my mind *before* I ever set foot in August Dove. And I let him think that because there's no need for him to know the rest. It's done, and he'd just worry."

"If you say so, but—"

"No, Shane. I can't have any *buts* in this situation." She pauses to kiss the top of Aria's head. As she does, the baby babbles a few loud syllables while banging her rattle on Celia's leg. "Dad knows enough, and it's all true," Celia goes on. "I also asked him to please accept my decision and *not* reach out to Heather. Told him that I'm just moving on and leaving well enough alone. That … I'm good."

Shane tips his head and squints at her. "Are you, Celia?"

"What?"

"Are you good?" Shane tips up his newsboy cap to better see her. "I mean, after what I saw in San Francisco?

After what you told me while leaning against a brick building on the streets? That you couldn't get past your mother not including you in her own dreams."

"What are you saying, Shane?"

"Nothing. Well, something. I'm just checking to be sure you're *really* good with how things ended in August Dove. I mean, you asked me in California why Heather couldn't ever have things *both* ways—her passion *and* you."

"I did."

"Well maybe your mother couldn't—for whatever reason—include you in her dreams back *then*, but what if she could now? You didn't stick around to even give that possibility a chance."

Celia says nothing. She looks from him to the gentle lapping waves at their feet. She rocks Aria a little, too, swaying with her baby.

"So … what if it's *not* too late?" Shane presses. "What if Heather can do that *now*? Have both worlds *now*?"

Celia shakes her head. She also tickles Aria's face with the fluffy fur of her lion rattle. Takes a quick breath, too, before looking at Shane again. "Granted, Shane, you *did* catch me in a fraught frame of mind on the streets of San Francisco. And I *don't* deny how I felt. Those awful feelings were very real. But I also have distance from that moment now. Clarity. I've done lots of thinking. On the plane. Unpacking. Being home." Celia nudges off her sneakers, stands with Aria and walks to the small, splashing waves.

Shane only watches for a second before joining her. He takes Aria and holds the baby to his shoulder. "I'm listening," he quietly tells Celia.

Celia nods, then dips her fingers in the water and touches

a few drops to Aria's hand. Then she starts walking barefoot in the shallows. "Here's what I think, Shane. Here's where my thoughts went. My mother's jewelry boutique—"

"August Dove."

"Yes. August Dove is a beautiful *wonderland*. The wings—*everywhere*. The décor. That painted wall mural. How many customers step up to that dove mural with its outstretched wings and feel their own wings soar? Then there's the *incredible* jewelry, all of it their own pieces of art. And all of it set against the magic of those wings of peace. Of those framed musician posters. Walking into August Dove is like stepping into the pages of a fantastic fairy tale."

"I agree," Shane tells her, Aria still in his arms.

"And when I walked in, I knew."

"Knew what?"

"I knew how wrong it would be to deny Heather Gray *that* life. To cage *her*—in a way."

When Celia's quiet a moment, Shane is, too. He feels Aria's sleepy weight against his shoulder as the baby relaxes in the sunshine.

"Seeing Heather in her own element there," Celia finally continues as they slowly walk, "it was undeniable. *That* was her purpose—started all those years ago when her parents brought her to Woodstock as a child. When Heather became *transfixed* with what she saw: The people. The fashion. The music. The self-expression. It's also undeniable the amount of lives she *is* touching—doing what she's doing. The renowned musicians on the walls. Customers in and out of her jewelry boutique. But at the same time, I'm not in denial, Shane. Because I'm also saying this. Some white dove of hope *did* just fly out of my heart when I walked into that shop."

"So maybe you're still open—"

"No, Shane. If my mother had met me halfway … If she'd said *something*. Reached out to me. Well, things might have gone differently. But that didn't happen. For some reason, she couldn't. Or … wouldn't. Because she *did* recognize me. You know she did. And if she had just said, *Celia!* It's you."

"But she didn't." Shane turns now and walks toward Aria's stroller near the sand chairs.

"No," Celia says, catching up with him. "She didn't. And it is what it is. There was nothing to grasp on to from her." Shane puts the nearly sleeping baby into Celia's arms for her to settle in the stroller now. Celia fusses with her, then, as the drowsy baby falls asleep in the warm salt air. After she does, Celia sits beside Shane beneath the beach umbrella. "Sometimes?" she begins, her voice hushed as Aria dozes. "Not going to lie. Sometimes I regret that I even did it. Even *thought* to do it. Attempt some mother-daughter reunion. But if I didn't, Shane?" she says, stroking his arm. "I'd always wonder. So the whole situation was dual-edged."

"But did you give the situation *enough* of a chance?"

"Shane. You're relentless with me today. What's going on?"

"I just want to be sure you're *really* satisfied with the outcome." He blows out a breath. "And listen, don't get mad."

"Oh, no. What is it?"

"Before we left for California? When I told Jason I had to bail on the stairs a few days? He figured out why."

"Jason knows all this?" she whispers. *"Jesus, Shane. It's private!"*

"Celia. Jason Barlow's a smart man. He already knew about the California trip from Maris and put together the pieces. Hell, he knows everything now, okay? Called me a couple of times out west, just to check in. And I had breakfast with him yesterday morning."

"Which means Maris knows everything."

Shane nods. "I'm sure she does. But you know it'll stop there. They both want nothing but the best for us."

From her sand chair, Celia only watches him. "If you sought out Jason yesterday," she reasons, "you were looking for advice. So what'd he say?"

Shane hesitates. "He told me how in his mind, Ted Sullivan—for ten years—was the enemy."

"I can get that."

"Me, too. But Jason went on to say how once he got to know Ted, that the man's become a great friend. One of the very *few* people Jason can always count on. And he wondered if we might—just *might*—be wrong. If it's possible for you to have a relationship with Heather in some different capacity. To have her in your life in some way we're just not seeing."

"Like how, Shane?" Celia quietly asks.

"Don't know." In his pause, a salty breeze whispers off Long Island Sound. "But that's *why* I'm pressing you. To be sure this all gets resolved in the way you really want."

"It doesn't matter what I want. It's just how it went. And I'm not going to try again."

Shane doesn't say anything. He looks directly to Celia beside him. In his silence, there's only that light October breeze and the lapping waves. Water and air. Salt. Warmth.

"Shane," Celia gently says. "After that morning in August Dove, I know who matters in my life. And that I already *have* the kind of relationship I was seeking."

"With Elsa."

"That's right. *Her* wings have buoyed me more than once. Things are good with my father, too. And with *you*." Celia stretches close, strokes his face and kisses him. "Am I disappointed in how some things went? Yes. Am I embarrassed that you had to witness me coming undone on the city streets? Yes, I am. I don't want you to see me that way."

"What way?"

"Like someone who doesn't really deserve this," Celia says, lightly tugging the short gold mariner necklace he gave her. "Like someone who *isn't* the strongest person you know—as strong as a boat's anchor chain."

Shane won't hear of it, shaking his head. "Celia. Don't."

"No. I feel like I let you down. For starting something with my mother that I couldn't finish. And it straight up *sucks* that, unfortunately, it took me walking into August Dove and going through that whole crappy experience to realize all the beautiful goodness I already *have*. But please trust me when I tell you any curiosity, or false hope, I might've had … is behind me. I'm good. *We're* good. It's all good." She gives him a smile, leans to him and squeezes his forearm.

Shane sits back in his sand chair. He resettles his newsboy cap on his head. Leans forward and loops his arms around his knees, then looks back at Celia—beautiful Celia—sitting there. An escaped wisp of her auburn hair blows in the breeze. Her face is calm. Her hazel eyes watch his. And Shane can't help but think of all the people he was testy with up north the past two days. His boss. Fishermen in Red Boat Tavern. Drivers on the highway, even. Okay, God, maybe.

"What is it, Shane?" Celia asks.

"Jesus, Celia." He takes her hand in his and kisses the back of it. "If you'd just told me all this sooner, I would've pissed off a lot less people this week."

eighteen

ALL CLIFF HEARS ARE VOICES.

They come from the other side of the privacy panels around the newly painted guard shack. So many voices are chatting, laughing, yelling, he can only imagine the crowds lining the street. But *behind* the privacy panels, there's silent—almost manic—last-minute prep this Friday afternoon. Nick's stringing white twinkle lights along the shack's roofline. Carol's doing the same to the new bushes she added to the landscaping. The lights are all battery operated, and it's Flynn's responsibility to flick the remote upon command. In the meantime, he's chowing down a large chocolate-chip cookie—part of the refreshments his mother arranged for the event.

Cliff steps out of the guard shack just then and straightens a *Welcome* mat at the door. After all the pondering and planning and voting and painting this past month—this is it. The Guard Shack Color Reveal is really happening. It's just minutes away now.

"Hey, Cliff," Carol says. She's beside that shack door and stringing tiny lights on the last shrub. "How's your son doing?" she asks. "Will he be here for this?"

"No," Cliff tells her. "I'm actually seeing Denny this weekend, though. I'll tell him you asked about him."

"Oh, please do." Carol wraps lights around and around the small Alberta spruce. "I quite enjoyed that Nova ride on Labor Day weekend."

Cliff glances to Flynn when he hears him loudly whisper, *Whoa. What are you … jealous?* Which gets Cliff to look at the question's recipient. It's Nick, twisted around on his stepladder and watching Carol inquire about Denny.

But more noise drowns out any further behind-the-partitions chatting. There's the rhythmic thump of heavy pellet bags landing on cornhole boards. There's the *Woots!* when a tossed bag slides into the hole.

There's the noise of not tailgate-grilling, but something more like sand-chair-grilling. Portable grills are fired up; steaks are sizzling; burgers are charring; buns, toasting. Large scoops of macaroni salad are being thunked on dishes. Soda can tops are being popped.

Then there's the talk.

The color-debating that hasn't let up in weeks is still going strong.

Navy and white. Can't get more coastal than that.

Sure can. How about silvery gray?

With navy shutters, yeah!

You want summer sand tan? Yep, beige and boring.

But Cliff hears something else, too. He hears Elsa's name being mentioned. So he ventures around the privacy panels and looks at the front row of sand chairs. Her chair's been reserved with a custom sash. He plans on asking her to be the guest-of-honor shack-countdown emcee. A megaphone waits on her empty chair.

Empty.

Thus people mentioning her name. Wondering where she is. There's Celia with Aria. Nearby, the Gallaghers are set up with Matt grilling. And the whole Bradford clan—Shane included—is off to the other side. Eva's wandered over to where Maris sits with Jason.

And they all keep looking over their shoulders. They search the crowds on the street. Now Lauren's walking to Celia.

"Did you see Elsa at the inn?" Lauren asks.

"No. No, I was busy with this little pumpkin," Celia says, bouncing Aria on her lap.

"Oh, you cutie." Lauren bends and tickles Aria's chin. *"Coochie-coo!"*

"Can you hold her, Lauren?" Celia asks. "I'm going to text Elsa."

Cliff looks to Maris and Eva now. Both women are also intently texting. Cliff's sure it's Elsa they're after.

Even Kyle, also texting, asks Shane something beside him. Shane looks around, then shakes his head. So Kyle keeps thumb-typing.

And Elsa's reserved seat is still glaringly empty.

All as the cornhole games continue. And the street tic-tac-toe competition heats up. As do the smokin' grills.

But now, Cliff's concerned. So he joins the others. Yes, he does. He pulls his cell phone from his pocket, then moves back behind the privacy partitions. Does something else, too. *He* starts texting, his fingers moving rapidly over his phone.

⁓

Well now, this is something Elsa never saw coming. Her cell phone's lighting up like a Christmas tree. It's dinging and flashing out of control. Even worse, it happened as soon as she kicked off her sneakers and settled on her nautical-striped sofa this afternoon. Put up her feet, lay back and just … closed her eyes.

Until her phone gets them open—pronto!

So she reaches for that phone on the coffee table and brings it closer. Squints at the screen, too. Why, there are text messages from everyone! Eva. Maris. Lauren, too. *And* Kyle. Celia. *All* of them are asking after her. *Where are you?* And, *Is everything okay?* And, *Aria's missing her nonna! Hurry down.* And one more, *Don't want you to miss the shack's big unveiling!*

Elsa sighs. It seems Mitch was onto something earlier this morning. And if she couldn't hide her sadness from *him*, certainly everyone else would pick up on it, too. Which is exactly why she's been hiding herself—behind sunglasses, home alone on her sofa—all day long.

But there's no escaping this texting crew. Her phone dings over and over again. The senders won't relent without some answer. So Elsa sits up, reaches for her spare reading glasses on the end table and begins quieting the crowd. Her fingers type responses for each.

To Celia: *Headache. Staying in. Talk soon.*

To Maris: *Tired. Bit of headache, too. My regards to all.*

To Eva: *Oh, this jet lag. Taking a pass on reveal.*

To Lauren: *No worries. Just resting post-trip.*

To Kyle: *Thanks for checking. Fine, just fatigued. Need another jet lag tip!*

Right as Elsa goes to set her phone down, one more text arrives. It's from Cliff. Cliff—telling her he's waiting for his guest of honor. Not only that, he sends a photo of her empty seat with a *Reserved* sash slung across it.

"Ah, Cliff," she whispers as she lies back again, phone in hand. She knows how important this event is to him. He's worked on it for weeks now. So as not to worry him, she keeps her answer vague and touches upon her jet lag. *Good luck*, she finally ends her message. *I'll come by tomorrow to see the shack.*

Done. But she still holds her phone—because she knows. She's *not* done with it. Lying on her sofa and waiting for more *dings*, she sees Sal's old rowboat oars mounted over her fireplace. On the driftwood mantel, she sees her happiness jar. There's the seagull feather Cliff dropped in it last month, after she officiated Kyle and Lauren's vow renewal.

And right on schedule, her cell phone dings again.

Plans this weekend with Denny, Cliff's text reads. *Some house projects at his place. Catch up with you next week.*

Next week.

Maybe by then she won't feel so sad.

Maybe by then she'll have answers.

Answers about the distraught scene she witnessed on the San Francisco streets.

Answers about Celia Gray and Shane Bradford.

"I'm just not buying it, Maris," Jason says. He leans close to her in their sand chairs at the Guard Shack Paint Reveal event. The racket around them—between the lawn games' hoots and hollers and the sizzling grills and the laughs and talking—is kept to a dull roar. Which is why he's leaning close to Maris. It's the only way she'll hear him.

"Buying what?" she asks back.

"Your aunt's excuses. She's *so* into these things, she'd never miss it—jet lag or not. So I'm going to call her." Jason starts to stand, telling Maris, "Be right back."

Problem is, he has to take a hike just to find a quiet-enough spot to talk. Finally, he walks beneath the trestle and heads out the other side. There's a grassy area there with crumbling concrete steps leading up to the Scoop Shop plaza. So he sits on one of those steps and makes his phone call.

"Elsa," he says when she picks up.

"Jason?" she answers. "Didn't Maris get my text?"

"Yeah, and that's enough from you. Cut the bullshit already."

As he expected, at first Elsa resists. She tells him she's at the inn. The place is all buttoned up for the night. That she's tired.

"Not buying it, Elsa. You *never* miss an event like this."

There's a pause—and he knows. She's giving in.

"To be honest, Jason," Elsa begins, "I just didn't want to see everyone today."

"Okay," he reasons. "And why's that?"

"It's just that something's happened—"

"Elsa," he interrupts. "What's going on? You can tell me."

She sighs then. "Listen. So maybe I *don't* have a headache, okay?" her voice comes through the phone. "Or maybe it's more of an emotional headache. But Jason? I *really* need some space today. I'm fine, but something's on my mind that I'm *not* getting into right now."

When he still presses her, it's Elsa who interrupts this time.

"It's pretty personal, Jason. And I need to think some things through. So promise to cover for me at that guard shack? You *know* I'd do the same for you."

He does know that—without a doubt. So he gives Elsa his word. Hangs up, too. And doesn't say the rest until he stands and pockets his phone.

Says it while descending those dilapidated concrete steps.

Says quietly, to himself, *"Son of a bitch."*

⁓

So this is it, Shane thinks.

Americana.

A community gathered for a worthwhile event. For something … symbolic. Something that represents one and all. Like the American flag. Or a holiday parade. A patriotic concert on a town green. A baseball game or farmers' market.

And for Stony Point? A Guard Shack Color Reveal.

Roadside spectators, lawn games, barbecues. It's all here. Yes, pure Americana.

Sitting in his sand chair, Shane shoots the shit with his brother. He tosses a Frisbee with his nephew, Evan. He stealthily reaches behind his little niece, Hailey, and taps her *other* shoulder. When she turns that way, then this way, he tickles her cheek. "Gotcha!" he says.

He also finds himself in a recently familiar quandary. One in which difficult questions present themselves.

Americana? Or the sea?

Stony Point? Or a lobster boat on the Atlantic Ocean?

The *best* harborside house in Rockport? Or a shabby cottage rental here?

On an afternoon like this, he can't help but think those questions. Here, there. North, south. Atlantic Ocean, Long Island Sound. Boys in the crew. Old beach gang.

No one?

Celia.

Before he can ponder enough to eventually keep him awake at night, Cliff interrupts everything. A call for attention through his megaphone does it. Standing in front of the guard shack's privacy panels, he gives a really brief speech, too. It's a speech of gratitude, mostly.

"To Nick, Flynn and Carol for making this happen," Cliff says, motioning to his three team members standing beside him. "This past week, they went above and beyond to beautify this Stony Point landmark."

A round of polite applause rises.

"Thanks to all our residents, too, for your enthusiastic votes," Cliff continues. "It's *really* good to see the outpouring of love for Stony Point!"

More applause, this time with a raucous bent.

"So without further ado, allow me to hand over the ceremony to Carol, Nick and Flynn."

Nick and Flynn both take their positions at either end

164

of the large privacy panel directly in front of the guard shack. Carol picks up the megaphone and begins the countdown at ten. By the time she gets to five, every sand-chair occupant is chiming in with her.

"Three … Two … *One!*" the voices ring out—then go silent.

Shane watches with amusement as this pin-drop silence falls on the entire block. It happens as Nick and Flynn pull the privacy barriers apart. Flynn then flicks a remote on hundreds of twinkling white lights.

Then—a collective gasp.

Because there it is.

The little guard shack nicely painted. It looks pretty sweet, actually. In the dusky late-afternoon sunshine, those tiny white lights twinkle on the shack's roofline. The shrubs planted beside the entrance door twinkle, too. And the paint? All the shingles are perfectly coated. There's no variation in the shade. A new brass doorknob glimmers on the shack's Dutch door. The roof shingles have even been power washed.

There's a hushed minute of *oohing* and *aahing* as people take in the sight. And realize just what they're seeing.

Which is when things fall apart.

First, there's a chorus of, *"Green?"*

Kyle shoves Shane. "Look at that," he says.

So does everyone. They shove and point and squint. They say more, too.

Green wasn't on the ballot.

The vote was for navy, gray or tan.

This isn't right.

How'd they get … green?

When Cliff raises the megaphone and tries to appease

165

the crowd, he dodges a thrown tomato before folks settle down.

"Thank you," he says then, pacing in front of all the occupied sand chairs. "Now, there *was* an error—as you can see. A mix-up with the paint colors at the hardware store. And once that error happened, well, my team and I made it official. We put the unexpected color to the vote ... and it was unanimous. Green!" He holds up his hand to squelch some verbal resistance. "Please, if I may continue." Another pause for silence, then, "Green," Cliff goes on. "The color of *tranquility*. Of harmony. Of nature—which makes it very calming. And that is something this entire community often needs to do. *Calm down*."

"Hear, hear!" a voice rings out.

"Yeah, Commish! You got that right," another chimes in.

Cliff nods. "So our green landmark that is the first thing you see when arriving beneath the trestle? Let it serve as a reminder. *Calm down*. Be *tranquil. Breathe*. That's the point of this wonderful place after all, isn't it?"

As he says it, folks get up and approach the freshly painted guard shack. Shane thinks they seem mesmerized by it, actually. Some gingerly touch it. Some take selfies near it. Kyle and Lauren tell him they like it, too. All the while Nick's trying to get a photo of the paint team for the Stony Point newsletter. He's got Carol, Flynn and Cliff lined up, but Nick's not in the shot. So Shane takes the camera and gives Nick a shove.

"Get in the picture, guy. I'll grab some photos," Shane tells him.

"Job well done, young man," Cliff tells Flynn on the first camera snap.

166

"Well, *anybody* can paint," Flynn mutters from beneath moppy bangs sweeping his face.

Snap.

"But it came out so good!" Carol tells Flynn. "That careful second coat made all the difference."

"You've fulfilled your community service, Flynn." Cliff shakes Flynn's hand for a picture as he says this. "I hope you see the reward of respecting this place *and* the people here."

"I guess," Flynn answers while turning the handshake into a ladder shake. He extends first his right hand, then his left. Cliff reciprocates as Flynn crouches further and further down with each handshake until they both do a do-si-do at the end.

Snap.

Cliff, laughing, tells Flynn, "The trailer will be awfully quiet without your keen remarks. You feel free to stop by anytime."

The thing is, as Shane snaps the pictures, he can't miss new chatter rising from the crowd behind him. So he turns to take pictures of the fine Stony Point citizens celebrating their tranquil landmark. *Snap ... snap*, as he pans the crowd. And one more *snap* as he meets Celia's eye, too. All while rising murmurs grow.

I like it.
All that time we wasted voting?
Not a waste—look what came of it!
It's beautiful.
And all because of a paint mix-up.
A mistake.
Yeah. One lucky mistake.

167

Lucky mistake.

Lucky mistake.

Celia repeats the words in her mind.

Lucky mistake.

That's how she's come to think of the missed opportunity with her mother in San Francisco.

A lucky mistake.

In the twilight hour now, as tiny white lights twinkle on the charming green guard shack beyond, Celia looks at Aria in her lap. Bounces and coos to her precious baby.

She looks at all the people around her. Folks talking, eating, laughing.

She looks at the people who've *never* walked out on her.

Her neighbors. Her friends here. All of them.

She catches Shane's eye.

Catches his wink before he takes her and Aria's picture.

Oh, yes. All that *didn't* happen in that boutique? In August Dove?

It's hard, but Celia knows.

One lucky mistake, indeed.

nineteen

THE NEARLY FULL MOON HANGS low. It drops a swath of silver on Long Island Sound. In its light, Jason makes out familiar coastal markers: the big rock; the last cottage on the far point; the old pier leading to the boat basin. A slow-moving barge is being tugged past Gull Island Lighthouse.

It all situates him, too.

Casting his fishing line out from the rocks. Breathing the misty evening air. Seeing the landmarks. It's all part of his home.

So is what he's listening to.

Easy familiar talk, like Kyle announcing that his new mega riding mower was delivered yesterday.

"They say midmorning is the optimal time to mow a lawn," Kyle declares now, then casts his fishing line. It whizzes over the dark water. "By midmorning, the dew's evaporated so wet grass won't clog the blades. The temps are still cool, too."

"I thought midday was best," Shane counters.

"Eh. Maybe now, in the fall. But in the summer?" Kyle muses. "It's too hot midday, which makes mowing feel like hard work. And if you really shear the grass on top of that heat? Then you're inviting turf stress."

"What the hell?" Jason asks. "The *grass* gets stressed?"

Kyle nods. "Which is when you get those dry, bare patches."

They go on a little more while Shane toys with a fish nibbling at his line. *"Come on, sucker,"* he whispers, trying to hook it.

Kyle, meanwhile, lists *late*-afternoon mowing merits. "The grass has time to recover before nightfall," he explains. "Which is when lawns are prone to fungus."

They quiet then. And sip from beer cans. They thought they'd grab some Friday night fishing after the Guard Shack Color Reveal. Now Kyle extends an invite to them—a lawn mower invite. "Come and check it out sometime, guys."

"Will do," Shane tells him, still frustrated with the evasive fish at his line. "What's running through here these days? Do you know?"

"Why? You got a nibble?" Jason asks from a nearby boulder.

"Something's toying with me." Shane's taut line goes slack just then. "It's not that big. Can't hook it, though."

"Too small for a bluefish," Kyle remarks. "The reports say porgy are biting."

"Maybe that's it," Jason says while giving his fishing line a tug.

Shane partially reels in his slack line. "Hey, Nick's not fishing tonight?"

"No. Neither is Matt," Jason answers. "They're helping the commish with cleanup."

"Yeah, getting those dividers down," Kyle says. "The sawhorses packed away. Extra chairs folded."

With that heavy moon rising higher, Jason reels in his line and now pushes off that boulder. "Well, fellas. I'm gonna take off. Haven't had dinner yet and am *so* friggin' hungry."

"Me, too." Kyle packs a few things—small scissors, an extra sinker—into his tackle box. "Need a lift, Barlow? I've got my golf cart."

"Yeah." Jason leans his fishing pole over his shoulder and carefully maneuvers off the rocks in the moonlight.

"What about you, Shane?" Kyle asks.

Shane gives his still-slack fishing line a tug. "I'm hanging out here a little longer. See you tomorrow night, brother."

"What's happening tomorrow?" Jason calls back.

"Dinner at The Dockside. After Shane here busted his ass on the Atlantic all week," Kyle explains, "I'm feeding him a good, healthy meal. At that Harvest Night I told you about."

"The one I picked up your pumpkins for?" Jason asks, just stepping onto the sand now.

Kyle's right behind him. "Sure is. You and Maris gonna make it?"

Jason shrugs. "We'll try."

"Hey," Kyle says, turning to Shane out on the rocks. "How long you sticking around this beach town anyway, bro?"

"By contract, end of October." Shane casts his fishing line again, setting it flying over the water. "That's when my cottage rental's up."

Jason walks back a few steps and stops beside Kyle. "Coming up fast. You got a plan after that?"

"Not really." Shane toys with his fishing pole, moving the line some. "Shit, that's my life lately," he calls to them. "I go a week at a time. Month by month. How far ahead can I really look?"

Jason and Kyle give a wave and head out to where Kyle's golf cart is parked on Champion Road. But Jason throws one glance back toward the rocks. Shane's just standing idle, his fishing line seeming afloat.

⁓

Maris hears a noise.

She was just switching on the two small crystal chandeliers above her denim-blue kitchen island. But the noise came from behind her. So she walks to the deck slider and squints out into the darkness. There's Jason. Wearing an old sweatshirt with faded jeans and beat-up fishing-night hikers, he's sitting at the patio table and brushing the dog.

So Maris flips on the deck light and opens the slider screen. "I didn't hear you come home."

"Got here a few minutes ago. Maddy was outside, so I thought I'd brush her for your Christmas card photo."

"Oh." Maris joins him at the table. "Fishing broke up early?"

"Yeah. No one had dinner yet. And with the guard shack thing, Kyle didn't have time to bring his portable grill and cook us up something there."

"Who went, anyway?"

Jason nudges Maddy to turn. "Just Kyle and his brother.

Shane stayed behind. He's still fishing."

"Hey, and what about Elsa? Fill me in on what she said on the phone."

"Something's definitely up," Jason says, pulling the de-shedder brush over Maddy's shoulder. The brush lifts a clump of dry fur. "But I couldn't get much out of her. She said it's personal."

"Personal?"

Jason glances at her and nods. "And she pretty much wanted me to respect her privacy. Which means to mind my own business."

"Wow. She seemed *fine* earlier, when she picked up her watering can," Maris notes. "How about when she saw you for her inn keys?"

"She didn't."

"What? But I told her you were in the barn studio—"

"And I was, but Elsa never came by."

"Huh. So she's been bothered all day by something."

"Seems it."

"Listen," Maris says, leaning over and touching Jason's arm. "Do you think this could have anything to do with Shane and Celia? And what happened in California?"

"Not sure. All I know is that Shane *insisted* at breakfast yesterday that all was kept under wraps with him. And with the whole Celia's mother thing. So I don't think Elsa is aware of *any* of that."

"Great. Now I'm *really* worried about my aunt." Maris sits back in her chair and eyes Jason. He's leaning over the dog and working that fur-filled brush down her flank. "Would you go to the inn and check on her?"

"Me?"

"Yes."

Jason sits up and looks at Maris. *"Tonight?"*

"Yes." She sees his hesitation. "I'll never sleep otherwise, worrying. It'll have me tossing and turning and up all hours."

"Well … Why don't you come with me?"

Maris shakes her head. "She'll talk more to you alone—always has. And it's early still. Just seven-thirty."

Jason resumes his dog-grooming. He tugs the brush through Maddy's thick undercoat. "What about dinner?" he asks. "I'm starved."

"Oh, I'm sure Elsa will have *something* there to feed you. So just change out of that ratty sweatshirt and go. I'll finish with the dog," Maris says when she stands, walks around the table and gives Jason a gentle shove. "Go!"

twenty

ONCE THE GUYS LEAVE, SHANE sits alone on a boulder. Small waves splash at the rocks and tidal pools down below. No matter where he is—here or out on the Atlantic—he never tires of that rhythmic sound of the sea. Lapping onshore or lapping the side of an anchored lobster boat. He could just listen to that splashing and let his mind wander.

Which he does now. Above, that big old moon is higher in the sky. Its pale lunar light falls on the earth. He looks back at Elsa's inn beyond the dune grasses. A few lights are on; she's there. Shane squints down the length of the beach, too. It's empty this evening. He wouldn't be surprised if folks are lingering at their grills and lawn games at the guard shack shindig. It was that good of a time.

On the rocks, though? Quiet. Whispers of the sea. Of those beach grasses up on the sand. The hushed coastal sounds are like the thoughts worrying him still. Thoughts

175

of Celia. Of what he didn't do for her in her mother's jewelry boutique. His worries rise and fade like the waves. Whisper in his mind. Still agitate him with regret at all he *didn't* do. With regret that he didn't veer off-script—even after Celia had walked out of August Dove with Aria.

Regret that he didn't give a piece of his mind to Heather. In retrospect, he owed Celia that much.

He reels in his line now, packs up his few things and walks back to his cottage. It's quiet there, too. There are only *his* sounds inside.

His dropping his keys on the counter.

His washing up at the kitchen sink.

His pulling a flat griddle pan from the cupboard and setting it on the stove. A small pot, too.

His getting knives from the drawer.

Pulling American and cheddar cheese and butter from the fridge; a carton of organic tomato-and-Parmesan soup, too.

Cutting thick tomato slices.

Opening the plastic around a loaf of bread and pulling out three slices.

Dumping the creamy tomato soup into the pot.

Clicking on stove burners to heat the soup and the griddle pan.

Buttering the bread slices.

Setting two sizzling on the hot griddle.

Adding American cheese, tomato.

Stirring a spoon through his warming soup.

Flipping the sandwich once, then again.

Adding shredded cheddar cheese, more tomato and the third slice of buttered bread atop his sandwich.

Flipping it and toasting that side.

Sliding an old tarnished spatula beneath his double-decker grilled cheese sandwich and dropping it on his chipped dish.

Setting the lone dish on his wooden kitchen table.

Flicking on the dull light above the table.

Pouring an ice-cold glass of chocolate milk from a small carton he'd bought.

Pouring his soup directly from the pot into a large bowl before setting the empty pot back on the stove.

Finally, he sits and lets his sandwich cool for a few minutes. When he does, there are no more noises in the old cottage. There are just shadows. Dim lighting. Old furniture. Crappy paned windows that don't want to open. So he opens the kitchen door to the back porch. Cool autumn air drifts in through the screen door now.

Then Shane sits again while shoving up his flannel shirtsleeves. Next he sips a spoonful of soup and digs into his sandwich. Takes a hefty bite. Tastes the melted cheese, the warmed tomato. Dips a corner of the sandwich into his soup and takes another bite. Drinks a long swallow of chocolate milk. Leans his elbows on the table and just finishes his inadequate meal—dipping and chewing and sipping until it's gone.

Afterward, he pushes off his chair and washes everything: plate, glass, pan, pot, utensils, and sets them dripping in the dish drainer. As he's stacking it all, the silver arm cuff he bought for Celia at August Dove catches his eye. The cuff is near his keys further down the kitchen counter. So he dries his hands on a towel and picks up the piece of jewelry. Sitting at the table again, he toys with the thin cuff. Feels the carved dove. Drags a finger around the silver cuff itself. Turns it. Spins it.

And jumps at a knock on the screen door behind him.

~

When Shane turns, Celia's standing there with Aria.

"Celia," he says before getting up and walking to the door.

As he undoes the hook lock, Celia's watching him closely. "You seemed lost in thought," she softly says. "Didn't even hear me climb those seven steps?"

"No." Shane looks at her through the screen. Her auburn hair is down; her face is relaxed; her smile, questioning. "What are you doing here?" he asks, opening the squeaking door with one hand while his other hand really discreetly holds that damn silver cuff.

"The baby was so fussy," she whispers now as Aria nearly dozes in her hold. *"I took her for a walk, that's all."*

"We'll sit on the porch," Shane says, grabbing his sweatshirt from a chairback and stepping outside now. He's also tucking that piece of jewelry deep into a sweatshirt pocket. "Salt air will be good for the little one."

Holding Aria against her shoulder, Celia leans on the half-wall. She waits while Shane slips his sweatshirt on over his flannel shirt, then carries Aria's stroller up the stairs and onto the porch.

"Thanks," Celia murmurs before settling Aria there. She lays her down and pulls a light blanket over her. Whispers sweet nothings and lightly kisses the baby, too. After wheeling the stroller across the porch floorboards, Celia

hoists herself up on the half-wall and leans against a roof post. In the distance beyond her, through the porch's open-air view, Long Island Sound glimmers beneath the moon's silver light.

Shane, meanwhile, notices the half-strung orange harvest lights clumped in a pile on the faded white porch table. He'd started hanging them earlier today and never finished. So he flicks them on, picks them up and slowly loops them around hooks on the roof overhang. "I'm glad you stopped by," he says when he nears Celia with his glowing lights. "So I can be sure you're okay."

"Shane. Of *course* I am. I already told you that. Not only am I *fine*, I'm busy, too."

He throws her a glance while manipulating the string of glimmering orange lights on the overhang right above where she sits. "What do you mean, busy?" he asks, hooking a light, then bending and kissing the top of her head.

"I *mean* … I'll be busy singing at Kyle's Harvest Night tomorrow."

"Seriously?" Now Shane backs up, those orange lights still in hand. "My brother's locked me in to dinner there tomorrow."

"Good. You'll catch my act, then."

"That I will." As he moves past her, he strings more lights. They cast a golden orange glow around the porch roofline. Her gentle voice reaches him as he raises his arms and keeps stringing.

"Your porch lights are so pretty, Shane. I could stay out here for hours."

He doesn't say anything, just keeps stringing those lights.

"Hey," he barely hears. *"I'm really fine."*

Now, he pauses his orange-light-stringing and looks over at her. In her jeans and a thick sweater, she's beautiful in the moonlight. He can hardly believe how beautiful. "I'm not saying you're not fine, Celia. But I saw the pain that came out on that San Francisco street. So I'm glad you came by." He takes two steps back to her, bends and kisses her—right where she sits on the half-wall, her knees drawn up close. *"I wanted to see you again,"* he murmurs. *"It's really impossible, but hell do I wish we could be together tonight."*

"Me, too."

He stops stringing his twinkling orange lights then. Instead, he sets them aside before sitting himself on that half-wall, too. Straddles it right in front of her—as close as he can sit. He touches her silky hair. Her face. "If you'd spent the night," his low voice goes on, "I would've held you close."

"Oh, Shane," she whispers, her voice as soft as the splash of small waves below. *"I would've loved to be held in your arms."*

So he reaches around her on that half-wall and does just that. Holds her so close. His hands loop around her back and press her body to his. When he does, she adjusts her position on the porch ledge—relaxing her bent knees and moving her legs right around his hips. His face is near her ear, so he nuzzles her hair and whispers, *"I would've kissed you."* He does that then, too. Shifts his hold and kisses her forehead, her cheeks, her lips. When he does, she cradles his jaw and deepens the kiss. Her legs lock around his hips now. They keep at it—urgently wanting more.

If only, Shane thinks.

No time, wrong place, some other life.

So when they reluctantly separate, he tucks back her hair, rests a hand on her face and sees her eyes tearing up. *"I would've loved you, Celia Gray. All night,"* he still whispers.

As the moon rises above.

As the salty breeze hitches.

As the orange lights glow misty.

As the sea spreads beyond them and they kiss more. Small, tender kisses this time. He feels her soft lips on his mouth, his jaw, his neck—all while they both straddle that half-wall as they face each other. As his hands loosely clasp around her backside. As their mouths meet. As her arms hook beneath his shoulders. As more words are whispered into kisses.

As Shane loves her with restraint.

With brief kisses, over and over, while both his hands cradle her neck now and she sighs into the night.

When Celia eventually tells him she has to get Aria home, it's hard to pull away. But Shane does. He carefully lowers the stroller with the sleeping baby in it down the porch stairs. Gently then, Celia takes the stroller and wheels it along the planked walkway to his front yard.

When she stops and looks back at him, he motions to her. "Come here," his low voice says in the shadows.

She does. Celia puts on the stroller brake, then walks the few steps to him, to his open arms. She presses her body right against his as his arms envelop her. Closer still, he hugs her. In the night, there's no room for her to even move in his hold. There's just the darkness and distant waves and the two of them breathing. His face presses to the side of her head. Her hair is silky against his cheek, his jaw. When they separate, he puts a finger to her lips, then runs the back of his hand along her cheek, to her throat.

So that—as she walks the sandy beach roads home—the last thing she'll remember is his touch.

～

When he returns to the back porch, Shane finishes stringing those twinkling orange lights before sitting there on the half-wall by himself. It could almost seem like the past twenty minutes didn't even happen—the way some stillness sweeps back in. Out past his yard, he senses the vast water of Long Island Sound in the night. But he doesn't look out at it.

Instead, he pulls that silver dove cuff from his sweatshirt pocket and moves it so that it shimmers in the glow of the porch's tiny orange lights.

twenty-one

LATER THAT EVENING, JASON'S CROSSING the crushed-stone walkway at the Ocean Star Inn. As he approaches the front wraparound porch, he sees that lights are on. Windows are illuminated in the night. Decorative white starfish lean in random panes. He climbs the porch steps, swipes a hand through his unkempt hair—wavy from being out on the damp rocks, fishing—and gives a few good knocks.

It doesn't take long for Elsa to open the door. She's got on black jogger pants with a fitted cream top and is holding some tool. There are no greetings. No surprised *Hello!* Just this. "I knew you'd show up."

Jason casually shrugs. "Here I am. And here are your inn keys you didn't pick up earlier because you were avoiding me." He holds out her keys.

"Oh, *basta!*" Elsa says, pocketing the keys. "Now, I'm in the middle of a project I want to get done. And since you *are* here …" She motions him inside. "I'm putting you to work."

Jason nods. "Doing what?" he asks while walking beneath the Mason-jar chandelier near the reservation desk.

"Hanging a tapestry in the dining room."

"In the dining room," he repeats while following her down the inn's hallway. "Where you won't be having any more Sunday dinners?"

"What?" she asks, glancing back at him.

"Because you no longer care about your family?"

"Why would you say that?"

"Because I'm guessing you're maybe packing up and moving to California?" When Jason turns into the dining room, he sees her tapestry laid out across the table there. Gives a low whistle, too. The tapestry's woven threads swirl in varying shades of blues and greens. Golds, too. "That's some piece of art, Elsa." As he says it, he takes off his jacket and hangs it on a chairback.

"Yes. It's psychedelic." Elsa stands at the table and ponders the elaborate tapestry. "Celia, the baby and I took a tour of San Francisco in a true 1970s hippie van. We chugged up and down all those hilly streets. Saw some of my old college haunts. Bought souvenirs at little shops. Saw the *iconic* murals painted on buildings. And, ha! We even took a picture at the Grateful Dead house. Oh, we had so much fun," she wistfully says with a glance to Jason. "And I bought this tapestry that day. At the time, the blues and greens reminded me of the beautiful sea. But now?" She shrugs. "Now those woven colors mirror what my thoughts have been lately. A tapestry of doubts and uncertainties."

"I figured. That's why I'm here." Jason takes the

screwdriver Elsa holds. "Now where are we hanging this thing?"

Elsa turns and points to a spot above her dining room server. "There. On this decorative rod." She touches a long, burnished-gold curtain rod atop the server. "I already marked the bracket holes on the wall."

So Jason gets to work. He stands on a stepstool and mounts those brackets. Carefully, he turns the screws. "So *is* it true?" he asks while working. "You moving to California?"

"Jason!"

"What else *can* I assume?" he asks over his shoulder. Elsa, hands on hips, is standing at the table and glares at him. "You came back from San Francisco all clammed up. So it makes sense that California had some effect on you," he reasons. "Are you maybe leaving everyone behind to join your friend out there?" he goes on, turning in another screw. "To start a new life? Reopen your boutique?"

"That's just crazy."

"Is it?" He moves the stepstool to the far side of the server and works on the other rod bracket. "With your emotional headache? And then you were a no-show at the biggest event to hit this beach since Kyle and Lauren's vow renewal?" He bends, plucks a screw off the server and mounts this second bracket to the wall. Slowly, he twists, twists the screwdriver. "But if you're moving, Elsa, there's one thing you're forgetting that's right here in Stony Point."

"And what's that?" she asks, pressing a wrinkle out of her tapestry.

"*Famiglia.* Your sister's daughters, Maris and Eva. Who you just *love.* Celia and your granddaughter. Hell," he says,

185

working on the final screw now. "Your favorite nephew-in-law."

"Just cool it, Jason. Anyway ..." Elsa picks up that decorative rod and works it through the long pocket on the back of her tapestry. "How *was* the shack reveal?"

Jason steps off the stool and walks to the other side of the dining room table. "Not the same without *you* there," he answers, lifting the tapestry as she maneuvers the rod through the pocket. When she's done, he takes the decorative rod while Elsa scoops the tapestry fabric beneath it. Together, they walk it to the wall.

"So what paint color actually won the vote?" Elsa presses.

"You'll see. After this." As he says it, Jason snaps one end of the tapestry rod into the bracket. "When we drive by the shack on the way to The Sand Bar." While he moves that stepstool to the other side of the server, Elsa holds the rod. He takes the end of the decorative rod from her then, and steps up on the stool.

"The Sand Bar?" Elsa asks.

"Yep, I'm starved." With that, he snaps the rod in the bracket, fusses with the tapestry so that it hangs straight on the wall, then steps down. "I need a good meal," he says, handing Elsa her screwdriver. "And you need a good, stiff drink to numb that emotional headache of yours." Wasting no time, he lifts his jacket off her dining room chair and slips it on. "Come on," he tells her. "Let's go."

⁓

And after Elsa tells Jason, *Hold on a minute, buster;* and brushes her hair; and changes out of her cream top and

186

black joggers into a black mockneck and leopard-print maxi skirt with a wide copper-colored belt and black suede booties; and puts on her gold bangle and gold necklace chains; and tops off the ensemble with a cropped denim jacket, off they *do* go.

Elsa settles into the passenger seat of Jason's SUV. In the dusky evening light, they cruise the beach roads toward the trestle. Many of the shingled cottages are buttoned up tight for the season. Others are the stuff of daydreams— little bungalows and shanties with golden light shining in the windows; red and yellow autumn leaves swirling around illuminated lampposts; tendrils of smoke rising from chimneys. They round a gentle curve, and up ahead? Elsa squints to see the guard shack. Why, it's delightful! There are tiny lights twinkling on its roofline. And on the shrubs in front of it. As they drive, the SUV slows.

"Jason!" Elsa says as he now stops the vehicle. "Wait a minute. Is that shack … *green*?"

Jason leans forward and looks out her passenger window to the shack. "It is."

To better see this, Elsa turns in her seat. Squints her eyes. Tips her head. Yes, the entire shack is painted that color. "But green wasn't on the ballot," she says, whipping around to Jason. "How did this happen?"

"You missed it, Elsa. The whole darn thing."

"Oh, come on." She turns to the shack once more. "But … that's a *lot* of green. There must've been a *riot* here seeing that color!"

"No. Everybody actually liked it. Do you?"

She considers the twinkle-light-illuminated guard shack. "Well. Maybe." She looks again. "It's … calming."

"Yeah," Jason says as he puts the SUV in gear, waves to one of the part-time guards and starts driving again. "And you *soak* that calm in, Elsa. You seem to need it."

Elsa brushes him off and settles in her seat. A moment later, through the shadowy, dank stone trestle they go. Oh, she knows the folklore well, too. You leave beneath the trestle with one of three things: a ring, a baby, or a broken heart.

Actually, as Jason exits the tunnel and drives the winding road, and as silver moonlight falls onto a nearby saltwater marsh, Elsa thinks she maybe has all three.

A ring, a baby, *and* a broken heart.

Stands of trees loom roadside in the dark now; evening shadows grow long. All as Elsa silently tallies her life—her ring, a baby, and her broken heart.

First there's that gorgeous diamond ring in the hidden confines of Cliff's trailer—if he ever finds his way to proposing to her.

And, a baby? Well, she has a beautiful grandbaby she now fears one day losing to the coast of Maine—if Celia and Shane are together.

And a broken heart? Definitely. After witnessing Celia's heartache on the San Francisco streets and not making any sense of it—of Shane, broken-down Celia and Aria all together—*Elsa's* heart is broken, too.

And apparently, as she's whisked away from it all for an hour or two, Jason Barlow damn well knows it.

twenty-two

TORMENT.

The whole ride to The Sand Bar, Elsa felt it. Torment. Because, heck—it's Jason she's with. And she'd trust her nephew-in-law with her life. So *can* she tell him what's on her mind? Would her story of a distraught Shane and Celia be safe with him? Jason's always been good for his word.

Then—torment. Because what if Jason went straight to Shane with that news? His and Shane's friendship goes way back—thirty years—to when they met as kids at the beach. And Elsa can't be sure of the sway *that* kind of brotherhood has.

But still.

Sitting in a dark booth in The Sand Bar now, she looks around and still wonders. Decorative wood pilings tied with nautical rope are at either end of the long bar—where nearly every stool is occupied tonight. Illuminated twig pumpkins twinkle near those roped pilings. The bar's door

189

is propped open to the evening. Salty air drifts in and mingles with the hum of easy talk and laughs. Blends with some rockin' tune cranking on the jukebox. With Patrick greeting them at their booth now. He stands there in his black pants and white button-down with a black vest open over it. Those shirtsleeves are cuffed back, too.

"Hey, my friends. Elsa. Jason. What's happening?" he asks, shaking Jason's hand.

"Patrick," Jason says. "Good to see you. Place is *hopping.*"

"Sure is." Patrick glances over his shoulder toward that open door. "And where's the rest of your posse?" he asks.

"Just us tonight," Jason tells him, motioning between him and Elsa.

"Okay, then," Patrick says. "What can I start you with?"

Jason nods to Elsa, who tells Patrick, "I'll have a Scotch and soda."

"Make it two," Jason adds. "And after working up an appetite Friday night fishing, how about dinner?"

"What'll it be?" Patrick asks.

"Give me your smoked turkey on ciabatta. All the fillings. Tomato, spinach, provolone. The works. Sweet-potato fries on the side." Jason looks across the table to Elsa. "What about you?"

Elsa shakes her head. "Nothing tonight."

Jason looks long at her, then to Patrick. "Throw in an appetizer, guy. How about those stuffed mushrooms?"

"Got it, kids." Patrick knocks on their table, turns and heads to the bar with their order.

So Elsa sits back in the booth while Jason takes off that jacket he wears—a short, hooded gray fleece number with leather toggle buttons. He folds the jacket beside him on the booth seat, then cuffs back the sleeves of a plaid flannel he's got on over some black thermal tee and faded jeans with beat-up boots. Fishing clothes, apparently. His father's Vietnam War dog tags hang against that tee.

They make small talk now. Jason mentions work; Maris. Candles flicker in red globes in the booths—theirs included. The jukebox plays a melancholy tune. A silhouette of two people dancing close moves across the small dance floor.

Finally, their appetizer and drinks are delivered.

But Elsa knows she won't get much more chitchat out of Jason. He's waiting her out. Waiting for *her* to talk. So she takes a swallow of her Scotch and soda. Then another. "After being in California," she finally begins, setting down her liquor glass. "After seeing my old college friend, and after being in that bustling, artistic city … I guess I came home feeling blue."

"Blue?" Jason lifts a stuffed mushroom and takes a bite. "Why, for God's sake?"

Elsa shrugs. "It's one of those moods I just can't shake." She forks a mushroom for a nibble, too. It's stuffed with seafood and tastes divine. "After catching up with Wren and where her life had taken her? It made me miss my Milan boutique—which all *started* with my college heydays. And that hippie name Wren gave me—"

"Miss Moonchild Starbeam," Jason says, then takes a swallow of his drink.

"Yes. That name *inspired* my shop name—*Many Moons Ago*. So now? Now I guess I'm feeling very far from the person I used to be."

"But Elsa, you weren't going to stay that same person

forever. We change over the years."

"We do. You're right. But honestly? I'm actually doubting my decision to uproot here to Stony Point for a life plan I *still* haven't been able to commit to."

"What do you mean? Your inn?"

She nods. "Let's face it, I seem to use *any* excuse not to open it. And I *also* can't go on tying Celia to that stalled inn. This wasn't *her* life."

"But it is now."

"Is it? Really?" Elsa sips her Scotch and soda. "Living a stone's throw from her almost mother-in-law?"

Jason tosses up a hand. "Come on, Elsa."

"Sorry, Jason. That trip west brought to light doubts I'd buried. Maybe since Sal died." *Doubts that came to the surface after seeing Shane and Celia on those city streets,* she thinks—and can't-can't-*can't* say. "Doubts for a year now," she says instead.

"Maybe you're just jet-lagged." Jason pauses and leans back as a waitress delivers his meal. The ciabatta is toasted golden. Between the bread slices, thin-sliced turkey is piled high with tomato, spinach, provolone. The sandwich drips with dressings, too. Jason thanks the waitress, first. Then he wastes no time slicing that sandwich, reaching his hands around half and lifting it. "Give yourself some time before jumping to conclusions."

"Time?" Elsa forks off another bite of stuffed mushroom, then sets her fork on a small plate in front of her. "Time I had plenty of in California—and I never felt better. I *liked* my old self there. And am glad I got to see *that* person again. I think I've really missed her."

"Well," Jason reasons around a mouthful of sandwich.

192

"You can still be that person here."

"No. It's not the same. But don't worry … I'm not going to do anything drastic. Maybe it'll all blow over, what I'm feeling," she tells him. *Depending on if things blow over with Shane and Celia, too,* she only thinks.

Jason lifts a few sweet-potato fries. "What can I do to help?"

"Nothing." Elsa finishes that stuffed mushroom. Around her, folks are having a good time. Friday night's really kicking in this coastal bar. Someone's always dropping coins in the retro jukebox. The table two over from them sings along to a song playing now. Patrick's pulling a draft at the bar. Servers carry trays of food and drinks all around them.

"Nothing?" Jason persists. "What about—"

"Listen," Elsa cuts him off. "I *had* help last year, and it didn't work."

"What are you talking about?"

"When I put the inn up for sale. Without my son there to run it with me, I felt like it was time for me to go. And it *was* my decision to do just that—until I was stopped."

"By everyone around you."

Elsa nods. "The thing is? Back then, I *also* felt it was time for *you* all to go on with your own lives—without worrying about me."

Jason says nothing. He takes a bite of his ciabatta sandwich, wipes a spot of dressing from his chin and just listens.

So she shrugs. "Sometimes I guess there's still this awful doubt … *here*," Elsa says while patting her heart.

Their waitress swings by just then. "Can I get you anything else?" she asks.

Elsa lifts her now-empty glass. "A refill, please. Scotch and soda."

"Me, too," Jason says, nodding to his glass, then turning to Elsa. "I don't get it. I thought things were pretty good with you. So *something's* happened. Especially if you're now telling me you have awful *doubts*?"

"Yes. In my heart."

"Doubts? Or is it fear?"

"What?"

"Fear. My father used to talk about that. About having fear in those jungles in 'Nam. And how fear would keep him frozen in place."

Elsa listens as Jason grows very serious now in the shadowed bar.

"In the war," Jason explains, "my father said that fear made him not even want to move. Fear of stepping on a stick. Or … or of swatting a jungle spider. Because *moving* could give away his presence to the VC. To the enemy. So he'd freeze in place—out of only fear." Again Jason pauses as their second round is delivered. When it is, he picks up his glass for a swallow, then continues. "Is that what *you've* been doing, Elsa? Staying frozen here at your beachside inn for a *year* now? By some *fear*?"

Elsa can't even talk. There's a knot in her throat she can't get any words around. But, oh, the words flow in her mind. Her mind is actually screaming. It wants to let *out* her words. Wants to say that something *is* going on—with Shane and Celia. Something big. Something kept from her.

To share that, though, feels wrong … like a betrayal of their privacy. Or worse yet—gossip.

"What's *scaring* you, Elsa?" Jason asks—as if reading her

mind. "And holding you back?"

What am I afraid of? she only thinks. *Everything that stopped me in my tracks on Wednesday. In San Francisco. I'm afraid that Celia has some terrible news. I'm afraid she's going to move on, move away, and start fresh—maybe with Shane, maybe not—and that she can't bear to tell me. If that's the case, I also fear I'm going to* lose *beautiful Celia* and *my precious granddaughter. And that's just one too many things to lose in my life.*

What would Jason say to that? What would he say about Celia being devastated on the city streets? Would he know what could have caused her distress? Does he have thoughts on Shane and Celia? Oh, Elsa would *love* to hear his take on them—because he *would* have a take. How she wishes she could hear it.

Instead, she only gives a sad smile and turns up her hands.

Jason scrutinizes her. "It's really that bad?"

"It is. And unfortunately, it's a private matter I have to work out alone."

"I hate to see that, Elsa."

"I hate to feel it."

Jason takes a long drink of his Scotch and soda, then sets that glass down. "It's that bad that you can't even tell *me*?" he asks, his voice low. "You can tell me anything, you know that."

She sips her drink and touches her glass to his. "Not this."

While sitting there, his tired eyes watch hers. His dark hair is kind of a mess. A few days' whiskers shadow his face. Finally, he shakes his head—right as a real oldie starts up on the jukebox. One so recognizable, so fun, someone turns up the volume. So now there's just that steady, pulsing drumbeat opening of *Devil with a Blue Dress On*, with the keyboardist flying a hand down octaves of jangling piano keys, as the organ and a jammin' tambourine build that beat to a crescendo—right as the singer screams "*Hey*, hey! All right." It seems half the bar crowds the dance floor then—drawn by the pounding *will* of Mitch Ryder and the Detroit Wheels.

Jason is drawn there, too. "Let me distract you then, Elsa. Come on, I've got the cure for your blues. At least for a little while." He swallows another mouthful of his Scotch before standing and taking her hand. "Dance with me."

～

And dance they do.

It's all Jason could come up with. They'd hit a roadblock in that bar booth. A roadblock there was no getting around. Elsa's emotions are barricaded—for whatever reason. Well, if he can't get the story out of her, he can at least have her *forget* the story.

For a song or two, anyway.

So he cuts loose on the dance floor. Which slowly gets Elsa to. Oh, he sees it. He sees her reserved swaying grow more into a shimmy. Sees her body pick up on that pounding beat. Her booted feet tapping beneath her flowing leopard-print skirt.

And what does he do? He eggs her on. Really gets into the dance—almost exaggeratedly so. Jason bends at the waist, extends his right leg and slap-kicks it repeatedly on the floor—all to that song's driving beat. He straightens with a sharp clap and marches—his arms pumping—right to Elsa. He's got a move to *every* beat of that music.

Smiling now, Elsa sashays right past him. Her dancing is understated as she spins around in that long skirt, bops to the right, then to the left. Her bent arms pump the beat; her thick brown hair falls forward, then back, with her every step. Oh, she meets him—move for rockin' move—as though *she's* got on the high heels and alligator hat, oh yeah.

Yes, Elsa takes his dancing dare.

She finally just gets down.

Jason does, too.

With a hand held to the back of his head, he struts right to her. In his jeans and loosened flannel shirt, he twists; he keeps his feet stepping forward, then back—clapping his hands on beat with each changeup.

Yeah, they bring it down.

They sweat.

They laugh.

And Elsa shakes it out. He sees it. Instead of *walking* real cool, she shows him. She *dances* real cool. Through her outstretched arms moving with the beat to her shuffling booted feet, every worry is tossed aside.

So Jason keeps going. He stands in front of her with some *attitude*, hands on his hips, and slaps his right foot on the floor. Straightens with a clap. Dances around her. In the warm, shadowed bar now, he takes Elsa in his arms and gives a spin before they gyrate, twist and stomp while throwing caution—and every worry imaginable—to the wind.

Funny thing is, the other dancers get into it, too. Some

do *The Monkey*. Some do *The Jerk*. The dance floor, well, it's practically electric with song and motion.

Hell, Jason is, too. He sees Elsa bring some subtle 1960s go-go moves. So he bends and holds his fists in a loose boxing position, pumps those folded arms with each step toward her, then claps, throws his head back and just grooves to the music, the beat. The night.

Maybe they both needed this, actually.

This letting loose.

twenty-three

IT WORKED.

Jason getting a drink in Elsa and a dance out of her did the trick.

Early Saturday, she wakes up having made a decision. For much of the week, she's been weighing her options. Confront Celia? Or leave well enough alone.

All morning now, as she has her breakfast, and does a load of laundry, and pays a bill—but especially after her time at The Sand Bar with Jason last night—Elsa's feeling differently about things. She supposes it's because she did what Jason suggested.

She danced it out.

Did she ever. Shimmying to a couple of oldies was just the right medicine.

Because this morning, her decision's made. Oh, she'll do nothing extreme. She'll just do this—try to bridge the mystery *with* Celia. If they privately talk, maybe Celia will fill in some blanks. So Elsa belts a long sweater over her leggings and slip-on sneakers and heads out.

She doesn't have far to go, though. Just across the yard to Celia's gingerbread guest cottage. It looks straight out of a fairy tale with its pale yellow shingles and wide white trim edging the windows. Windows that let in soft sea breezes and birdsong. In a high peak on the cottage, a diamond-shaped stained-glass window glimmers in the morning sunshine.

And when Elsa knocks at the front door, Celia's voice carries through one of the living room's open windows. "Come on in, Elsa."

So when she walks in, it's no surprise that Celia's sitting right there. Wearing a loose burgundy flannel over cropped jeans with moccasin slippers, she's on the couch. Her flannel shirtsleeves are cuffed back as she's bent over the guitar on her lap while repeatedly strumming just one string.

Until she looks up at Elsa. "Hey! We missed you at the shack unveiling yesterday!" Celia says, then turns one of the guitar's tuning pegs while plucking that one string. "Hope you're feeling better today?"

"I am." Elsa moves some loose pillows on the far end of the couch and sits while Celia's apparently tuning her guitar. "Can't believe the shack is green, though!"

"I know. What a surprise, right?"

"Definitely," Elsa says, thinking surprises are aplenty in Stony Point. "Is Aria napping?"

Celia only nods, moving to another guitar string and plucking that one now.

"Celia." Elsa waits until she looks over at her. "Now that we're back," she explains, "I thought we could …

reminisce about last week. And talk a little about what's coming up for us."

"Absolutely." Celia, her guitar still resting on her crossed legs, tips her head down and turns another tuning peg while briefly plucking a string.

Elsa nods. Good. This is good. Celia's receptive.

"But I really don't have the time right now," Celia's saying, moving her fingers to a higher string on her guitar. She plucks it, then tries two bars of some riff. Her head is tipped to the instrument as she's clearly intent on this tuning. She manages a glance at Elsa. "I'm polishing up my set list for a Harvest Night gig later." Another plucked string while simultaneously turning a tuning peg. The note wavers. "At Kyle's diner."

"You're *playing* there?" Elsa asks, watching Celia so focused on her tuning. "I didn't know this," Elsa says. And thinks, *I don't seem to know a lot of things lately.*

"It was spur of the moment." Celia tucks her hair behind an ear and listens to another brief riff, once—then again—before turning another peg. "Kyle asked me yesterday when I stopped in the diner with Aria. So now I have to tweak my set list."

"Okay," Elsa says. And the thing is? Celia looks … fine. Happy, even. She manages easy smiles while chatting with Elsa. She's also very into her music. So what the heck was that San Francisco morning all about? Elsa, well, she just about gives up wondering anymore and stands now. "I'll leave you to your music, then. We can talk some other time." It isn't until Elsa takes a step or two toward the door, all while Celia keeps tuning—*pluck, pluck, thrummm*—that Celia calls her back.

"No, wait," Celia says. "I have an idea." Her hand is splayed over the six guitar strings now. "Come hear me sing tonight and we can talk afterward. Because there's actually something important I want to tell *you*."

Elsa turns back. This is the first whisper of hope she's felt in days. Celia's trusting her. She wants to let on about her relationship with Shane, maybe. And the cause of her California tears. *Finally*, Elsa will get to the bottom of this.

"So come *with* me to the diner?" Celia asks now.

"Well ... I know you like to go on your own and do your thing. And we probably won't be able to talk there. I'm sure the place will be mobbed."

"But I'm working really hard and have some California songs I want to sing. *And* want you to hear!" Celia draws her fingers softly across the guitar strings as she leans close to the instrument. "So just come. Relax and have a nice time. Afterward, we'll talk back here." Again, she plucks a string and tunes. "I like to calm down after a set."

Still, Elsa hasn't moved. "Who's watching Aria?"

"Maris. She's coming by later. And *you* come here for tea tonight—after my show," Celia says with another easy smile. Her eyes watch Elsa standing near the front door. Her fingers pluck out a little ditty now, too. "We'll talk then."

~

Saturday morning, Jason's rushing through the upstairs hallway. But he skids to a stop when he turns into his bedroom. Standing in the doorway, all he sees are clothes. A mess of clothes. Summer clothes piled high on the bed.

Winter clothes spilling from plastic totes. Dresser drawers are open. Clothes half hang out of them. There are small clothing piles on the scuffed-up hardwood floor outside the closet.

"Shit," Jason whispers. He knows just what this is.

It's Maris' semi-annual changing of the clothes—this time, summer to winter. And the *last* thing he needs is to be dragged into this project, especially with a CT-TV meet-and-greet to get to. Maris is standing at her dresser mirror where she's trying on some faded linen vest.

So Jason quietly walks into the room to get himself changed.

"Argh," Maris says when she spots his reflection in her mirror. "I wore this a lot during the summer. Keep?" she asks, turning to him. "Or toss."

He looks at her in her fitted vest buttoned over, well, nothing but her bra as she stands there in her old silver-paint-speckled jeans. "Keep," he says, then approaches, cradles her face and kisses her. "You look great," he goes on, nuzzling her neck now.

"Jason!" She spins back to the mirror. "I'm trying to get our summer clothes put away."

"I know." Yep, kissing over. So he heads to his own partially emptied dresser, then turns to a tote on the floor.

"I still can't believe what Elsa told you last night," Maris is saying now, standing sideways in front of her mirror.

"Which would be not much," Jason answers while brushing through a tote of his clothes. He needs something to go with the black jeans he's got on.

"So whatever's bothering her, she's *not* saying," Maris' semi-distracted voice reaches him.

"All I know …" He pauses while pulling a dark gray Henley top from that tote. "Is that Elsa came back from San Francisco feeling blue." He peels off the loose flannel shirt he had on and pulls the gray Henley over his head. "That's it."

"Which I still don't get. Because when she picked up her watering can, Elsa told me that her trip was great. A fabulous … blur, is how she put it."

"Apparently it *wasn't* great. Seems something happened out there."

"Could she have *ever* caught wind of Shane and Celia?"

Jason looks over as he tucks his father's dog tags beneath his shirt collar. "No. Shane said everything was done by the book and that he was *long* gone once Elsa left her friend's house."

Maris unbuttons and removes that vest, folds it and tucks it in a summer tote. "Well," she says, standing there in only her bra and jeans. "Should *I* talk to Elsa?"

"No. From what I saw?" Jason grabs his wristwatch from his dresser top. "She'll work it out. Just give her space." He looks up from clasping the watchband. "She got better as the night went on. Heckuva dance partner, too, getting down with some pretty funky moves."

"I'll bet." Maris pulls a thin V-neck sweater on over her head. "But I still feel bad for her."

"And *I* told her we're here for her." Jason crosses the room and cracks open a window. The room's feeling dusty with all the clothes swapping. "Anytime."

As he's been talking, Maris is lifting jeans out of her tote and laying them across the bed. Distressed jeans, dark jeans, faded jeans, cropped jeans. "Sometimes when I'd come home from my denim inspiration trips abroad, I'd feel that way," she's saying—as though talking out Elsa's problem. "I'd be a little down. You know …" Maris turns as Jason approaches and takes her in his arms. "All that *zest* and *excitement* overseas, then just regular life again."

"Maybe that's all it is." Jason kisses her neck. "Hell, regular life is okay by me." He lifts her hair and leaves more kisses on her skin there.

Maris briefly closes her eyes and tips her head to the side, then pulls away and scans the messy bedroom. The clothes strewn everywhere. Her own disheveled reflection. Then him standing there all dressed to go out. "You're distracting me, Jason Barlow."

"That was my intent."

Maris waves him off and pulls an armful of summer tees out of his dresser.

"Listen," Jason says, walking around a spare prosthetic leg in the closet and grabbing his olive trucker jacket there. "I saw Shane's truck outside. I'm going to check on him at the stairs, then I'm off to my meet-and-greet."

"Where to this time?"

"Close by. Old Saybrook. There's an art fair going on. Trent booked us a tent."

Without turning, Maris vaguely says, "Pick up something out for dinner later. There's nothing here."

"What are *you* eating?"

"I'm babysitting Aria and eating there."

"What?" Jason asks while putting one arm, then the other in that denim jacket's sleeves.

"I'm watching the baby at Celia's," Maris explains, stacking that pile of tees on the bed. "She has a singing gig at the diner."

"Oh, for that Harvest Night. Right." As they both crisscross the room, Jason grabs his keys off his dresser valet. "I'll have Kyle make me something, then. You don't want a dinner, too?"

"No." Maris is bent to a lower dresser drawer as she talks. "Celia's leaving me a pizza."

Hmm. Something's caught Jason's eye now. It's in a messy pile of clothes near the door. He reaches down and picks it up. "Maris, I *love* these shorts."

She straightens, brushes a strand of hair from her face and eyes the faded denim shorts he holds. "*Ugh.* Those baggy things?"

"They're for yard work," he insists, dropping them atop the bed before glancing at the time. "Don't be throwing away all my good stuff."

"Don't worry," she says as he walks out of the bedroom. "I won't."

But one glance back says otherwise as Jason spots her—dropping those very same shorts back in the *toss* pile.

twenty-four

FUCK!" SHANE GRIPES.

In the late-morning sunlight Saturday, he drops his hammer and quickly shakes out his hand. The finger he just whacked is throbbing—but good—after he hit it *with* that damn hammer. Standing there on one of the lower rotten steps of the Barlow stairway, he tightly clasps his stinging finger. "Fuck, fuck, fuck."

"Most commonly used word in Vietnam. During the war," a voice calls from behind him.

Shane turns and squints up to see Jason standing near the top of the stairs. "Fuck is?" Shane asks.

"Yep. Said in just about every other sentence, from mundane bullshit to do-or-die combat situations."

"Most used word here, too," Shane says, shaking out his whacked hand again. "Especially when I hit a finger with the hammer."

"Your hand okay?"

"Yeah. Nerves just got to calm down."

Jason walks several steps lower and leans on the frayed-rope railing. "My father said when fuck wouldn't do, some variation—or acronym—of the word stepped right in for soldiers fighting over there."

"No shit." Shane shifts the tool belt slung around his hips and sits sideways on a rotten stair. "Like what?" he asks, hooking an arm around a bent knee.

"Well, acronyms like … FUBAR. Which is Fucked Up Beyond All Recognition. Whether it was an impossible situation battling a hilltop, a person, didn't matter."

"FUBAR."

"Yep. Or … then there's something *all* the guys in the jungle waited to become. A PFC."

"Private first class?" Shane asks.

"No. Private Fuckin' Civilian again once their tour was done. They lived and *breathed* for the day."

"Jesus, I'll bet."

"Yeah. Or how about SNAFU?"

"What's that? Some bad, messed up situation?"

"Close. Situation Normal: All Fucked Up."

"Hey, I like that one. *Situation Normal: All Fucked Up*," Shane quietly repeats. In a few seconds' pause, the golden October beach grasses whisper in the sand beside him. "Damn sure had my share of those over the years. SNAFUs."

"Yeah, bro. Me, too."

Standing there in some black jeans, hiking boots and his trucker jacket, Jason shifts against that railing. "Then there's the FNG. Which you were when you arrived here in August."

"The fun new guy?"

"Try the Fuckin' New Guy." Jason walks down to where

208

Shane's been working. "Which you are on *this* job, too."

"No, man." Shane picks up that tossed hammer and stands. "Here I'm the F-O-G. Fuckin' Only Guy."

There's a crowbar leaning against one of the nearby railing posts. Jason takes that crowbar and pries up a rotten step. The old, splitting wood creaks beneath the pressure. "Well listen, FNG. You almost wrapping it here?"

"I am, boss. Got a few more new stairs to cut on the worktable and get installed. Once that's done, double-check EFS once more."

"Come again?"

"EFS, man." Shane motions down to the fifty or so newly installed wooden steps leading to a small beach and Long Island Sound. "Every Fuckin' Stair."

"Wiseass."

"That I am. Then I'll install new rope in the railings and we're good. Should be done next week."

"Okay, guy," Jason says, setting the crowbar aside.

And Shane sees it. He sees it on everyone who stops by these mystical stairs. That pause. Jason looks out at the Sound spreading blue to the horizon. Sunlight glimmers on the rippling water. And he takes a long breath of the salt-heavy air. Everyone does—just like that.

Then Jason looks at him and gives a wave. "I'm off."

"Where you headed today?"

"Another meet-and-greet."

"Behave yourself, Barlow. Don't need you bumping into any more blonde beauties."

"Shut up, Bradford. And it's one of the last fair stops. Almost wrapping those, too," Jason says, turning and climbing up the stairs.

209

"Yo, Barlow!" Shane folds back his flannel shirtsleeves. "Just so you know. I'm leaving half-day. Got a boatload of errands since my trip out west."

Jason turns again. "Dealing with your landlubber life?"

"Pretty much. Buy groceries. Gas up the truck. Post office stop. And, oh yeah. Get this." Shane tips up his newsboy cap and squints at Jason near the top stair. "I actually have a roll of film that belonged to your brother."

"What? To *Neil*?"

Shane nods. "It's been sitting in my junk drawer in Maine for ten years now. He left it behind last trip, and I saw it the other day. So I brought it back."

Jason looks long at him, then walks down a few steps. "Are there pictures on it?"

"Can't tell. Could be, or else it was a spare roll he never used. Either way, I'm dropping it off later to get it developed."

"Jesus." Jason gives a short laugh. "How do you like that?"

"Yeah. I'll let you know as soon as the pictures are ready—if there are any. Be interesting to see, no?"

"Shit, yeah. Appreciate it, man."

Shane tips his hat at him. "So I'll be busy running around this afternoon before heading over to The Dockside for that dinner my brother promised me."

Jason waves and heads up the stairs again. "Might see you there later. Grabbing supper on the way home," he calls over his shoulder.

Shane returns the wave, lifts that hammer and crowbar and gets back to work on the stubborn, rotten step he'd been tearing out when he whacked his hand. With the sun on his back, he hammers that crowbar beneath the step.

When he does, the wood splinters as the crowbar digs under the rotten pieces.

"Hey, Bradford," he hears Jason call down to him from the top. *"AMF!"*

Shane straightens, nudges back his cap and squints up at him again. "Now what's *that* code for?"

Jason gives a sharp salute. "Adios, motherfucker."

An hour later, Shane tarps the tools and worktable on the bluff and takes off. Drives back to his rented bungalow, unpacks a sweatshirt and empty water bottle from his work duffel, gets changed and scrounges together lunch. After being gone much of the week, the refrigerator is practically empty. Which is exactly *why* he took the afternoon off—to go grocery shopping.

And by midafternoon, he's checking off his landlubber-life list in earnest.

His gas tank is topped off. Some bills he paid in Maine are mailed here. Laundry's in progress—a load of his sweaty stair-work clothes and such. He'll swing by the laundromat for pickup on the way back to his cottage. Now, he wheels his stuffed Maritime Market grocery cart to his truck, errands complete. Problem is, those strings of old, faded lobster buoys are still piled in the back of the truck bed. He tries shoving them over to make room for his groceries, but there are too many buoys. Too many for his truck, and too many for Evan's classroom. But Shane actually has an idea now for *some* of those old roped buoys. It's pretty decent, too.

JOANNE DEMAIO

Meanwhile, he stacks his loaded grocery bags on the front passenger seat and floor of his pickup, grabs Neil's undeveloped roll of film from the glove box, then locks up the truck. There's one more stop to make in the shopping plaza. Joggling the film canister in his hand, he thinks about the last time Neil was in Maine. He wanted to go out on a lobster boat with Shane to clear his head. To decide what to do about Lauren. And Kyle.

But Shane wouldn't let him on the boat. Wouldn't even check with the captain. Said Neil would be so distracted aboard ship, he'd be a liability to the crew. Mess up. Someone could get hurt. Shane told Neil back then that he only had two choices, anyway. He had to either walk away from Lauren, get busy with his life, work like hell with Jason and someday meet some other broad. *Or* he could stay with Lauren but would have to fight the God damn fight—with Kyle.

That was the last Shane had heard from his old friend. Upon returning from a hard day on the lobster boat, he found Neil's jotted note saying he was headed home to fight that fight.

And a week later, apparently, Neil was dead. That hard fact Shane only learned this summer.

So now Shane's really curious about what—if anything—is on this roll of undeveloped film Neil left behind. Would it have some clue to Neil's life back then? Some images? Maybe of Neil. Maybe Lauren. Something, anything.

It's time to find out—after ten long years.

212

The local pharmacy here has a photo-processing department and should be able to help him. So he heads across the parking lot in its direction.

"It's really good you still do this," Shane says minutes later to the clerk behind the photo counter. He slides over the canister of undeveloped film. "People just use their phones for cameras now, but still. Every now and then, you come across film like this."

The clerk drops the canister in an envelope upon which Shane had written his name and contact information. "There's a renewed interest in film, definitely," the clerk says. "Plus we get lots of family negatives people bring in for duplicate pictures. For photo albums, you know."

"Roger that."

"What size prints do you want? Four by six?"

"Not sure. What's the next size up?"

"Five by seven."

"That's good. Go with that one."

The clerk nods and gives Shane his receipt.

"How long before they're ready?" Shane asks.

"About a week. Give or take."

⌒

A week, give or take, Shane thinks while crossing the parking lot to his pickup.

He couldn't figure *where* the hell the *last* week would take him, that's for damn sure.

And where that week would take Celia.

But for now? The *next* week's going to start by taking him straight back to his cottage to put away his groceries.

213

As he pulls out of the busy shopping plaza, he thinks the coming week will then have him take a nice hot shower and get ready for one hefty diner meal at Harvest Night later on.

After that, it's anybody's guess where the hell the week will dump him.

twenty-five

SHANE SENSES THE SEA EVERYWHERE.

Even here—at the Dockside Diner. It's early Saturday evening. Twilight. He just parked his pickup and takes in the sight. Further down the street, a nearly full moon hangs low over the harbor water, so there's that coastal backdrop. Stars start to emerge in the vast sky. And as Shane crosses the parking lot, glowing lanterns make the silver diner's windows look like portholes. So if he looks just right, the long diner could almost be a ship coming in from sea.

If he looks just right.

But hell, it's really an optical illusion. Especially when Shane sees the outdoor patio. Kyle went *all* out for his Harvest Night. Mini faux pumpkins dangle from nearby tree branches. A portable trellis stands at the patio entrance. The trellis is woven with twig vines and paper lanterns of gold and yellow. Around the patio perimeter, heavy rope is looped from dock post to dock post. Globe lights are strung above, too.

Shane wanders beneath the trellis to the diner patio now. Wispy-topped cornstalks are tied to lampposts there. Pumpkins sit on banded whiskey barrels. Hay bales are scattered here, stacked there. People mill about in corduroy jackets and fleece vests. Candles flicker on outdoor tabletops laid with gold-and-navy plaid tablecloths. Folks at those tables lean close; laugh. They eat hearty dinners—stuffed peppers and chili and potpies. There's a dessert table where candied and caramel apples are lined up beneath the glass dome of a pastry case. A large twig pumpkin is on that dessert table, too. After their dinner, patrons can reach into that pumpkin and pull out their harvest fortune written on folded orange notecards.

And there. Over to the side. Shane veers in that direction, where there's a lattice-type fence panel draped with fishnet. And in front of that panel? Kyle's live-music stage. An empty stool—*Celia's* stool—is set near a microphone stand and a few small amplifiers.

Break a leg, Cee, Shane thinks.

He keeps walking, too. Beyond the dessert table, there's an opening in the dock-rope fencing. That's where a galvanized aluminum tub is stocked with burning logs. The flame there crackles and sparks as it flickers skyward. More hay bales are set out nearby. Bags of marshmallows and roasting twigs are arranged on a small table there.

"Hey, glad you made it," a voice says.

Shane turns to see Kyle. He's in full work mode—dressed in his black shirt, black pants and an orange chef apron tonight. "Kyle," Shane says back, shaking his brother's hand. "What a gig you got going on."

"Yeah, thanks." They stand near the aluminum-tub firepit as Kyle points out the stage area; a small dance space; the game zone in the parking lot. "We've got a candy-corn ring toss," he explains, pointing to a stack of plastic rings and mini orange-and-white traffic cones arranged on the pavement. "Or you can shoot some hoops, there." He points to a mounted basketball hoop and a box of stuffed pumpkins for making hook shots. "Or just sit back and enjoy the food and entertainment. Speaking of which," Kyle remarks, "nice threads."

Shane glances down at his own black vest over a gray flannel button-down, dark jeans and trail shoes. His black twill bomber is loose over it all. "Sounded like a snazzy night planned here," Shane says. "Thought I'd upgrade my look."

"Well, come on," Kyle tells him. "I got your table all set up for you, man."

As Kyle leads the way, they wind themselves back to the patio area; squeeze around packed tables; wave to Carol selling fall flowers off her portable cart.

And Shane is just happy to be among it all. To be able to sit with a big meal, clear his head and rest his weary bones.

Just then, Kyle turns and pulls him aside. "Listen, bro. There's … well, I got something to tell you." He hitches his head to a nearby table. "Got somebody I want you to meet."

Shane looks to the table set over on the side. An orange-globe candle flickers atop it beside a small basket of assorted gourds. There's that blue-and-gold tablecloth draped over the table where … *two* place settings are arranged. And at one of those place settings, a woman sits. She's probably in her mid-thirties. Her smooth blonde hair is shoulder-length with a deep side part. "Who is that?" Shane asks his brother.

Kyle grabs Shane's arm and pulls him back a few steps toward his outdoor grill. "Your date," he tells Shane.

Shane quickly looks from Kyle, to the woman, then back to Kyle—who might be perspiring now. "Jesus Christ, Kyle."

"Wait. Just hold on. Lauren and I kind of arranged a *little* something for you tonight."

"No, you didn't."

"Yeah, we did." Kyle grabs a napkin at his grill station and dabs his forehead. "You mentioned some recent breakup with a broad with a baby. So we figured … what the hell. This just felt like something me and Ell could do for you. And we thought you and Quinn might hit it off, you know?" Kyle motions to this Quinn. "She's a yoga instructor."

"*Tell* me you *didn't* do this," Shane slowly says without looking at Quinn.

"I *did*. Because you seem a little lonely lately. And it's a good night to sit with someone. To meet a nice lady over that dinner I made you."

"Didn't know it came with strings," Shane says while giving his brother a discreet shove. "Shit, Kyle." And it suddenly hits Shane. He's on a blind date now. So he drags a hand through his hair. Straightens his vest beneath his bomber jacket. Clears his throat. "What the hell's the matter with you?" he asks Kyle. "I'm not *looking* to get involved with someone right now."

218

Kyle pauses to high-five one of his passing customers, then turns back to Shane. "It's just a *dinner*. So relax." With that, he shoves Shane now—in the direction of this blind-date table. "Come on, she's waiting."

"I'm going to fucking kill you," Shane grumbles over his shoulder to Kyle behind him.

"Let's see how tonight goes first. Maybe you'll actually thank me, bro."

∼

When Elsa and Celia arrive at Harvest Night, Elsa floats around some while Celia freshens her makeup in the diner restroom. Elsa looks at the beautiful patio twinkling beneath lights and candles. She stops at Carol's flower cart, chats some and buys a little bouquet. While looking for an empty patio table then, she stops Celia heading to the stage area. Elsa plucks a flower from her bouquet and says it'll help Celia channel California as she sings. Celia takes the flower and right away tucks it into the side braid of her auburn hair. Lauren swings past just then, too. She's carrying a tray of dinners and manages to *briefly* pause with a quick greeting.

The whole place is just a whir of energy like that. Finally, Elsa finds a lone, empty table on the patio outskirts and sets her flowers there. She sits then, too, and loosens the camel-colored barn jacket she wears over a sweater and cuffed jeans. Flips her hair out of the jacket's collar and sits back.

This is nice now.

This sitting.

This relaxing on a cool evening.

It's pretty unbelievable how Kyle and Lauren have transformed the diner patio for this Harvest Night. The lights, and pumpkins, and paper lanterns, and candles. It's just a magical sight, especially with that nearly full moon hanging over the horizon.

～

"Celia! Glad you're here," Kyle says as Celia approaches the stage area.

"Me, too. Seems like a really lively crowd tonight."

"It is. And hey, guess what I did?" Kyle asks as she sets down her guitar case and takes in the busy patio.

Celia turns to him now. "What?"

"Set up my brother on a blind date. Surprised him, actually. He had no idea."

"You *did*?" Celia leans past Kyle and scans the tables. "Where are they?"

Kyle points out Shane and some blonde woman seated at a small table at the edge of the patio. "They look good together, no?" Kyle asks.

Celia squints at Shane. He's got on his black vest over some button-down and dark jeans. His black bomber jacket is slung over the back of his chair. He had no idea this date was happening? Oh, Celia can just *imagine* Shane's thoughts on this … *surprise*. She smiles widely when she turns to Kyle. "They *do* look good," she tells him while bending to open her guitar case. "Not bad at all."

"Yeah. I thought so." Kyle starts walking toward his grill station. "Maybe in your set later? You can dedicate a song to

Shane. And Quinn, that's his date. Sing something special for them."

⁓

At her table in the shadows, Elsa sets aside her special Harvest Night menu. Celia's taken the stage and is ready to begin. She looks stunning in a pale gray woven poncho over silver metallic skinny jeans and open-toe black booties. The poncho is cropped; a fitted black top with three-quarter sleeves is visible beneath the poncho's loopy stitches. Celia's all settled now on that stool on the small stage. She's also fussing with her guitar, tuning a string or two. Finally, she leans to the mic.

"On this gorgeous autumn night," Celia says to the crowd, "beneath the light of that golden moon, I'm not here as Celia Gray. No. Tonight? Tonight I'm channeling the mystical magic in the air and am … *Lady Blue Heart.*" As she says it, she first looks to Elsa and gives a slight wink. After all, Lady Blue Heart *is* the hippie name they came up with on their jet airliner flying six miles over the earth. Destination? San Francisco.

But Elsa notices something else. Celia's gaze quickly moves. She scans the patio and with the *briefest* of smiles— one no one would notice except Elsa—her gaze stops on someone else. For a mere second.

Elsa looks that way and the only familiar face she sees there is Shane's. But, wait. He's sitting with someone at a small table on the fringe of the patio.

"Huh," Elsa says to herself, squinting at an unfamiliar blonde accompanying Shane. The pretty woman leans

across the table while chatting—though Shane does seem a little awkward. If Elsa's not mistaken, it looks like the two of them might be … *on a date.*

Once Celia begins serenading the Harvest Night diners, the place changes from magical to mesmerizing. Celia's soothing voice carries like a mist floating past the tables. She opens her set with an original song she wrote late this summer called *The Moon Knew.*

And Elsa's entranced by it all. By the sultry atmosphere; by Shane laughing now with the mystery woman he's with; by the lyrics Celia sings—evocative phrases holding secret meaning if Elsa reads between the lines.

But it's when Kyle stops by to personally take Elsa's dinner order that, heck, a real bomb is dropped.

"Hey, Elsa," Kyle says after she orders the veggie-burger basket. "Get a load of Shane."

Elsa turns in her seat. "Shane?" she asks upon seeing him telling some seafaring tale, she's sure, to that woman.

"Yeah." Kyle looks over, too. "Check it out. I set him up on a blind date. It seems like they're hitting it off, no?" Kyle asks, then swings away to his grill while keeping an eye on the fixed-up couple.

Hitting it off? Elsa glances to Kyle departing, then to Shane again. All while hearing Celia's suggestive song lyrics.

The moon knew, didn't it? Celia's voice teases. *Smiling down on our midnight walk.*

And the stars, they knew too … wisely winking at our talk.

Oh, the twisted, silent tales weaving through this October night. *Did* Celia take midnight walks with Shane this summer? Elsa wonders now. Moonlit strolls together? Because what about San Francisco—just days ago—when

Celia was *devastated* on the street? *Crushed.* And what about Shane embracing her and Aria there?

Where did *that* all go?

And now Shane's dating *this* woman?

All around us, yes, the magical night-world knew, Celia sings on, *that I … yes I … was so in love with you.*

Oh, that does it. Elsa's more confused on this *mysterious* autumn night—than *ever.*

⁓

By the time Jason gets himself away from his meet-and-greet and arrives at Dockside Diner's Harvest Night, the place is packed. He finds only one empty parking space way in the back. But on his walk across the parking lot to the patio—where music and the aroma of a smoking grill and people's talking voices and floating paper lanterns and flickering candles fill the space—he has a chance to take it all in.

He doesn't take in much, though. Not when he happens to see Shane. He's sitting at a small table with … a blonde woman. They're laughing. And leaning close. All while Shane's digging into some abundant dinner plate his brother served up for him. Shane raises his loaded fork, chews that mouthful of food, dabs his face with a napkin and picks up some private convo going down.

Okay. So where the *hell's* Kyle? Because, shit. Jason came here for a mouthful of amazing food—not an eyeful of something *dangerously* interesting.

He finds Kyle at his grill in full chef mode, right down to a long orange apron over black threads. Tongs in one hand, spatula in another, he's turning steaks, flipping burgers, handing plates to the waitresses.

"Yo, Bradford," Jason says, slapping Kyle's back when he nears.

"Hey, glad you made it, Barlow."

"I did. Maris is watching Aria, so it's just me," Jason explains, scanning the patio. "The joint is *jumping*, man."

"Yeah. Couldn't ask for a better night."

Jason shifts around to get Shane in his sights. "What's going on with your brother?" Jason asks Kyle, all while nodding in Shane's direction.

"Ha! Listen, dude. Me and Ell *did* it. We set him up."

"What?"

"Yeah. Remember when you came in the diner? And we were working on finding some dame for him?"

"You were *serious*?"

"You bet we were." Kyle nods to Shane's table. "And there she is. Name's Quinn. She's my mother-in-law's yoga instructor."

"No shit," Jason laughs. But oh, he can figure Shane did the furthest *thing* from laugh when he walked in on some secretly prearranged blind date tonight. "How'd the guy take it?" Jason asks now.

"Well." Kyle lifts a juicy steak onto a plate. "Guess he's going to kill me later on. So … nice knowing you, Barlow."

Jason squints over at the couple. The woman's straight blonde hair is shoulder-length. She's very pretty and seems engaged while talking with Shane. Relaxed. "Looks like Shane's enjoying himself, though," Jason vaguely says.

Kyle leans over for a look. "Yeah. Quinn, too. Me and Ell did all right, no? I think they're really hitting it off."

"Time will tell," Jason says. "Listen, Kyle. I'm going to find a table … but maybe I'll pay Shane a visit first."

⁓

He does just that, too.

Jason, on his way inside the diner to use the restroom, briefly stops at Shane's table. He comes up behind him and clasps his shoulder. "Hey, Shane. Good seeing you." Oh, he *knows*, too—as does Shane—he's just busting his chops. Putting him on the friggin' spot.

Shane spins around. "*Jason*, my man. Hey," he says, then clears his throat. "What's happening?"

"Finished at my meet-and-greet." Jason steps back and eyes the busy patio. "Stopping by the diner for some supper now. I won't keep you, though," he adds, looking at the blonde woman with Shane.

"Oh, hell. Where are my manners?" Shane puts down his fork and turns in his chair. "Quinn, this is a friend of mine. Jason. Jason Barlow."

"Nice to meet you, Jason," she says, reaching over her salad plate and extending a hand.

"Likewise." Jason shakes her hand. "Great night to be outdoors. Good food, music," Jason says, motioning to the love of Shane's life—Celia.

"I just *adore* her way," Quinn says, squeezing Shane's arm as she does. "Her voice is *so* captivating."

"That it is," Shane agrees—all while trying to communicate some shit to Jason with just a look. Maybe to save him? To help him through this awkward situation? "Have a seat, Barlow, why don't you?"

225

Ha. Jason's not biting. It'll be more interesting watching Shane sweat through this date from a distance. "Thanks, but some other time, maybe. I'll just leave you two lovebirds be," Jason says with a wink to Quinn and a wave to Shane as he heads inside the diner.

Oh, and knowing one thing for certain the whole way there. Which would be this: Shane's going to kill *him* now, too.

~

And it doesn't take long.

That murder might be going down within minutes. Because as Jason's standing at the mirror over the restroom sink, he hears the door open behind him. He glances at the reflection in the mirror to see who walked in.

Safe. It's some other dude heading straight to the urinals.

So Jason soaps up his hands—right as that restroom door *whips* open behind him. In the mirror reflection? This time it's Shane.

Shane, who's bypassing the urinals and walking straight to him at the sinks. He's got on his black vest over a gray plaid button-down and dark jeans. Surely he elevated his look with that vest for one reason tonight—Celia. Maybe even with the intent of jamming with her on his harmonica during one of her songs.

"What are you doing out there?" Jason asks, rinsing his hands now.

Shane stops beside Jason. "My brother and sister-in-law fucking set me up. So what *could* I do?"

226

"Yeah?" Jason pulls a length of paper towel from the dispenser. "And how is she? Your date."

"You son of a bitch, giving me a hard time."

"Well?"

"Fine. She's not bad, if I was available."

"And you're aware *Celia's* witnessing this mega match?"

"Guess she would be." Shane turns to the mirror and dabs at his hair. "Hell, I didn't know *what* I was walking into tonight. Definitely a rogue wave—if ever there was one."

"No shit." Jason tosses his paper towels into the trash. "Well, you can rest assured that Celia's going to *enjoy* seeing you handle this. She'll be watching a show of her own."

Shane looks at Jason. "Yeah," he says with a half laugh, then turns and walks away. "Gonna be a helluva night," he says over his shoulder as he pushes through the door and heads back out.

Carol's garden cart is set up near the game area. The yellow wire cart with two big, spoked wheels and three mesh shelves is well-stocked. Good thing, too. Carol's got a steady stream of customers buying a painted rock, or a bunch of autumn blossoms in cans or tucked in plaid craft paper and tied with twine. There are marigolds, faded hydrangeas, sedum, zinnias, mini sunflowers.

"This for your lady?" Carol asks when Shane chooses a tin-can bouquet.

Shane squints at her. "Pardon me?"

"I asked you out earlier this summer." Carol shrugs. "You said you were seeing someone."

227

"Right."

Carol nods to the table where Quinn is sitting. "That who you turned me down for?"

"No." Shane looks over to Quinn, then to Carol. "That's Kyle's version of a good idea."

"What?"

Shane's thumbing through his wallet now. "My brother set me up."

"Did he now ... So what's wrong with that?" Carol asks while taking a few dollar bills from him.

"Nothing. Problem is, I *am* seeing someone. Except Kyle doesn't know it."

"Oh yeah? Why not?" As she asks, Carol ties an extra rust-colored bow around Shane's tin-can bouquet.

"It's complicated, Carol." Shane looks over to Quinn before picking up the bouquet he just bought. "*Ridiculously* complicated."

More customers idle around Shane now. They browse the flowers, turning this bouquet, picking up that one. So Carol gives him a wave as he heads back to his table.

"Good luck to you, Shane," he hears her call after him.

Oh, he hears something else, too. A dedication is being made from the stage. It stops him in his tracks and gets him turning to Celia there.

"This song goes out to a special couple in the audience tonight," she's saying, sitting sideways on her stool and leaning to the mic. Okay, and he knows *damn* well where Celia's going with this. The spotlight shines on her so that her fitted silver jeans glimmer in the evening. A flower's woven into her side braid. And her smile is subtly apologetic as she looks right at him pathetically standing

228

there with his tin-can bouquet.

"Yes, this next song is for Shane and Quinn," she softly says into the mic. "The dedication request comes from Kyle, our chef and host tonight. It also comes with wishes from the stars above shining down on new love." Celia's fingers strum a soft chord now. "Oh, there's nothing like new love, is there?" she asks, her voice serious in the shadows.

And Shane knows. Celia was put on the spot as much as he was tonight. She with a dedication; he with a date.

Random applause and whistles rise from the patio tables.

Shane looks at Celia a moment longer. But as she starts singing her beautifully rendered song of stolen glances and clandestine touches silently capturing the heart, he turns to his table. After one glance back, he sits with Quinn and gently sets the tin-can bouquet in front of her.

"Hey, there you are!" Quinn turns to Shane settling in his seat. "Guess we've got a song now?" She hitches her head to the stage, a small smile on her face.

"Quinn," he says with a slow shake of his head. "Please accept these flowers as an apology."

"Apology?" She squints at him across their candlelit table.

"Yeah," Shane answers, blowing out a breath. "My *sincere* apology. Because my brother, Kyle … his intentions were good, you know? But unfortunately, he's not well-versed in the realities of sea life."

"Which would be?"

Shane looks long at Quinn. Then, while sitting at their table on the patio outskirts, in the shadows of the October evening, he leans closer and tells her. Tells her the reality of long winter weeks out on the Atlantic in federal waters a hundred fifty miles offshore. The reality of a three-hundred-mile commute from here to Maine. The reality of having a week left in Stony Point at best, before his life gets hauled back to the water. The reality that it would be unfair to pursue *anything* more than a few hours of conversation tonight.

As for the reality of Lady Blue Heart onstage *having* his whole heart? That reality Shane leaves out.

Thankfully, Quinn is totally understanding. She nods and loosens up somehow with the knowledge that … this is it.

Maybe they both do.

They relax knowing they'll chat this one time, wish each other well, and go their separate ways. So now? They relish their dinners. And their conversation is more forthcoming. More frank.

All as Celia plays on.

~~

Celia didn't want to do it. She really didn't. But heck, when Kyle asked her to dedicate a song to Shane and his date, what could she say? That there could *be* no dedication? That she and Shane are actually head over heels for each other? Madly in love? Drop *that* bombshell on Kyle and have it ricochet to everyone she knows—including Elsa? That is *not* how she'd *ever* want to go public with her and Shane Bradford's relationship.

So she politely obliges Kyle's request. When she finishes that romantic dedication to Shane and his date, her heart's a little sad for the predicament they're both in tonight.

Lady Blue Heart, indeed.

It all has her setting aside her guitar and leaving the stage for a break. Elsa must notice, because Celia sees her stand at her table and motion her over.

～

"Celia," Elsa says, waving to her leaving the stage. "Over here!"

Celia nods and works her way around the crowded tables. She also bends and thanks diners stopping her and complimenting her performance. Some shake her hand; others give a thumbs-up. All of them smile. Reach out and pat her arm.

But eventually, Celia makes it to Elsa's table—and sits with a long sigh. She nibbles at the onion rings in Elsa's veggie-burger basket. They chat about the night. About the songs Celia's sung. About the rowdy turnout for this second Harvest Night.

Kyle brings Celia a glass of cold water with a lemon twist and thanks her for the dedication. "Oh, man," he says, standing there and looking across the patio to Shane and Quinn. "Your song was *really* sweet."

Celia nods to him. "Anytime," she quietly says, giving a wave when Kyle returns to his grilling station.

A few minutes pass when Celia just sits back and catches her breath. Cools off. Sips her water. Picks up Elsa's craft-paper-wrapped bouquet and smells the blossoms. Reads aloud Elsa's harvest fortune, too: *"Everything's coming up pumpkins for you!"*

Yes, Celia seems glad for this brief respite—chatting

with Jason, too, when he arrives at their table. He's carrying a plate of food in one hand, some drink in the other.

"Mind if I grab a seat here, ladies?" he asks.

"By all means, Jason." Elsa motions to an empty chair.

"Great show, Celia," he says, putting his things on the table and sitting with them now.

"Thanks. The amazing energy here makes performing easy. Which," Celia says while standing, "I better get on with." She turns back, though, after a few steps. "Maris was a lifesaver, babysitting Aria tonight," she calls.

Jason nods with a wave before turning to Elsa.

"Surprised to see you here," she tells him.

"Yeah. Swung by for dinner after another meet-and-greet. For CT-TV, you know?"

Elsa nods. "Close by?"

"Old Saybrook." Jason aligns his flatware alongside his heaping plate of food. "At an art festival there."

Elsa leans over the table to better see his meal. It's some creamy orange concoction topped with sprigs of green herbs. A few hunks of fresh-sliced Italian bread are perched on his plate, too. "What *is* that you're eating?"

Jason lifts his fork. "Butternut squash gnocchi." He drags his fork through it, finally lifting a mouthful. "With Italian sausage mixed in."

"*Mmm.* Looks like some *good* comfort food," Elsa says, then takes a bite of her veggie burger.

"Speaking of comfort," Jason says around his gnocchi and sausage. "You feeling any better today? How's that emotional headache of yours?"

"It's fading," Elsa quietly answers. But she doesn't tell him that's because she's likely getting answers from Celia after her show here. "Bopping around The Sand Bar last night helped. Just shook it off some."

Jason lifts a hunk of bread. "Still not going to tell me, are you?"

Elsa shakes her head, then plucks an onion ring from her food basket. And wastes no time bringing up Shane's date now. "They look well together, don't you think?" she asks, biting into that loaded onion ring.

"They really do." Jason glances their way while dragging that hunk of bread through his butternut squash gnocchi.

"I'm going over to say hello," Elsa says. She pats a napkin to her mouth and suddenly stands. "Would you actually watch my things?" she asks, motioning to her purse and jacket on a chair beside her.

"Of course. But Shane's not going to be too happy. I *just* crashed their table, and now you?"

Elsa gives an innocent shrug as she gets up and pushes in her chair.

"Well," Jason says, hovering his creamy gnocchi-filled fork midair. "Get me the dirt, would you?"

If there's one thing Shane's perfected during his twenty years of lobstering, it's this. Having eyes on the back of his head—most of the time, anyway. On the boats, there's either an uncoiling rope he has to sidestep. Or a sudden wave needing dodging as it washes over the deck. Or a heavy lobster trap come loose and dangerously propelling toward any target—himself included.

So he doesn't miss, not for a second now, Elsa DeLuca.

Her approach to his table feels just as dangerous. She's on the hunt for the lowdown here, no doubt.

Shane clears his throat. Stands briefly, too, before sitting and introducing Quinn. Of course, Elsa relishes the intro. She sits for a few moments and makes friendly talk with Quinn—the way she does with anyone new she meets. Quinn tells her about being a yoga instructor. About her love of travel and how she explores yoga studios wherever she goes.

As they talk, Shane sits back, crosses his arms and lets them have at it.

"Maybe you'll take a class of mine?" Quinn is asking Elsa now.

Elsa smiles. "If I can fit it in. I've got a seaside inn I'm trying to open, and … yoga would probably help to stay Zen."

"Ah, so *you're* the innkeeper. Shane mentioned that. I guess Celia," Quinn says, nodding to Celia singing onstage, "works with you?"

"She does. So Shane mentioned that, too?"

"I did, Elsa," Shane manages to get in. "A little bit."

And when Elsa stands to return to her table then, Shane's somehow relieved. He subtly blows out a breath, actually. Oddly, it's the same relief he gets upon doing fancy footwork to avoid getting trapped *in* that uncoiling rope. Or the relief that floods him upon ducking *beneath* a swinging lobster pot. He breathes easy now. Sweats a little. Briefly closes his eyes, too. Like he just escaped a real predicament.

Hell, here or out on the Atlantic, it's all relief—one and the same.

twenty-six

CELIA SEES IT ALL.

From where she's playing her guitar, and singing into the mic, she leans this way. That way. Turns sideways. Stands for a faster number, for a song where she goes off on an impromptu guitar jam and gives a few slap strums for a drumbeat feel. But always, she keeps a clear view of her audience.

Well, the audience that matters anyway.

She sees Elsa swinging by Shane's table. Sees the introductions being made, the hands being shaken. Sees Elsa and pretty Quinn talk, smile. Sees Shane patiently wait out Elsa's visit with his date. Sees him sit back with relief afterward. That much can't be missed.

As she's ending a song, Celia turns on her stool. Her eyes follow Elsa now. There. She's back at her table with Jason. Elsa's leaning close and talking. Jason's just listening, and nodding, while he eats. Oh, the talk is of Shane, no doubt. Shane and his date.

Well, it's time to put a stop to it—and Celia knows just how. She'll give them something *else* to think about.

So after her song, Celia waits until the applause fades, then adjusts the microphone. Shifts on her stool. And introduces her final number. The audience quiets as she talks.

"This past week," she begins, "I had the distinct pleasure of visiting a renowned landmark. It was on the streets of San Francisco. In Haight-Ashbury. Twelve steps led up to a gorgeous portico on an old Victorian home. At the Grateful Dead house." She pauses while a few sharp whistles and *Woots!* ring out in the evening. "I stood there," she goes on then, "and took it in. *Absorbed* the creative maelstrom that happened at that address. And tonight here, as Lady Blue Heart? I'm paying homage." Another pause as random cheers rise from the patio tables. "I'm closing the evening with a song the Dead has performed many, many times. Tonight's version is different, though. I've blended in my *own* lyrics and hope you enjoy them. Also … this special song has quite a history, and a message we can all relate to at some time in our lives," she softly explains to the listening crowd. She can sense it—that they're listening. In the shadows, the tables are all still. So she stands now and begins lightly strumming her guitar. With just a feather touch. She plays the opening riffs of her song, once—then again, all while talking. "This song—originally titled *Lonesome Road Blues*—is one *hundred* years old. Well," she says, her fingers working those strings. As she pares the music intro down to just the song's raw melody, she looks out beyond the patio, toward the distant harbor, then back at her audience—Shane included. "Being lonesome knows no time limit, right?"

Jason's got a feeling about this song.

Still at Elsa's table, he sits back, crosses his arms and just listens. Celia's got the crowd riveted with the way her fingers are working that guitar. She's deftly culling some epic tune that's already hinting at the blues—in a modern way. So, a California-influenced song? With Celia's own words? *And* the blues? Jason pays attention as she begins to sing.

Oh, I'm goin' down this road, feeling bad.
Goin' down this road, a-feelin' bad.
Thinking all the things I wished I sa-a-a-aid.
And I ain't gonna be treated this a-way.

Shit. Jason glances over at Shane, then back to Celia.

Celia—who's obviously telling her whole sad August Dove story to the night.

～

Elsa's captivated.

She knows. Here it is, damn it. *Here's* what happened to Celia and Shane in San Francisco—in Celia's *own* words. If only Elsa could figure them out. Could make sense of Celia's song.

My hopes were high, but oh … those lows.
Silly me, I stood there … and just froze.
Yeah … I stood there and just froze, froze, froze.
Don't wanna be treated this a-way.

The thing is, the way Celia rips into her guitar now, between verses, Elsa hears it. And it alarms her.

She hears the rage.

～

Shane's choked up.

Leaning his elbows on the table, he carefully watches Celia. Because he *never* saw this coming. Hell, he's caught so off guard. Because Celia, whether anyone knows it or not, is *broadcasting* her devastating woes of the week. Just belting them out to the night.

So I'm ... goin' where the ocean laps the shore.
Goin' where the ocean laps the shore.
Headed where the pain's no more, more, more.
Don't wanna be treated this a-way.

When her fingers pluck out the interlude, damn if Shane doesn't hear it. Doesn't hear her crying through those guitar strings. It's like he's right back outside that brick storefront with her. Especially with the way her anger rises with each successive verse.

Goin' where the salt air always blows.
Well, I'm goin' where the salt air always blows.
Stickin' to this life I alone chose, chose, chose.
Don't wanna be treated this a-way.

Oh, if he could ... Wouldn't he just grab his harmonica and jam with her. Right now. Stand with Celia, take that pain of hers, blow it out of his harmonica and *wail* it to the fuckin' skies.

～

Celia goes off on her own private jam. Her fingers find the sorrow, the anger, and they strum, pluck, *slap* it out of her guitar. It doesn't go without her notice, either, the way some folks have stood. Have started clapping along. A few couples get down on the dance area. Whistles rise. They're with her all the way. She feels it as she sings her last verse. As her whole body moves with the song. As her braid loosens and she gets into the music, the moment, beneath the God damn night skies and sings her song's end.

But she can't stop, either. So she goes in for that last verse—*again*—one last time.

With everything she's got.

Her foot's keeping a steady, rockin' beat. Her body pulses. And half singing, half yelling, her voice gives its all.

So I'm … goin' down this road, feelin' bad.
Oh I'm … goin' down this road, feelin' sad.
Now I'm … goin' down this road, feelin' mad, mad, mad.
I ain't gonna be treated this a-way.

And the way her voice rises up in pitch, and her sheer, bloody insistence laces the words before bringing the last line down to nearly a whisper, when she's done singing, that's it. It's all she can do to have her fingers drop it way down and let that guitar slowly, exhaustedly, walk her out of the song until it's lost in the crowd's ripping applause.

twenty-seven

MARIS HAD A PLAN.

Had being the key word.

Saturday evening, she *thought* she'd get some sewing done while babysitting. That she could work on the secret project she's crafting for Celia. That little Aria would sit in her baby swing while Maris pulled a denim jacket from her big tote. That the baby would coo while Maris selected a few spots to distress on the blue denim. That the baby would wave her fuzzy lion rattle while Maris dragged the blade of her razor knife in narrow slits through denim fabric. Maris thought that while she said sweet nothings to Aria, the soft, ragged sound of ripping denim would fill the room.

As if.

Because how could Maris resist that sweetie pie's charms? Instead of shaping a distressed patch or two on the denim jacket, Maris held Aria. Combed her silky hair. Counted her fingers. Turned the cardboard pages of a baby animal book and touched Aria's tiny fingers to the fluff and fur and cotton on the illustrated animals. Dipped and flew a stuffed seagull over the baby as she laughed and pumped her fisted hands. Maris held Aria in her lap and watched TV. Swayed with her while singing a lullaby. And finally, she gently clattered Aria's seashell wind chime hanging in the nursery window as the baby fell asleep.

Which is when Maris thought she might try again. She could pull that denim jacket from her tote and do some distressing.

And she *would've*—if she hadn't come across a worn scrapbook in Celia's living room. It's on the bottom shelf of an end table near the sofa. And once Maris starts thumbing through that scrapbook, the denim jacket stays put.

All sewing is shelved.

Shelved in place of research for her and Neil's novel.

For *Driftline*.

Because what she landed on is a historic treasure trove.

Sitting on the sofa in the quiet of Celia's cottage now, Maris thumbs through that scrapbook. On each page, there's another photograph of Celia's mother—Heather Gray. Many images are circa 1969 at Woodstock.

There's Heather as a little girl spinning around in the crowd. She's maybe seven or eight years old and wearing a short-sleeve, flower-printed dress. A bandana scarf is looped around her neck; a bangle bracelet is on her wrist; her blonde hair is flyaway.

And there's her father beside her. His dark hair is shoulder-length. His clothes are pure hippie—fringed vest over a loose shirt, bell-bottom jeans and pointed leather boots. A cigarette dangles from his fingers as he watches

Heather mid-spin beside him.

The thing is, as Maris browses these Woodstock images, she sees more than Heather and her parents.

She sees her *Driftline* characters in the crowds.

"Yes," she whispers now, bent over that open scrapbook in her lap. *"Yes,"* she whispers about a woman in black hip-hugger bell-bottoms with a black cropped tank top showing much of her fit torso. *"That could be Princess."*

Quickly, Maris turns the pages. The images are amazing. The woman in a form-fitting, fringed beige maxi dress clinging to her every curve, her braless breasts. A leather cuff wraps around her wrist. Stone pendants hang from her neck. Her long blonde center-parted hair falls stick-straight. She has an arm slung around a shirtless man wearing cutoff jeans. His black hair is a wild mess of curls; his face, unshaven.

He could be the fireplace chef in her novel.

And it goes on enough—this seeing her characters in Celia's scrapbook—for Maris to do this: She gets her cell phone and starts taking pictures of these old photographs. It's the denim designer in her coming out. For so many years when she had her own denim line at Saybrooks, her work was visual. *Understand the body first.* She had to perceive a body's curves beneath the designs she drew. Her hand and a piece of charcoal, or colored pencil, or pastel would capture the denim designs her mind visualized. Visual sketches filled her notebooks. Her chic pencil figures were posed casually in denim jackets and jeans in shades of blues and grays.

Visual, visual.

In her corporate studio, tall and lean mannequins wore

her designs in the mock stage: a sleeveless maxi dress patched together with mere pieces of denim. A bandana halter top over high-waisted, acid-washed jeans.

Visual. Visual.

It's incredible how she taps into that art of fashion design, the *attitude* of fashion design, as she completes Neil's novel.

Even now—sitting on this sofa with an old scrapbook in her lap.

Ultimately, she's building a *visual* file of the Woodstock attendees and their hip 1960s style.

Snap. The utterly cool lady with long, long bangs brushing her heavily lined eyes. A coin-choker wraps around her thin neck. A fringed, flower-printed shawl drapes over her chain-mesh bikini top and baggy jeans tied with a tapestry-woven leather belt. Massive silver rings adorn each of her fingers loosely hooked into her pants pockets.

She's inspiration for her character sitting cross-legged as hot dogs are roasted in the fireplace.

Snap. The man with shaggy brown hair and a smug expression. He wears only a vest open over loose jeans.

He's Driftline's younger, drafted brother, maybe.

Snap. The lone woman *standing* in a sea of sitting people. She wears a skimpy halter over white denim cutoffs. Rings on her fingers; leather cuffs on her wrists. Beaded headband wrapped around her long black hair as she grooves to the music.

The girlfriend of *Driftline*'s younger brother?

Snap, snap, snap.

Maris photographs all this vivid inspiration. The flower crowns and bandana headwraps and beaded necklaces and turquoise chokers. The ultra-mini dresses paired with tall, beat-up leather boots. The fringed bags. Tinted circle sunglasses. Tie-dye dresses. Sheer, embroidered peasant tops. The lowest of hip-huggers. Leather sandals. Brimmed hats.

Hell, it's her novel's characters come to life.

She's so drawn in that, for a moment, doesn't she get it. Doesn't she get Heather Gray also tapping into this monumental 1969 event and making it *her* life. It must've been almost impossible not to.

But when Maris hears Celia at the door, she closes that scrapbook and sets it aside. A minute later, Celia breezes into the living room and they chat about the night. Maris fills her in on what an angel Aria has been. Celia talks about her gig, about the people there for Harvest Night.

"What a crowd showed up—two people in particular," Celia says as she drops her keys and purse on a living room chair. "Shane and his date."

"What?" Maris squints across the room at her. *"Date?"*

Celia nods, laughs and tells Maris about the blind date Shane walked straight into—unawares. A fix-up Kyle and Lauren arranged. "His date, Quinn, was very pretty. And seemed nice enough. I'm sure Shane would've hit it off with her if … well, you know."

Maris laughs, too. "Poor Shane. I'll have to get the scoop from Jason," she says while collecting her tote and jacket. Before leaving, though, Maris mentions Celia's scrapbook and the really historical images in it. "I actually took pictures of some of the pages. Of the incredible fashion back then. Would you mind if I incorporated those into my novel?"

"Oh, please do. It'd be nice to have *something* good come from those pictures."

244

Which leads them to talk of Celia's encounter with her mother in San Francisco.

"Jason told me some things," Maris lets on. "He'd called Shane during the trip. Had breakfast with him, too, once Shane got back."

Celia nods. And elaborates on how it didn't go well with her mother. That Celia's plan that morning actually fell apart.

"It was a tough time," Celia admits. "I'm still working through some feelings."

"I'm sure you are. And listen, Celia. I lost my mother at a really young age, too. I know the situation's *so* different, but if you ever want to talk …"

"Thanks, hon," Celia softly says. "I'll keep that in mind."

"Regardless, Jason and I are glad you and Shane are back home, safe and sound," Maris says, giving Celia a brief hug before hiking her tote on her shoulder. "And now you must be tired, so I'll be on my way."

Celia walks her to the door while telling her Elsa's actually stopping by with tea. "I like to unwind, you know?" Celia explains while in the front doorway as Maris leaves. "Kick back after having a gig. And what a gig it was."

⁓

Shane bowed out early.

He walked Quinn to her car, thanked her for her understanding and for her company, and they parted ways.

At his cottage now, he turns on the orange harvest lights and rusty lanterns on his back porch. Grabs a beer and his harmonica, too, then sits himself on the porch half-wall.

He hikes his booted feet up and leans against a roof post. It feels like he's got to shake off the night. Shake off feeling awkward. Shake off being watched. Not to mention shake off feeling bad for Quinn. The poor woman got kind of caught up in his messy life.

When he takes a long swallow of that cold beer, it goes down damn easy. Out beyond his yard, Long Island Sound looks black beneath the starlit sky. There's only a streak of silvery light dropping on it from that nearly full moon, but the rest is dark. Neighboring cottages are, too. They're just hulking shadows in the night.

He takes another swig of his beer before setting it aside.

Now? Now he thinks of Celia. Thinks of how he'd have loved jamming with her on that last song. But like so much in his life, his hands were tied. He couldn't take his harmonica to the small stage area. Couldn't look at her, wait for her cue, and bring in his own blues. Couldn't stomp around, meet her eyes, and accompany her on her song the way he accompanied her into August Dove one San Francisco morning.

Tonight, she was alone with her emotion.

So is he.

Even now as he pulls his harmonica from his shirt pocket. For a long moment, he just sits still in the night. Feels the sea damp rising. Smells the salt air.

Finally, he brings the harmonica to his mouth and riffs on Celia's last song. As he does, he hears her words in his mind. Pictures her alone on that stage. Closes his eyes, sends his own song into the night and remembers Celia's emotional voice.

Oh, I'm goin' down this road, feeling bad.
Goin' down this road, a-feelin' bad.

246

Which is exactly how he felt driving under the trestle a little while ago.

Bad.

He suddenly puts his harmonica down.

Looks out at Long Island Sound.

Whispers, *"God damn it all."*

⌒∿

Elsa gets her answer.

Sitting in the painted wicker chairs on Celia's back porch, she gets it.

With cool salt air drifting in the screen of an open porch window.

With solar garden lights glimmering near potted mums on the stone patio outside.

With a massive Boston fern spilling from a nearby plant stand.

With a vintage lantern flickering atop the long table abutting the far wall.

With a bulb dimly glowing beneath the natural fiber shade of a lamp on a small table between them.

With night having softly fallen.

Peace, peacefulness all around them.

As Elsa lifts the knitted cosy from her teapot.

As Celia slips off her shoes and puts on fluffy slippers.

As Elsa pours tea into Celia's china cups.

As they sip.

As Elsa silently nods.

And listens.

Listens.

Celia's low and steady voice delivers Elsa's answer.

Steady, without interruption, Celia's words come.

Those words talk about a woman named Heather Gray. About Celia's mother.

And the tainted morning on the last day of their California trip.

Celia's still talking. Telling Elsa every detail. About Heather. And her significant accomplishments. Her noted fame in the music world. In the jewelry world. Celia talks about walking into her mother's jewelry boutique. Describes the shop in its every winged and feathered detail.

And talks of her encounter there.

Of her instant regret.

Of Heather being taken with little Aria.

Of Celia not admitting her identity.

Of the awkward fumbling as Celia felt faint.

Of seeing growing recognition in her mother's eyes. Recognition gone unheeded.

Of Celia managing to exit the store, albeit gracelessly.

Of the emotion and distress of *everything*—hopes and plans and sad reality—hitting her full force on the streets of San Francisco.

"I knew your mother left you as a child," Elsa says now. "That you don't even know her, really. You mentioned that to me last summer. But I had no idea she lived out there."

"Mm-hmm. And when *our* California trip began to crystallize? So did my hopes. But, oh, they were such false hopes," Celia's saying. "Being a mother myself now, and loving Aria with everything I've got? Well, I thought things could be different with my own mother." She pauses with a regretful smile. A sad smile, maybe? "But they can't."

248

"You're sure, Celia? Maybe Heather needed some time. To grasp the situation. To realize—"

Celia shakes her head. "She *did* realize. She knew who I was. That much was clear. She needed no more time. And truly, Elsa. I learned that morning, with much difficulty, that things are actually better this way."

"You won't try again?"

"No." On her cell phone, Celia pulls up a website. "There will never be another morning when I get myself all dressed, Aria too, with the intent of walking into August Dove." As she says it, she hands Elsa her phone. Elsa looks at the beautiful shop pictures. Of the wings—sequined and beaded and feathered. Of the striking, spread-winged dove wall mural. Of the poster-sized rock star photographs. When she flips to a photo of the outside of the boutique, Elsa gasps.

"What's wrong?" Celia asks.

Elsa looks at the feathered wings propped in the display window. At the murals of wings painted high on the window's glass. At the words *Peace, Love & Jewelry* painted along the bottom of the glass. Then she looks at Celia. *"I was there,"* Elsa whispers. *"That same morning."*

"What?" Celia takes the phone and looks at the picture. "You were? You actually went in the shop?"

Elsa shakes her head. "No, no. My driver, Toby, was bringing me back to the hotel. And … and we were stuck in traffic. Right there," she says, nodding to the phone. "The shop looked so intriguing with all those wings, I actually *thought* of stopping in." Elsa leans over to see that image on the phone again. *"That's* your mother's jewelry store?"

"Has been for decades. Ever since she left me and my father."

"Oh, Celia." Elsa reaches over and squeezes her arm. "I'm really sorry you went through that. Then—*and* now. This had to be weighing on you heavily our whole trip! And that last day?"

Celia only nods.

"It must've been devastating," Elsa quietly realizes.

"At the time, it was. The morning ended with me fully defeated. I had nothing left inside. Which is why, when I got Aria back to the hotel room, I actually fell fast asleep."

Elsa gives an ironic smile. "And then I knocked on the door with a balloon bouquet."

"You did." Celia lifts her china teacup and clasps it close. "And I'm not sure my expression hid all that had just happened."

"Sometimes I wondered ... But you never said a word!"

"I couldn't." In the low light, Celia curls her legs beneath her in the big wicker chair. She looks over her teacup at Elsa, too. "I just *couldn't* bring all that mess to your *beautiful* time with Wren. This was your trip—*yours*. And you deserved every special minute of it. But I wanted you to know about my mother ... now that we're back."

"I'm so sorry, Celia."

Celia shrugs in the shadows. Her voice is nearly a whisper. "What was I doing? What was I looking for? The mother I need is right here. Has been since the moment we met and you invited me over for lemonade. You've done *so* much, Elsa. Have been *so* generous. You opened up your *home* to me—your career, your whole ... life."

Well. By now Elsa's hand is clasped over her mouth—

just to hold back *her* emotion. To think of Celia, dear Celia, going through *all* this. Finally, Elsa gets up from her wicker porch chair. *"Celia,"* she whispers through her tears.

When Celia stands, Elsa opens her arms.

And Celia? She stifles a sob and walks right into them—without hesitation.

Which is when Elsa gives her the kind of hug that Celia's mother never could.

twenty-eight

LATE THAT NIGHT, JASON'S SITTING on the edge of the bathtub. He's in a tee and loose pajama shorts and is pulling off his prosthesis. His forearm crutches lean against the hamper. "I eventually felt bad for the guy," he's saying to Maris.

"For Shane?" she asks.

"Yeah." A salty breeze ripples in through the slightly open bathroom window. Jason sets down the prosthesis, turns sideways and leans against the tiled wall. "Kyle's gonna get his ass kicked, putting his brother in that situation. And I felt bad for Quinn, too. She seemed like a really nice lady."

Wearing her black nightshirt, Maris is sitting on the closed toilet while applying his good moisturizer to her elbows. Her hair's loosely tied back. "*Ach.* Being there on a blind date, both of them? And with a lot of eyes on them? Super awkward."

"No kidding. Celia say anything to you when she got home?"

"Little bit." Maris rubs the moisturizer on her hands now. "She didn't get much into it, but there *was* a twinkle in her eye talking about Shane's dilemma."

Jason leans forward on the tub edge and rolls the silicone liner off his stump. "Well, I'll tell you … it was like watching a tennis match," he says, holding the inside-out liner now. "I'd look away, but then have to check out that date again." Running the tub spigot, he rinses the liner beneath streaming warm water. That done, he spreads a few drops of soap over the liner and rubs it around. As he does, he tells Maris about Celia's gig. "That last song? Wow. She blended her own lyrics with the original of an old blues number. And *her* lyrics? No one would really know it," he says while rinsing the liner, then turning it right-side out, "but they were all about *whatever* went down with her mother in San Francisco. I could just tell," he says, then hangs that damp liner on a drying stand in the tub.

"Really?" Maris asks. She stands now and sets his tube of moisturizer on the tub edge. Brings him his towel, too. "And how'd it go over, that song?"

"Celia got a standing ovation. Her music's never sounded better." Straddling the tub, Jason swings his residual limb over the edge and soaps up the stump. He looks over as Maris heads out to the hallway. "Heartache's a helluva muse," Jason calls to her.

⌒

Elsa's back home after having tea with Celia. And talking with her.

Now Elsa changes into navy pajamas with white piping. The capris are loose; the top, short sleeves. She heads to the bathroom to do her ear-care routine for her second piercings. First? Standing at the mirror, she dips a cotton swab into the cleaning solution on the sink top.

And *thinks* how much it meant to have Celia open up to her tonight. But still—*still*—Elsa grapples with the elephant in the room.

With Shane.

Carefully, she dabs the damp swab around the diamond stud in her left ear.

And *thinks* how Celia just told her everything—*except* why Shane was with her on the San Francisco streets. Was he there as a friend? Someone she'd opened up to? An unbiased ear? Elsa *could* buy that—if she hadn't witnessed the lover's kiss and intimate embrace, too. Even tonight, Elsa saw the same sad, faraway expression on Celia that she saw in San Francisco that morning. Elsa also saw Shane on a date with another woman.

Now she takes another cotton swab, dampens it with solution and cleans her other ear.

Saturate a cotton swab, dab it around the hole … and you'll be fine, the boutique attendant told her and Wren.

So Elsa does.

She dabs this ear now and only hopes Celia will be fine.

That maybe in a few weeks' time, like Elsa's twice-pierced ears, a heart will be healed, too.

When Elsa returns to her bedroom, she stops at a paned window and presses aside the curtain. The night beyond is dark. It seems very still out there. Like all the world's paused. Just breathing.

Or maybe that's just Elsa's own personal feeling—for Celia.

Celia's life seems paused.

Elsa feels that, yes, especially after witnessing Celia's powerful closing song tonight. Her performance was raw emotion—the personal lyrics *obviously* drawn from a few brief minutes inside August Dove. As though a part of Celia—in thoughts, in memories—is still struggling *inside* that shop. Paused right there.

"Dio ti benedica, Celia," Elsa whispers while looking up at the starlit sky. *"God bless you."*

The last thing Shane wanted tonight, especially at this late hour, was an argument. But hell, isn't that what you often get—the last thing you want.

The last thing you're in the mood for.

The thing that just pushes you over the edge.

So over the edge he goes—with Kyle.

Who not only had no business fixing him up, but has no business calling him now and looking for the post-date scoop. No business asking Shane if he had fun. Asking if he's going to call Quinn.

Then Lauren yells out from the background not to wait too long. *Text Quinn so she knows you're interested!*

All while Shane sits here on his inadequate cottage sofa and watches some old movie on the too-small TV.

Well, he wasn't really watching the movie. He was too busy still processing Celia's last song. Too busy worrying about her. Too busy thinking that even though she *says* she's okay—that she's good with how things ultimately happened—maybe she's not.

Maybe Heather Gray has gotten deep, deep under her skin.

Which is the last thorn, poison, shit Celia needs in her life.

So Shane lets his *brother* have it now—have his anger at being fixed up, and then some. Yep, some anger at Heather is sent his way, too.

It's all there in Shane's pissed-off words seriously telling Kyle off. Words insisting he didn't appreciate the pity date. That Kyle straight up overstepped.

"I'll live my *own* life, thank you very much," Shane warns, putting a booted foot on the painted trunk coffee table. "Just like I did the past fifteen years, okay? Maybe things were better that way. *Jesus*, and now? On top of it all? I'm about to go out on federal waters for weeks on end." Shane shakes his head, takes a breath, and lets his anger rip. Really low. Really restrained. "And *you* think I'm also going to get something off the ground with some lady? Get fuckin' real, Kyle," Shane tosses over the phone. "And back *off.*"

A few seconds of silence pass before Kyle answers. "Fine, I'll back off," he says, then hangs up.

Shane waits a few surprised moments to be sure. Yep. Dead silence.

So he tosses the cell phone aside on the sofa, gets up, shoves open a sticking living room window and gulps a breath of salt air.

Which is when his damn phone rings again.

He walks to the sofa, scoops up the phone without even a look and answers.

"What *now*?" he almost yells.

Silence, then, "*Shane?*" comes the sweetest whisper.

❧

Shane's eyes drop closed.

Celia, he thinks—then gets himself out to the back porch.

"Celia, *shit*. I thought you were Kyle," he says on the way. Pushing through the kitchen screen door, he goes on. "I just hung up with him."

"And sounding pretty tense."

"Yeah, I *was* tense. Still am." Shane sits himself on the faded white porch bench. Sits there in darkness. "I really let him have it for meddling in my life."

"Shane. He thought you weren't seeing anybody," Celia insists.

Insists gently, Shane notices. Insists with ease.

And it works. He takes a cleansing, salt-air breath and is just glad to have the two things he loves nearby: the sound of the sea—its small waves splashing on the nearby little beach—and the sound of Celia's calming voice in his ear.

"And maybe Kyle found you a good match," she softly says now. "Tell me about her."

"About Quinn?"

"Yes."

"Okay. Quinn. She's a nice lady, actually. Dedicated to her yoga studio and students—including Lauren's mother. Passionate about traveling and daily acts of meditation. She enjoys cooking. And renovating her cramped but cozy Cape Cod, as well as walking her rescue dog Ruby."

"Oh my gosh, Shane!"

"What?" Shane sits straight on the porch bench.

"Quinn sounds really cool. So … are *we* done?" Celia asks, defusing the situation in her own way. "Are you leaving me for her?"

Shane goes with it. Breathes easier. Manages to smile. "At least I have options now."

"*Ah.* Decisions, decisions."

"Seriously?" Shane drags a hand through his hair as he sits there on the bench. "That's why I ripped into my brother. Because I had to backpedal out of things with perfectly innocent Quinn—who also didn't ask for any of this. So I had to tell her *my* story."

"Which is?"

"That I'll be out to sea and unavailable. That Kyle didn't understand, but I hoped she did. And I told her early on, so we just enjoyed the evening afterward with no stress. More like … friends."

"Shane. If you'd just waited, *I* could've made things easy and done the backpedaling. Just walked right out of the picture and become Lady Blue Heart forever."

"Celia. That's enough."

"But I saw the kiss Quinn gave you at the end of the night. She was all in."

"No. That was a friend kiss—on the cheek. A kiss that let me off the hook with her understanding."

"Okay." Celia's tone gets more serious. "Did you at least have *some* fun?"

"No. I didn't. All I wanted tonight was to eat my dinner in peace there and listen to you sing."

A pause comes until Celia's low voice responds. "We

don't always *get* what we want, do we?"

"Ain't that the truth," Shane murmurs back.

He also stands and walks to the porch half-wall as they say their good-nights. Small ripples of Long Island Sound barely glimmer in a wide swath of moonlight now.

Celia's dead right. We *don't* always get what we want in life. How many times has Shane been dealt *that* hand? Hell, too many. He didn't get to be around when his father died in Maine. He didn't get to have a brother for fifteen long years. He didn't get to save poor Shiloh on the lobster boat. He doesn't get to have Celia here with him right now. On this porch. Close. Doesn't get to touch her hair. Her face. To see her.

He didn't get something else he wanted, either.

Wanted badly.

This one's a big one.

This week, he didn't get to tell Heather Gray what he *really* thought of her.

What he thought of her watching her brave daughter walk into her jewelry boutique.

What he thought of her letting her daughter just go— letting Celia walk out onto the city streets—without a word. Without a hug. Nothing.

Didn't get to tell Heather Gray what a blessed fool she was.

Didn't get to tell Heather Gray what *he* thought of *beautiful* Celia Gray.

Damn it.

In the one, single last fleeting chance he had alone in August Dove? He didn't get to go off-script.

twenty-nine

SOMETIMES THEY DON'T TALK.

Oh, it's paradise nonetheless—Jason's Sunday mornings in bed.

Through the open window, a sea breeze always drifts in and brushes his skin just the same. The edge of the window curtains, as usual, lightens with the rising sun.

But on some Sundays, he and Maris love each other silently.

It starts with a wordless touch. Today, it's hers on his jaw. Just a brush of her fingertips that gets him to open his eyes. And he knows then that she's been watching him. Watching him breathe. Dream. Sleep.

He touches her in return. His hand strokes her face, skims her hair, before she presses closer and kisses him. Gently tugs off his tee.

No words come, though.

None.

Instead, there are the squawks of seagulls feeding out on the bluff.

There's the slosh of waves breaking onto the rocky landscape below.

There's the whisper of that sea breeze lifting off Long Island Sound.

Wild, it's all wild. Wild and free.

They're a part of all that, too. In their wordless sighs, their moans, their touches.

Jason feels the salt air graze upon the room now, upon his skin. Feels it dampen Maris' thick, brown hair. Behind her neck, his hands lift through that hair as she kisses him. As they don't talk. As her mouth toys with his. As she deepens their kiss in such a way that he can't wait. Lying beside her, he takes hold of her mid-thigh-length black nightshirt with its lacy short sleeves. Gathers the silky fabric in his hands and hikes it up.

And she does the same.

Her hands drag down his pajama shorts and slip them off beneath the sheet.

With their touches, there are no words still. Sighs, yes. Low moans, too, when Jason hikes that nightshirt up higher, presses her onto her back and moves on top of her. His hands reach beneath that bunched-up nightshirt fabric and feel her breasts. He pushes the nightshirt higher still and brings his mouth to her belly, the soft skin of her breasts, her nipples. Their breaths quicken now. The sighs are gone as Maris raises her legs around him.

Yes, wild and free.

Urgent, too. Her sighs become throaty. His grunts, muffled, as the sex comes fast now. Their night clothes are twisted around them. His mouth kisses hers, moves to her neck. She raises her legs even higher around his hips and clings tight. And gasps with his every thrust, his every husky breath.

When they separate, they lie on their backs. Their chests rise and fall. Jason tosses an arm over his face. And for ten minutes, maybe fifteen, they slow. They doze. There's only the Sunday morning sounds they began with—waves splashing down on the bluff; feeding gulls squawking there; a sea breeze whispering.

Until Maris murmurs, *"Good morning."*

And Jason tells her he loves her. Puts his arm around her shoulders and pulls her close. Kisses the top of her head. Dozes. Wakes up. Dozes again.

And wakes for good when he remembers something he'd forgotten to tell her yesterday.

"Maris," he whispers and waits for her reply, a whisper back, a touch. Something.

But nothing comes.

"Sweetheart," he says, then keeps talking. Because he can figure she's awake. It's just that her every muscle, every fiber, is slack with relaxation. "I meant to tell you something," he goes on, reaching beneath the sheet now for his pajama shorts. "Shane's got a roll of film. Of Neil's," Jason says while slipping on those shorts. "Neil left it behind in Maine ten years ago."

"What?" Maris whispers. She straightens her nightshirt and looks up at him.

Jason nods. "My brother left it behind when he visited Shane. It was the same month Neil died."

"Are you kidding me?"

"Nope."

"I thought Neil already had pictures from Maine. That shot he took of Shane at the beach binoculars, right?"

"That was from a different roll. Because Shane's got one more."

Now Maris sits against the headboard and draws up her knees. "Oh my God, Jason."

"I know. Neil always had that camera with him, documenting everything." Jason sits up, too. But he swings his legs over the side of the mattress and reaches for his forearm crutches. "I can't *imagine* what's on that roll of film."

Sitting there for a few minutes, with his crutches looped on his forearms, he doesn't stand, though. Instead, as the morning takes hold, and the sun lightens the windows, they toss ideas back and forth.

Guesses of what photographs Neil might've taken.

Possibilities of some of the pictures being *of* Neil.

Wonderings of this briefest unknown part of his brother's life—the amount that would've taken up a single roll of film.

thirty

ONE THING SHANE BRADFORD KNOWS about his brother is this: Kyle's an early bird.

Just like his lobsterman brother.

Hell, they're both up at the crack of dawn, if not earlier.

So Shane wastes no part of his Sunday morning. He's got an apology to make and has no time to spare. Has to catch Kyle before he leaves for the diner. So after a quick shower, Shane puts on jeans and a flannel shirt over his tee, grabs his zip sweatshirt and heads over to Kyle's house on the bay.

But today? Shane foregoes his truck and walks.

He has to. It's the only way to shake off his anxiety. To calm some shaking nerves as he attempts to patch things up with his brother. He's so lost in thought, Shane doesn't pay the sunrise much mind. Doesn't appreciate the orange globe cresting the eastern horizon as he walks along Sea View Road. Doesn't admire the way the sun casts gold light on dawn's dark blue Long Island Sound. The way seagulls swoop beneath that early-morning light.

Instead, he keeps walking, putting one booted foot in front of the other to Bayside Road—to his brother's silver-shingled house in the turnaround at the end.

Okay, go time.

But as he crosses Kyle's dewy front lawn, and as leaves crunch beneath his step, Kyle's voice comes from a front porch window.

"What are *you* here for, loser?"

Shane squints to make out his brother on the still-dark porch. "To see your new mower."

A few seconds later, the screen door opens and Kyle leans out. "Seriously?"

"Yeah. And to apologize. I was out of line, bro, telling you off on the phone last night." Shane stops and tosses his hands in the air. "You meant well fixing me up with Quinn—"

"I did."

"You just caught me at the end of a *really* long week."

"Hope you were nicer to the lady."

"Of course I was."

"All right, then. Apology accepted."

"Just like that?"

"Yep." Kyle opens that screen door even further. "You want a coffee?"

"No. I can't stay long."

"Why not?" Kyle asks as he steps outside. He's got on jeans, scuffed-up, greasy work boots and a pullover sweatshirt. He's sipping his own coffee, too.

"I'm doing my part sprucing up that newly painted guard

shack," Shane explains. "Got some old salty buoys in my truck bed. Brought them down for Evan's class visit this week. But I have a ton of them, more than I need for my talk."

"So … what?" Kyle asks, then sips his steaming coffee. "You're hanging them on the guard shack?"

"Going to try. Thought I'd bring some coffee and eats to the trailer and see what's up with Cliff. Nick. Get some help hanging the buoys. Give the shack a true coastal feel."

"Awesome, man." Kyle takes a deep breath of the damp bayside air. Across the street, beyond some wild dune grasses, the bay is glass calm. "Nothing says New England like old salt-worn buoys."

"Roger that. But heck, show me your new machine first, brother."

"All right. Let's do this." Kyle tips up his mug and finishes the last of his coffee. He also opens the porch door and sets the mug inside. "Ell," he calls into the house. "I'm going out to the garage. Firing up my new mower for Shane!"

"Don't be long," Lauren's voice comes back. "Kids want breakfast!"

When he and Shane walk around the house, Shane tells Kyle, "Didn't know if I'd catch you. If you'd be at work already, cooking up some morning grub."

"Nah, it was a late night for me yesterday. You know, with Harvest Night. Took today off to actually *do* my yard work," Kyle says on the way to his garage. "Jerry's running the stoves."

"Nice of him."

"Yeah." As Kyle opens his garage and turns on the lights there, he asks Shane if he's really serious about not seeing Quinn again.

"I am," Shane says from behind him. He leans against Kyle's gray, four-door pickup parked there. The garage is huge, with more than enough space for two vehicles. There's a small workshop in the back. Gray cabinets are mounted above and below a counter. Hand tools—hammers, pliers, wrenches, screwdrivers—hang on the wall there. Lengths of extension cord are neatly looped over hooks. Folded-up sawhorses lean against the back wall. And everything is neat as a pin. Tidy. Spit-shined. "I told Quinn last night things wouldn't work—but that it was all me," Shane explains now. "That too much was going on with my job, and being out at sea, to start up a relationship. Because … you know, I didn't want her to feel it was something about her. She was very nice. Pretty—"

"See, man?"

"No, Kyle. Maybe in a different life. But not mine, not now."

"Why not?" Kyle asks in all seriousness. "You yourself mentioned changes in lobstering and wondering how long you wanted to push it. And you're here more and more—"

"I am. But there's shit going on that you're not aware of. I told Quinn that and asked her not to hold anything against you."

"So *tell* me about your shit." Kyle's moving a red gas can out of the way. He sets it beneath those folded sawhorses. "What's happening?" he asks over his shoulder.

Shane blows out a breath. "Long story short?" He grabs a dusty push broom leaning against the wall and roughly gives the worn bristles a few hard sweeps on the garage floor. "Been talking with that woman I was seeing."

"The one with the baby?"

"Yeah."

Kyle moves to his new mower parked between his truck and Lauren's car. "You getting back together?"

"I don't know." Shane sweeps some dry leaves, some pieces of dirt, into a small pile. "We'll see," he lies.

"Wow. Okay. Well … good luck, guy." Kyle bends and releases the mower's parking brake. "Maybe she's the one for you."

"Maybe," Shane says while sweeping his debris pile out to the driveway.

"Great. So *I* feel like the ass now. Setting up poor Quinn."

Shane leans that push broom against the wall. "You've been an ass since you were born," he says, then gives Kyle a shove.

"Shut up." Kyle shoves him back. "Now let me wheel my mower out to the yard."

Shane follows him outside. "You think Lauren will ever talk to me again?"

"I'll work on her," Kyle says—right as he rolls the lawn mower onto the driveway.

"Pretty damn impressive." Shane gives a low whistle at the machine glistening in the morning sun now. He circles the fully decked-out, zero-turn riding mower. As he does, Kyle points out the rear hitch, and the little trailer he also bought for yard work. Starts the mower up, too. Gets on, gives Shane a demo right there in the front yard.

"Let me take a spin, bro," Shane says.

Kyle hesitates until Shane *promises* he'll drive it with care.

So with trepidation, Kyle demonstrates first how to work the control levers. To move *both* forward—gently—to drive it straight. How to make smooth turns manipulating the levers. Turn left by pulling back on the right lever, and vice versa.

And yeah. Shane does it all. He shoves up his sweatshirt sleeves and takes off across Kyle's front lawn—just fine. Nice and easy. Moves the drive sticks out of neutral and *goes*. The mower gives a smooth ride across the lush yard. The engine purrs. And when Shane carefully, slowly turns, Kyle's looking on from the driveway. Looking mighty proud, too.

Until Shane riles him with a few full-spin turns and smokes it up some before coming to a stop at his brother's feet.

"You *scoundrel*," Kyle tells him then. Doesn't give him a good shove, though, until Shane's climbed *off* the mean machine.

Shane laughs, recovers his footing and heads for the street. "Hey, bro," he calls back. "Sweet wheels, man."

Goodness, goodness.

That's all Celia's feeling today.

Pure goodness.

After breakfast, and after Aria has her bottle, she puts on the baby's little jacket and hat and wheels her to the Stony Point playground. They spend a half hour there in the morning sunshine. That golden light glints off the changing foliage. It shines on Aria's laughing face as Celia gently, gently pushes her in the baby swing there. The salt air is sweet; the air, crisp. In her wavering swing, the baby coos and smiles at Celia. Celia coos and smiles right back at her, too.

269

Yes, all's good.

Even more? Celia really feels now that it's *good* she went to California. It's *good* that she went into August Dove. Because today? She has no regrets. Here she is, back home. Happy. Safe in her own world. And loving it, actually. It's crystal clear right now that she *had* to go through that San Francisco heartache—just to get to this place in her own mind. A place where she loves Shane even *more* for how he was there for her. A place where she loves Elsa even more now, too. Especially after Elsa fully listened to the whole story about Heather last night. What a blessing Elsa is in her life.

How much more do I need? Celia thinks as she swings her baby. *How much more does one even get?*

So she relishes things like this—thirty minutes at a beach playground. It's early still, so she and Aria have the place to themselves. And on this beautiful Sunday morning, Celia cherishes every second with her baby. Every murmur. Every little kiss she leaves on Aria's cheek. Every gentle push that gets Aria swinging through the sweet salt air.

"La dolce aria salata," Celia murmurs near Aria's ear. And lightly swings her again beneath the red, yellow and orange leaves drifting … drifting … from the trees. It's like they're in a colorful autumn fairy tale.

Once she buckles Aria back into her stroller, Celia takes the long way home. Yes, she veers right—instead of left—and walks down Sea View Road.

Walks to one particular shabby beach bungalow.

Wheels the stroller—*thumpity-thump*—down the planked walkway edged with sweeping beach grasses. The soft autumn-gold blades swish beside them, all the way to Shane's back porch. There, Celia applies the stroller brake, quickly takes the seven stairs to the porch and knocks on the back door. When there's no answer, she pulls a pen and paper from her tote, jots a note and nudges it under the old porch door.

And by the time she's back home at her gingerbread cottage, Celia feels like something else—something *real*—has also happened these past few days.

She's made peace with herself.

She's worked through her upset feelings with her songs; with quiet, reflective moments. There's no more beating herself up for how things went in August Dove. For how she behaved in that jewelry boutique.

"All was meant to be," she whispers to Aria as she puts her in for her morning nap.

Life, sooner than Celia'd thought it would, feels fine.

So there's only one thing left to do. One thing to close out that *chapter* of her life. To turn the page on it and move on—for good.

"And it's right here," Celia tells herself as she reaches to the closet shelf in her own bedroom. Her hands pull down the large, flowered trinket box there. *This* is where pieces of her heart stay. Pieces she sometimes takes a glimpse at, runs a finger over. Remembers.

Sitting on her bed then, Celia opens the box lid. Inside are mementos from her time with Sal: some summer photographs; an ice-cream stand menu; the platinum sea-glass engagement ring he'd given her.

And now, this.

Now, two more items to add to her trinket box. To become only memories.

First, she unwraps the twined-and-netted sea glass

pieces Shane gave her in California. It was on the morning they went to August Dove. He told her then how time *does* soften things, like it does to sea glass. *And I really hope*, he'd said, *that time has softened things for you and your mother, too.* That morning, at her hotel's courtyard, Celia's fingers toyed with the salty pieces as Shane's voice reassured her.

And her fingers toy with those glass pieces now. Their edges are dull. Soft. The saltiness of the sea coats them, it seems.

But suddenly, while joggling the loose pieces, the thought of putting them away forever actually alarms her. She touches each cool piece, brushes a few against her cheek while closing her eyes. Adds them—clinking and tumbling—to others in a crystal dish on her bedside table. She does *not* put the sea glass in the trinket box. Because there's no part of Shane that she wants to pack away.

The second item, though? She does.

She lifts it now. It's the turquoise pendant her mother gave her upon graduating from high school. The pendant Celia's worn on and off throughout the years. The pendant that she'd clung to the same way she'd clung to some faint hope. A beautiful turquoise pendant set in silver that her own mother's hands must've soldered. Shaped. Set the hand-polished stone into. A pendant she must've crafted with Celia in her thoughts.

And now, Celia sets that pendant in the trinket box with Heather in *her* thoughts.

Heather and a private farewell as she closes the box lid, lifts the box to her top closet shelf, pushes it to the back, then closes the closet door.

On the way home from Kyle's, Shane spots his rented cottage up ahead. He takes in the sight of it as he nears. The old beach house is seaworn. Its shingles are weathered. The cream trim paint is peeling. Salt water and damp sea air show their mighty presence here. Yes, Long Island Sound's close proximity has certainly left its briny mark on the cottage. But with the scrubby beach grasses alongside it, and with its boardwalk-planked walkway, the cottage also fits right into its surroundings. Becomes one with them, Shane thinks now as he climbs the few steps to his front porch. There, he spruces up the scarecrow tied to a porch post. Lifts a half-filled watering can and gives his few mum plants of yellow and red a drink. Then goes inside.

If he wants to hang some buoys on the guard shack, he can't have Cliff resisting the idea. So Shane will bring *everything* necessary to get the job done—including a small toolbox. Walking through the living room and straight to the cottage kitchen, he heads toward the back porch.

And stops in his tracks.

There, on his kitchen floor, is a folded piece of paper. *Ha.*

It must've been slipped right beneath his back porch door. And there's only one person on the entire planet who would've done just that. So Shane picks up the paper and taps it on his hand. Standing right there then, he opens the note. Reads the very familiar, unmistakable handwriting.

Smiling because I know you're reading these words right now.
—Celia

Yep, and *he's* smiling now, too. Man, he's so glad to have her in his life. Hell, who knew he'd *ever* feel like this? The way his life *was* going, he'd pretty much written himself off as some crotchety old salt of the sea.

"Not anymore," he says, then pushes open the squeaking screen door, walks to his backyard shed and finds the grimy toolbox there. Opens it to see some nails. Wall hooks. A hammer. All he'll need for his Stony Point buoy mission.

Finally, he's at his pickup and dropping that toolbox in the truck bed. Really, Cliff will have no reason to decline his guard shack offer. Shane's got the tools and will supply the labor to get the job done, and done well.

He checks the buoys now—rattling them around, lifting and untangling them.

They'll do—just fine.

He drives the dusty beach roads to the guard shack then. His truck tires take the curves and turn gritty on the pavement. Morning dew rises in a mist from front lawns. October sunlight dapples the shingled cottages. And a note from the love of his life is tucked into his flannel shirt pocket.

Shit, if Shane's not mistaken? All's pretty damn good with the world.

Good as it can be, anyway.

thirty-one

SHANE'S ALL LOADED DOWN.

Pushing through Scoop Shop's door later Sunday morning, he's got a four-coffee-cup carrier in one hand and a bag of fresh doughnuts in the other. And hell, who's he kidding? It's all a bribe, these sweet pastries. A manner of swaying opinions, decisions, viewpoints *his* way. He'll just soften Stony Point authority's ironfisted rule with junk food. That seems to do the trick around here. So he carefully gets to the parking lot and stashes the goods on his truck's front passenger seat.

Next up? Seek out Cliff Raines.

But Shane doesn't get far.

Not much farther than the stone train trestle, actually. After cruising through it, he's waved down at the stop sign near the guard post. So he pulls over to the side of the road, gets out and nods to Nick standing there in full uniform—from the khaki button-down and black pants to the *Security* cap on his head and walkie-talkie clipped to his belt.

"Where's the commish?" Shane asks as he lifts the coffee tray from his truck, then grabs the bag of doughnuts. "I got to ask him something."

"You're looking at him," Nick says. "I'm the *designated* commissioner in his absence."

"Absence?"

Nick nods. "He's with his son, Denny, back in Addison. Helping him out with some home projects this weekend."

"Okay." Shane sets the coffee tray and doughnut bag on a flat stone ledge off the side of the trestle. "You'll do, then. Have a coffee, why don't you?"

Nick does. So does Shane. They chow down on sugar doughnuts, too, the sugar grains dropping to the ground as they check out the newly painted guard shack.

"Have to admit, the new paint's pretty slick," Shane remarks, nodding to the shack. It sits on a little rise in the ground and is edged in black bark mulch. The midmorning sun's shining bright now, dropping rays of light on the green shingles. "And planting shrubs was a nice touch. But I still thought it was missing something."

"Oh yeah?" Nick, standing beside him, squints at the green guard shack with the new *Welcome* mat at the Dutch door. "Looks good to me, Bradford," he says, then takes a double bite of his doughnut. Dabs the back of his hand on sugar grains on his chin, too. "It's what they call ... *minimalist*. Has clean lines, you know?"

"I guess." Shane crosses the street to get closer to that green shack. There's a potted plant and stack of cheap white painter caps on the inside of its front window. He turns to Nick following him. "But come on, man. This is a beach community. And I'm not getting *beach* from solid green. I mean …" Shane elaborates while sipping his coffee, "green's a great color, I'll give you that. But it needs more … coastal New England flavor."

"*New England?* Like what?"

"As a matter of fact, I've got just the thing." Shane stuffs the rest of his doughnut in his mouth, washes it down with coffee and goes on. "Wanted to run it by Cliff."

"Run it by *me*," Nick insists, holding his coffee cup and half-eaten doughnut right there at the guard shack. "I'll decide for Cliff."

Just then, there's the sound of wheels propelled on the gritty road. The sound gets closer, the spinning wheels being rhythmically pushed over the pavement until a kid on a skateboard rolls into view. Those wheels grind along as he fast approaches Nick and Shane at the guard shack. Within feet of them, his skateboard comes to a clattering stop.

Shane steps back while eyeing a teen with curly black hair and an attitude to boot. It's that Flynn. He's got on a sweatshirt over a baggy tee and loose khaki shorts with some really beat-up leather sneakers.

"Sup, Nick?" Flynn asks, throwing in a nod to Shane.

"Hey." Nick casually raises his coffee cup to the kid, then turns to Shane. "This here's Flynn. Not sure if you've met."

"Not formally," Shane says, watching a nervous Flynn jam his hands in his pockets. "Just took your newsletter pictures at the shack reveal."

"Yeah," Nick elbows Shane. "This here's the punk that locked Cliff in the shed behind the Stony Point Beach Association trailer."

"That was *you*?" Shane asks.

"Yeah." Flynn kicks up his skateboard, grabs it and sets it aside. "Didn't really mean anything by it."

"Well, the boss thought so," Nick says around the last of his doughnut. "Flynn just completed his requisite community service painting the guard shack."

"That right?" Shane hitches his head at Flynn. "So what're you doing still loitering around here?"

"I don't know."

"Yeah, you do," Nick says, slapping Flynn's shoulder. "This is a happenin' place to be."

Flynn just shakes that moppy-haired head of his. "More like Carol asked me to water her new bushes this weekend."

"Okay, Flynn. That's decent, helping out Carol. My name's Shane, by the way," Shane says, shifting his coffee to his left hand and extending his right to this punk with an attitude. "And I guess you're the FNG."

"Huh?" Flynn asks.

"Fuckin' new guy," Shane dryly explains.

"Guess so." Flynn laughs and shakes Shane's hand. "FNG, *sheesh*."

"Ha!" Nick says, then finishes his coffee.

Shane turns and heads to his truck parked across the street. "Yo, Flynn!" he calls over his shoulder. "Grab me one of those painter hats in the shack window, would you? I got to work with Nick here on a project."

In no time, Flynn's wheeling his skateboard across the road. Shane looks up from his truck bed to catch the painter cap Flynn flings to him. "Thanks, dude." Shane pulls the cap low on his head. "Why don't you grab a coffee and doughnut," Shane says, nodding to the coffee tray and

Scoop Shop bag on the nearby stone ledge. "Hang out with the big boys this morning."

⁓

Shane explains the salt-worn buoys to Nick and Flynn at his truck. Tells them how the old fishing buoys are beyond repair, or just have seen their day and been replaced. He hauls out a string of them, grabs his toolbox and crosses the street again. He, Nick and Flynn study the front of the guard shack now, and the way the big Dutch door takes up the right side. To the door's left is a paned window, with empty shingle space to the left of that.

So it's decided. The string of faded buoys will get hung there. It's just the right spot.

They get busy then. The morning sun is warm, so Shane takes off his sweatshirt and has Flynn toss it in his pickup. On his way there, Flynn throws their coffee cups and doughnut bag in the trash. Nick grabs the large wall hooks from the toolbox, and they measure shack width and buoy-string length. They calculate; they hold the buoys here, there. Higher. Just beneath the roof overhang.

"Perfect. Just a little to the left," Flynn tells them from where he stands at a distance.

They all agree. So Shane shoves up his flannel shirtsleeves, grabs the hammer and gets a few big hooks nailed in the shingled shack wall. With more than one hook, they can distribute the weight of the buoys and make a legit arrangement. Nick steps away for a minute to sign in a visitor at the trestle. When he returns, Shane drapes the old buoy rope over just one of the hooks—to get a visual. The string of faded fishing buoys dangles against the shack's green shingles. And in the sunlight, it's funny how the buoys' time at sea is obvious. The seaworn blues and reds and oranges are distressed and scuffed and chipped. Anyone could just picture them bobbing in the ocean; can imagine the salt water tossing them against a lobster boat; can hear the slosh of the Atlantic, the cry of gulls.

"Hey, I have an idea," Nick says as he steps back and eyes the display.

"That'd be a first," Flynn tosses his way with some smart-aleck grin.

Ignoring the kid, Shane fusses with the buoys, this way … that way. "What've you got?" he asks Nick.

"There's some nautical rope at the boat basin," Nick suggests. "Someone left it behind at the end of the season."

While holding up the buoys, Shane looks over his shoulder at him. "Seriously?"

"I saw it, too," Flynn says. "All coiled up in the corner."

"Yeah … *yeah*," Nick tells Shane. "It'd look sweet strung here *with* the buoys."

Shane lowers the string of buoys now. "Go get it, Nick. We'll hang it right away."

Nick hesitates. Checks his watch, too. "Eh, not sure. Maybe I got to stay at my post."

"Me and Flynn will handle things here." Shane waves Nick away. "You won't be long. Just get a move on."

"All right. I'm on it. Back in a flash." Nick hesitates again, then reaches into the guard shack and lifts a security vest off a wall hook. "Flynn," he says, tossing him that vest. "You cover the guard post here at the trestle."

"Really?" Flynn takes that fluorescent-green vest and puts it on.

"Yeah. Log the deets if someone comes in." Now Nick's grabbing his gear from the green shack, then heading to Flynn. "Here's my clipboard. The log. A pen. If anyone drives in, just get their name, license plate—"

"I know. I know the drill," Flynn tells him with a glance at the clipboard. *"Where you headed? Which cottage you staying at? Visiting? Renting?"*

Nick's half listening, half jogging back to the guard shack for the security cruiser keys. As he gets in the car parked nearby, someone actually pulls under the trestle.

"That's Taylor," Nick calls out from the security car. "Wave her through. She lives here."

As Nick drives down the gritty beach road, Flynn does just that. And Shane can see he's taking his new job very seriously. Flynn steps aside, motions his hand, salutes Taylor as she slowly drives by in Eva's car.

It's quiet then. A few minutes pass. There's really only the sound of birdsong from the trees. A bicyclist pedals by, too. Calls a *Good morning!* And that's about it.

So Shane adjusts the string of buoys over two wall hooks and feels the sun warm on his back. He gives his flannel shirtsleeves another shove-up, then adjusts his white painter cap lower against the sunlight's glare. Meanwhile, Flynn's leaning against the shack. He's got a foot kicked up on it and holds that clipboard propped against his hip. Shane asks him about high school, and what classes he likes. Tells Flynn he's a lobsterman. That he brought the old buoys down from Maine.

They're interrupted when a car pulls under the trestle.

Flynn trots across the street and flags the driver to wait up. So Shane stays busy adjusting the buoys, hanging some higher, some tipped. The whole time, he can hear Flynn greeting the visitor at the trestle. When Shane glances back, Flynn's bent low on the passenger side as the driver leans over the front seat to answer his questions.

Satisfied Flynn's got it all under control, Shane gets back to hanging the buoys—still keeping an ear tuned to Flynn at the trestle.

"I'm renting a cottage," a woman's voice is telling Flynn now. "Staying on here for a little bit."

"Okay," Flynn's steady voice carries to Shane. "Let's see. Can I have your name?"

"Sure," the woman, friendly enough, says then. "It's Heather. Heather Gray."

Well, the damn planet might as well stop spinning with that one. Shane quickly looks back over his shoulder. Tips up his white painter cap, too. And can't miss a glimpse of blonde on the woman sitting in the sedan.

Problem is, it's not just Heather Gray steamrolling right into Shane's life just then. It's his whispered expletives. His elevated blood pressure. His tense memory. He might as well be sitting on a window-side stool in a little café in San Francisco. Might as well be watching Heather Gray walk across the street to her jewelry boutique.

To August Dove.

But he isn't.

He's standing at the newly painted green guard shack at Stony Point Beach—three thousand *miles* from California.

And now Celia's mother is *here*?

At the blessed stone train trestle?

Silent questions run rampant in his mind. *Why* is Heather Gray here? What the hell is she about to unleash on Celia's life? What good can come from any of it? Is Celia aware of this situation? What does Heather want?

Damn it.

Meanwhile, minutes feeling *dangerous* tick by as oblivious Flynn asks questions and jots down answers.

Street address?

Cottage name?

License plate number?

Hell, Heather met Shane. She *talked* to him in August Dove. He told her he was a quarryman from New Hampshire. Bought some of her jewelry.

Shit, shit, shit.

He can't risk being recognized. So he shifts his stance at the guard shack to keep his back to the street.

To Heather Gray.

But he manages to turn *some*, to look out from beneath the brim of his white cap just to be sure it's her.

And the sight he sees tells him damn well what he needs to know.

It is indeed Heather.

Heather, who is asking Flynn for directions to her rented cottage. Who momentarily gets out of her car and leans to the side to better see *where* Flynn is pointing. Who squints down the sandy beach road as Flynn tells her to go straight, then veer left at the fork.

Heather, who is carefully listening to Flynn direct her closer and closer to her cottage.

Closer and closer to Celia's life here.

Closer to Shane's life, too.

Hell, what did Jason *just* say yesterday on the stairs at the bluff? Something about a SNAFU?

Yep. That's what they've got right now—with Heather Gray arriving here in Stony Point.

A SNAFU.

One that's about to crash directly into Celia.

One that's about to toss a grenade into life as they know it.

As *Celia* ultimately chose it.

Standing at the shack with its buoys strung just so, Shane throws one more look Heather's way as her car slowly passes behind him.

That's what he's got on his hands to wrangle now.

A SNAFU.

A situation normal, all fucked up.

The beach friends' journey continues in

AUGUST DOVE

The next novel in The Seaside Saga from

New York Times Bestselling Author

JOANNE DEMAIO

Also by Joanne DeMaio

Also by Joanne DeMaio

Beach Cottage Series
(In order)
1) The Beach Cottage
2) Back to the Beach Cottage

Standalone Novels
True Blend
Whole Latte Life

The Winter Series
(In order)
1) Snowflakes and Coffee Cakes
2) Snow Deer and Cocoa Cheer
3) Cardinal Cabin
4) First Flurries
5) Eighteen Winters
6) Winter House
7) Winter Road
—And More Winter Books–

For a complete list of books by *New York Times* bestselling author Joanne DeMaio, visit:

Joannedemaio.com

About the Author

JOANNE DEMAIO is a *New York Times* and *USA Today* bestselling author of contemporary fiction. The novels of her ongoing and groundbreaking Seaside Saga journey with a group of beach friends, much the way a TV series does, continuing with the same cast of characters from book-to-book. In addition, she writes winter novels set in a quaint New England town. Joanne lives with her family in Connecticut.

For a complete list of books and for news on upcoming releases, visit Joanne's website. She also enjoys hearing from readers on Facebook.

Author Website:
Joannedemaio.com

Facebook:
Facebook.com/JoanneDeMaioAuthor

Made in United States
North Haven, CT
17 March 2025

66907234R00178